About the Author

Evie Woods is the author of The Lost Bookshop, the #1 *Wall Street Journal*, *Sunday Times* and Amazon Kindle bestseller, which was shortlisted for a British Book Award, and translated into 21 languages.

Evie lives on the West Coast of Ireland where she escapes the inclement weather by writing stories that push the boundary between what is real and what we wish were so. Drawing inspiration from the unseen forces that shape our lives and the healing power of storytelling, she invites the reader to embrace the magic that exists in our ordinary lives.

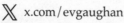

www.eviewoods.com

X x.com/evgaughan
instagram.com/evie.gaughan
tiktok.com/@eviewoods.author

Also by Evie Woods

The Lost Bookshop

THE STORY COLLECTOR

EVIE WOODS

One More Chapter
a division of HarperCollins*Publishers* Ltd
1 London Bridge Street
London SE1 9GF
www.harpercollins.co.uk
HarperCollins*Publishers*
Macken House, 39/40 Mayor Street Upper,
Dublin 1, D01 C9W8, Ireland

This paperback edition 2024

First published in Great Britain in ebook format
by HarperCollins*Publishers* 2024
Copyright © Evie Woods 2024
Evie Woods asserts the moral right to
be identified as the author of this work

A catalogue record of this book is available from the British Library

UK ISBN: 978-0-00-870667-8
US ISBN: 978-0-00-870746-0

Printed and bound in the United States

The woods are lovely, dark and deep,
But I have promises to keep,
And miles to go before I sleep,
And miles to go before I sleep.

Robert Frost

Thornwood House

Where Thornwood House now stands was once ancient woodland. It is said that when Lord Hawley purchased the estate in 1882, as a marriage gift for his wife, he ordered the entire site to be cleared before building works could commence. However, in the middle of this site grew a gnarled old hawthorn tree, a fairy tree, and 'twas said that misfortune would befall any man who so much as scarred the twisted bark. A seeress from the locality warned the Master not to touch it, saying that The Good People would have their revenge on anyone who tampered with their dwelling place.

But Lord Hawley was an educated man from Surrey, England and held no truck with local superstition. The plans were drawn up for his mansion house and he paid the workers handsomely to get the job done. Yet the local men still refused to be a part of it, and Hawley was forced to employ workers from his own homeland to cut the tree down. The seeress foretold no end of misery, but for the first few years, everything in Thornwood House seemed perfectly content.

However, when Lady Hawley fell pregnant with twins, she did become mightily sick and there was a fear for her life. Mercifully, she and the babies survived, but the real horror was yet to come.

A few weeks after they were born, the Mistress began to act very strangely and insisted that the children were not hers. A physician was sent for and rumours spread that the woman was suffering from hysteria.

The seeress, on the other hand, knew that it was not Lady Hawley's mind that had weakened. She knew that when a mother did not recognise her own child, it could only mean one thing: a changeling. The Good People had finally exacted their revenge by taking the human children and replacing them with evil, sickly souls. If they did not perish immediately, they would live to become mischievous and destructive individuals, intent on creating bitterness and hate wherever they went.

Before the Hawley twins ever saw their first birthday, Lady Hawley threw herself from the top window of Thornwood House.

Chapter One

New York

25th December 2010

Were it not for that tacky ceramic sheep in the gift shop, Sarah would never have even heard of Thornwood, much less got on a plane to Ireland and spent Christmas there.

'Have you got everything you need?' Jack had finally asked, after an hour of silently watching her reclaim all her worldly possessions.

'Um, yes, I think that's it,' Sarah said, looking about her at all the empty spaces she was leaving behind. Most of her belongings were already shipped and boxed in suspended animation in a Massachusetts storage unit. 'Well, at least now you can have that snooker table you always wanted in here,' she added, trying to sound cheery, but regretting it as soon as she heard it out loud. 'I'm sorry, I didn't mean—'

'It's okay,' he said, touching her lightly on the arm and giving her a crooked smile. 'I don't know what to say either, but you don't have to pretend, Sarah.'

The easiest thing would have been to fall into his arms and bury her pain somewhere neither of them could find it, but she'd tried that already and two years later, it still wasn't working. They were living in a house of unspoken needs and muffled emotions.

'Are you sure you want to leave today? I mean, it is Christmas, after all,' he said, nodding towards the lacklustre tree that blinked optimistically in the corner. 'You could wait till New Year's…'

'What difference does it make, really? We'd just be delaying the inevitable. I have to leave now or I never will. Besides, your family's expecting you for the big Natale Zaparelli, so you better get a move on too.'

He exhaled a long and weary sigh, stuffing his hands in his pockets. Sarah wondered bitterly what bothered him more: her absence from the Zaparelli family Christmas or him having to explain it.

'I wish it didn't have to be like this.' Jack shifted from one foot to the other. He didn't know where to place himself and finally, like an unwanted object in his gallery, he leaned against the nearest wall.

'Come on, Jack, it's taking all of my strength to do this. Please don't go soft on me now or I might just crack,' Sarah said, reaching for her purse and coat.

'All right then, beat it, lady and don't let the door hit you on the way out! Better?' he asked, with a half smile.

'Much.' She hugged him, briefly but fiercely, and turned on her heel, dragging her suitcase behind her. 'I'll call to let you know I've landed safely,' she called behind her.

'Maybe just a text message,' he said, adding in almost a whisper, 'I don't trust myself not to beg you to come back.'

Newark Airport had a sense of business as usual but with a halfhearted nod to the holidays. It reminded Sarah of when she was a child and spent Christmas in the hospital having her appendix removed. The worn-out decorations only served to remind her of where she wanted to be, but wasn't, and now the airport felt the same. Where were all of these people going? Were they all leaving their husbands? Most of them probably didn't even observe Christmas. Was all of this really going on every year while Sarah tucked into her turkey, naively assuming that everyone else had the same traditions?

Her sister, Meghan, would probably be serving her famous Christmas pudding about now. She wished she didn't have to impose on their holidays, but you can't always choose the timing of a marital breakdown. After three years of marriage, she had precious little to show for it. If anything, her life had shrunk since she'd met Jack. Her only option was to move back in with her parents or stay in her sister's spare room. It wasn't much of a choice: failed daughter or failed sister. Meghan's was the lesser of two evils.

Sarah absent-mindedly wandered through the gift shops, hoping to distract herself from recurring thoughts of what Jack would be doing now. He was putting on a brave face, like herself, but she was sure he would be feeling as lost as she was. At least she could go back to Boston, remove herself from the familiar, everyday things that would bring memories of their life together flooding back. Feeling certain that her hometown would act as some sort of a restorative, she booked the flight like a homing pigeon.

Coming back to herself, she realised she was standing in front of a display of ceramic sheep, in varying shapes and sizes. She must have been staring at them for quite some time, for the shop assistant stepped forward, sensing the possibility of a sale.

'They're super cute, right?' said the young girl with an overly painted face and nose ring.

'Uh, I suppose, if you like sheep,' Sarah replied, not wanting to offend. 'What shop is this?'

'The Emerald Isle Gift Store. You get a ten per cent discount with your Aer Lingus boarding pass,' she added, as if this would sway her decision. 'What part of Ireland are you going to?'

'Oh no, I'm not going to Ireland, just home to Boston,' Sarah assured her, deflecting the sales pitch. She grew up knowing that there was some Irish blood in her family tree (hardly a novelty in Boston) and had always promised herself that, if she ever had the money to do it, she would visit one day. Her honeymoon had seemed like the perfect opportunity, but Jack had argued that two weeks in the Maldives would be much more romantic than shivering in the damp and dreary Irish countryside. Perhaps he'd been right, but the mysticism and charm of the fairytale castles she'd saved on her phone called to her in a way that aquamarine waters never did.

The young assistant sat back behind the counter and was now testing the stretchability of her chewing gum. Given the day, Sarah took pity on her and picked up a rather startled-looking sheep and an Irish newspaper for good measure. She hardly registered tucking the half bottle of Irish whisky under her arm.

'Thank you ma'am and happy holidays!' The girl smiled as Sarah took her gift bag and headed for the departure gates.

Grabbing a cup of coffee to go, Sarah sat apart from the other passengers by the window, where she could see the aeroplanes being refuelled. A light flurry of snow had begun, illuminated by the airport lights to look like flecks of gold dancing through the air. Looking at the screen, she could see that her flight was delayed by two hours. Opening the screw cap, she nonchalantly poured a healthy measure of whisky into the paper cup. A medicinal measure. The coffee was bitter, but mixed with the whisky it flushed her bloodstream with a reassuring warmth. It all felt so surreal. Knowing that you're going to leave your husband and actually going through with it are two very different things. Her emotions were only now beginning to catch up with the reality of the situation. She twisted off the cap again and refilled her cup.

She wasn't getting much sleep since 'The Big Bad Thing' as she now referred to it. Somehow it was easier saying it that way, contained it somehow, so the feelings couldn't get out. Going to bed was like buying a lottery ticket; some nights you won and grabbed a few hours of sleep. Other nights, which were becoming more and more frequent, she woke in a blind panic, hardly able to breathe.

'You're suffering from an anxiety disorder,' her doctor had said, with her perfectly coiffed hair and rather inappropriate high-heeled shoes. I mean, how could you attend to an emergency in those heels? Sarah had wondered, while the doctor's explanation washed over her. Giving it a name didn't help matters. Pills were offered and refused. Jack had a lot to say about that. He had a lot to say about everything and often drowned any thoughts Sarah tried to have of her own. She was advised to cut down on the drinking. She didn't tell Jack about that part and had somehow managed to convince herself that this was a generic piece of advice that didn't really apply to her. She just knew that if she could be on her own for a while, she could sort herself out. Except she wouldn't be on her own in Boston. It was only now beginning to dawn on her that the price of familial support would be more interference. More well-meaning platitudes from people intent on 'fixing' her.

'Another coffee please,' Sarah said, standing at the Dunkin Donuts counter. She tried not to meet his eyes; surely he had smelled the whisky. Not that it mattered, she was well over the legal age. But there was a feeling of guilt there that she couldn't explain. She wasn't drinking for fun or because she had a fear of flying. She was trying to forget. She busied herself with her bag and spotted the Irish newspaper inside it. She took it out, just for something to look at, when a photo caught her attention on the back page. An image of a beautiful hawthorn tree, blooming with tiny white flowers, standing alone beside a busy road in the county of Clare in Ireland. The headline read: THE FAIRY TREE THAT MOVED A MOTORWAY.

'Huh!' Sarah said a little loudly, then bent her head to focus on the words.

Clare County Council finally bowed to local pressure to alter the proposed route of a major new motorway currently under construction, all in an effort to protect a very special hawthorn tree. Ned Delaney, a local folklorist and storyteller, lodged an objection, saying that the hawthorn tree was 'an important meeting place for the Connacht and Munster fairies'. Delaney (known locally as 'The Fairy Whisperer') insisted that to cut down the tree would 'vex' the little people and cause untold misfortune for anyone using the road.

Sarah felt as though she were suddenly back in her father's truck, as a teenager, driving through the countryside to gather bits of dead wood from the forest. He was a bit of a hippie, or a tree-hugger as the neighbours used to call him, and he instilled in her a great respect for nature. He would let her drive on the quieter roads and it felt so freeing, just the two of them, the road ahead and the trees lining the route. They would spend hours together in his workshop making impossibly crooked birdhouses and desk tidies and anything else that could be fashioned from rough wood and a few rusty nails. He always encouraged her and even got her to start sketching plans on paper for more sophisticated projects like coat racks and shelving units. It was thanks to those early days in the workshop that she finally decided to go to college and study art. She had such high hopes when she graduated, but New York didn't exactly work out as planned, on any level. Her working-class roots had always made her feel like an outsider in the galleries of New York, but now she felt like she didn't belong at home anymore either. Her stomach churned at the thought of setting up home in her sister's spare room. She turned her attention back to the newspaper.

Locals were hesitant to admit that they actually believed in fairies, but one resident summed up the general feeling when she said, 'It's better to be safe than sorry.'

Sarah blinked and shook her head. Could this be possible, in this day and age? She flipped the paper over and double-checked that it was in fact a genuine newspaper and not some kind of joke. Then she began to smile to herself and thought again of her father and what a kick he would get out of it. Her mother, on the other hand, had no time for such trivialities. Her mother and her sister Meghan were the practical ones, but Sarah and her father were the dreamers. Or at least she used to be. All of the magic seemed to seep out of her after The Big Bad Thing. Maybe Ireland was the place to find it again?

Glancing out over the concourse from her little table at Dunkin' Donuts, she realised she had walked quite far from her departure gate. In fact, she found herself slap-bang in front of the Aer Lingus departure lounge, with the flight number EI401 bound for Shannon flashing on the screen. An advertisement on a nearby wall showed the striking image of the Cliffs of Moher, standing majestically above the wild Atlantic Ocean, with the tagline, 'Ireland: The land of a thousand welcomes'.

Something inside her shifted, then settled. The decision was made. It was made the moment she saw that silly sheep.

Chapter Two

S arah woke with a jolt when the plane touched down on the tarmac. Peering out of the window, she couldn't tell if it was day or night, for torrential rain lashed the window in such persistent bursts that it was impossible to see out.

'You're lucky you slept through that,' came a lyrical Irish accent close to her ear.

Turning around, Sarah saw her neighbour smiling kindly at her, while wrapping up what appeared to be a hooked needle and a large ball of wool.

'I dropped a few stitches, I don't mind telling you!' confided the woman. 'I thought the wind would flip us over, but you slept soundly all the way through, you lucky duck.'

Sarah tried to compose herself and covertly wipe any drool from her face. She felt completely dehydrated and her head felt like it was being drilled at the temples.

'Sorry I wasn't much company,' she said, flattening her wayward hair into what should have been a bob.

'Oh, don't worry about that, you obviously needed the rest, and besides, my crochet always keeps me company. In fact,' she said, digging back into her bag, 'Happy Christmas!' She added, waving a hat. 'I crocheted eight of them during the flight.' It was a perfectly stitched beanie in a lovely berry shade and she handed it to Sarah.

'You're kidding me. You've been knitting these the whole time?'

'Oh I couldn't go anywhere without my crochet. It keeps me calm and Lord knows I hate flying, so this passes the time nicely.'

Sarah tried on the hat and it fitted perfectly.

'Thank you so much, that's really very kind of you.' Sarah realised that she really wasn't in New York anymore. People hardly made eye contact there, much less offered handmade gifts.

'Listen, my brother-in-law is picking me up so if you need a ride anywhere...' Sarah said, feeling seasonably charitable.

'Not at all. I'll get the bus straight from Shannon into Ennis so I'll be fine, dear,' she replied.

Sarah had no idea what the woman was talking about. Shannon and Ennis didn't sound very familiar. She must have been from out of state. But rather than get into a needless discussion, Sarah just nodded politely and fished for some tissues in her bag.

The pilot calmly announced that it was 06:45 a.m. local

time and a chilly three degrees Celsius (whatever that meant in Fahrenheit).

Rather oddly, he also mentioned something about Shannon.

'Holy shit!' she cried.

'Don't worry, love, it can't be much colder than New York,' her companion assured her.

'Where are we?' she gasped, grabbing the woman's arm.

'What? We're in Ireland, love, I told you, you slept right through!'

Sarah had that sickening feeling that was becoming all too familiar. The cold sweat and the uncanny sensation of popping candy in her bloodstream. It was starting to come back to her – the sheep; the whisky; the green shamrock logo on the plane. And something about a tree?

'We're not in Boston, are we?'

'Do you not remember, love? Well, I suppose you were a little worse for wear. I think that the air hostess only let you on to shut you up!'

'Oh God.' Sarah squeezed her eyes shut, trying to force the lock on her lost memories. She remembered laughing, possibly wishing people 'Top of the morning', but that was it.

'How did I even get a ticket?' Sarah shook her head, but still no memories came loose.

'You told me you were flying standby. Sure, they were only delighted to fill up the seats, weren't they? It's half empty as it is.' The woman was packing up her knitting and taking all of her valuable information with her.

Looking out the window, all Sarah could see was

darkness and the blurred lights of the airport through the rain. It was clearly not Logan International. She dug her cell phone out of her bag, powered it on and dialled Meghan's number immediately.

'I'm so sorry, Meghan,' she began remorsefully.

'And so you should be. Poor Greg was stuck waiting at the airport for you for hours last night. On Christmas Day, Sarah! What the hell happened to you? Didn't you get my messages? Are you staying with Jack?'

The plane finally came to a halt and the passengers began to unclick their seatbelts and open the overhead lockers. Sarah cupped her hand around her ear to block out the noise.

'No, I...' Sarah hesitated. She knew the least she owed her sister was an explanation, but she was almost embarrassed to admit what she had done. 'I'm not in New York,' was what she finally settled on.

'Well you're not in Boston, either, I can vouch for that!' Meghan snapped.

Meanwhile, the hat lady joined the line of passengers about to exit the plane, giving Sarah a supportive thumbs-up. She obviously had more faith in her than she had in herself.

'Look, Meghan, I really needed to get away. I thought it might be good to be on my own for a while, try and work things out in my own space.' This sounded good, Sarah assured herself. It sounded like a coherent plan.

'Well, I wish you would have thought of that before I spent all of Christmas Eve getting your room ready and half of Christmas Day calling the airline. How could you be so thoughtless? It's not like you,' Meghan replied.

'Okay, you're right, I deserve that. I just … I acted on a whim. I didn't even know what I was doing myself until I was on the flight and then I fell asleep and…'

'So you did take a flight, to where?'

'Um, well, I'm in Ireland.' The line went silent. 'If it makes you feel any better, I seem to have arrived in the middle of a hurricane,' she added, looking out at a stiffly horizontal windsock.

'Sarah, what are you doing?' came her sister's measured reply.

'Well, this is just a rough guess, but I might be having a midlife crisis.'

'This isn't funny.'

'I disagree. It's the first truly funny thing that has happened in the last two years. In fact, it's hilarious. I've just arrived in a country where I know nothing and no one, and it's Christmas, for God's sake. I haven't a clue where I'm going, or what I'm doing, and another thing…'

Sarah suddenly noticed that a flight attendant was standing by her seat, giving her a weary smile. Sarah raised herself up and realised that the entire plane was empty, save for her and the remaining crew. 'Listen, Meghan, I've got to disembark. I'll call you once I get settled.'

'Settled where?' Meghan shouted, exasperated.

'Well, in Ireland.'

'You mean you don't even know what part of Ireland you're in?' Meghan accused in a high-pitched voice.

'Sorry, you're breaking…' With that, she rang off to the

sound of her sister saying how they were all so worried about her. She instantly knew she had done the right thing.

Inside the terminal, Sarah dragged her lone sky-blue suitcase across the concourse. She'd packed the rest of her belongings in a removal van, which would probably be arriving at Meghan's house about now.

'What am I doing?' she whispered under her breath.

The place was deserted, apart from two tired-looking men in high visibility jackets leaning against the customs counter.

'Anything to declare, Madam?' the larger one asked in a deep baritone voice.

Sarah couldn't think of anything to declare, except that she was now officially homeless, so decided to keep her mouth shut. As the sliding doors opened, she felt the disappointment like a physical blow to her gut. Even though she hadn't been expecting anyone to be there, the sadness of knowing that nobody cared whether she was here or not still hurt. 'What kind of oddball travels abroad on their own for Christmas?' she wondered bitterly to herself. Still, there was nothing to do but get on with it now. A nice warm hotel room with a hot bath and some delicious food would make everything seem better, she assured herself.

Once outside, she struggled to button her coat against the wind and pulled her newly acquired beanie hat down over her ears.. She swiftly blew across the car park and into the reception of the airport hotel. To her relief, a tall, distinguished-looking gentleman sprang up to greet her with all the agility of Fred Astaire.

'You're very welcome to the Shannon Airport Hotel. How can I help you?' he rattled off with practised ease.

'Hey there, Marcus,' she said, reading his name badge. 'I just need a room for tonight, please, and if you can tell me where I can get some breakfast, that'd be great.'

'Ooh,' he said, sucking air through his teeth, 'unfortunately we don't have any rooms tonight, but I can offer you a twin room for tomorrow night?'

'You're kidding, right? How could you be booked up when this place is a ghost town?'

'Oh no, we're not booked up as such, but there's been a slight problem with the plumbing on two of the floors, so we've had to close up most of the bedrooms until we get it sorted,' he explained.

Sarah slumped into one of the leather tub chairs facing the view of the car park outside. Despite the fact that she had slept for most of the flight, she still felt like an emotional wreck. An emotional wreck with a raging hangover.

'I'm not normally…' She trailed off.

'Ah sure, it's the time of year, makes us all a bit funny, doesn't it?' He stepped out from behind the reception desk and made a swift appraisal of the situation. 'Right, follow me.'

'What? Where?' But he was already making great strides through the lobby and towards a door marked 'Dining Room'.

Once settled at a table with a large plate of bacon, sausage, egg and soda bread, Sarah began to relax a little.

Marcus joined her with a large pot of tea and two cups on a tray.

'Marcus O'Brien, at your service,' he said, introducing himself formally.

'Sarah Harper,' she replied, offering her hand. 'Where is everyone?'

'Skeleton staff at Christmas,' Marcus said as he poured a liquid black as tar into her cup. 'Anyway, what brings you to the Banner on this Stephen's Day?'

'The Banner?' she echoed. And who was Stephen, she wondered, the culture shock already setting in.

'Oh, it's a nickname really, UP THE BANNER!' he said, waving his gangly arms about. 'Never mind,' he said, on seeing her blank look.

'Would you believe me if I told you that it was a newspaper article about a fairy tree that brought me here?'

'The hawthorn, of course. Are you a journalist?'

Great, she thought, he did believe it. She had her cover story. Anything was better than the truth.

'Not exactly. This is delicious, by the way. I've never tasted anything like this back home,' she said, buttering her soda bread. It was magically curing her hangover, too.

'Well, if you can't get a good Irish breakfast here, we may as well all pack up and go home!' He excused himself with efficient courtesy and left to sort out some hotel business, wiping his finger along the tables checking for dust as he went.

Sarah took a moment to gather her thoughts, which basically consisted of how relieved she felt to have stumbled into the path of a man like Marcus. Sometimes you just needed to be looked after, especially after a night drinking whisky and buying a plane ticket to Ireland. She started to think that maybe this rash decision wasn't so bad after all. She could spend a week or two having a nice little holiday for herself; enjoying the country and its people (if they were all like Marcus), before returning home with a clear head.

'You're in luck,' Marcus said as he returned to the dining room. 'I've found you the perfect place to stay in the village,' he said, rubbing his hands together.

'The village?' Sarah wondered if he meant the New York or the Irish version.

'Thornwood. It's just a twenty-minute drive from here. It's what we would call in the business "a home away from home".'

All she could do was smile; a home away from home was just what she needed right now.

Breezing through a landscape of stone walls and green fields, Sarah couldn't help but smirk at Marcus's leather driving gloves. Everything he did was so correct and proper.

'You really didn't have to drive me, I could have taken a cab,' she said, as they glided around a roundabout.

'Not at all, we often send guests over here when the hotel is fully booked. It's a small village but it's also a popular spot for tourists, so we keep busy. And you said you were from Boston yourself?' he asked, shifting the gear stick with practised ease.

'Yep, although I've been living in Manhattan for a

couple of years with my…' She stumbled, memories flooding back. 'With my husband Jack.'

Marcus O'Brien had not spent the last thirty-odd years working as a hotel manager and learned nothing. He casually steered the conversation onto safer ground and chatted easily about all manner of subjects. Sarah marvelled at his ability to hold an entire conversation on his own, with little or no need for input from her.

Marcus wasn't exaggerating about the distance or the size of Thornwood. As the car rolled over a humpbacked bridge, Sarah was amazed to see that 'the village' was simply a cluster of houses, a shop and a pub, with a quaint little church overlooking the river. Instead of streetlamps, the village was lit by old-fashioned cast-iron lanterns, which were all festively dressed in red bows. The whole place looked so well maintained and cared for, with brightly painted shopfronts and window boxes bursting with evergreens.

'I have to give it to you, Marcus, this is one pretty little village,' she said finally.

'Well, we're very proud of it and we have a very successful Tidy Towns committee,' he replied.

'Let me guess, you must be president?' she joked genially.

'Vice president, but I've got my eye on the prize,' he said, tapping his nose.

'Now,' he announced, as they arrived at a pretty stone house, which was guarded by two bay trees lit up with fairy lights. 'It's not a hotel, but I'm hoping you'll be a bit open-minded.'

'It looks lovely, is it a guesthouse?'

'Oh, this isn't where you'll be staying, no, it's the owner that lives here,' he explained.

'The owner?' Nothing seemed to be straightforward in this place. You had to go from A to C, just to get to B, which probably wasn't the place you were looking for at all.

'Yes, Mr Sweeney, he rents out a gem of a little cottage down the road,' he said, checking her reaction.

'Sounds ... very ... authentic!' she said, secretly hoping that it would be plumbed with hot water.

'Oh, it is. Full of all those "original features".'

It sounded like a euphemism for cold and damp, but Sarah kept her reservations to herself.

Marcus insisted on taking her to the front door, which was adorned with a beautiful holly wreath. Sarah noticed the twinkling lights of a Christmas tree in the front window and she hoped they weren't disturbing these people. The shape of a person appeared in the coloured glass at the side of the door and they were greeted by a towering, grey-haired man with a ruddy face and a strong nose.

'Marcus,' he acknowledged, reaching out to shake his hand.

'Hello, Brian, how are you?' Marcus asked, but before the man had a chance to answer, he ploughed on. 'Listen, you're great to look after us at such short notice,' he said, touching Sarah's arm, 'and I'll leave ye to it now, you don't want to be overcrowded!'

While she shook hands with Mr Sweeney, Marcus had her suitcase out of the boot, insisting that no guest of his would carry their own luggage, not on his watch.

'You'll be all right now, won't you?' he asked, as though talking to a child. 'You will, of course,' he said, answering his own question.

Rather abruptly, the vital force that was Marcus disappeared back down the road, leaving Sarah and her new acquaintance in an awkward silence.

'I'll just get the keys,' Mr Sweeney said, lacking the vitality of her previous companion.

'I'm sorry, I'm interrupting your Christmas.'

'Ah sure, it's over now,' he said in a very practical way. 'It's not very far, but I doubt you don't fancy lugging your suitcase down an old boreen.'

Brian Sweeney was the polar opposite to Marcus. He was calm and unhurried, using his words only sparingly. There was a reserve there that made even small talk challenging.

They sat in a decrepit-looking jeep with mud and manure caked on the sides. After a sputtering start, the engine eventually agreed to turn over and they set off down the road, past the church and back over the humpbacked bridge. The road forked and he indicated to turn left onto the narrower road.

'Is this a one-way street?' Sarah asked, which earned her a hearty laugh from her driver. There were no road markings, just a barely visible ridge of tarmac that, over the years, had formed something of a spine in the centre of the road. Like a prehistoric animal, asleep for now. 'You can't be serious; how are two cars supposed to fit on this road?'

'They're not! One of you has to reverse until you come to

a layby or an entrance to a field,' he said, assuring Sarah that it was all perfectly normal in the country.

The car heater was furiously blowing out hot air, making Sarah feel drowsy and slightly queasy. Despite the bright sunshine, everything still glistened with a light whisper of frost. To the left, there was a large area of woodland, with the top of a hill peeking out above the conifers.

'What's up there?' Sarah asked, pointing up at the verdant hillside.

'That's Cnoc na Sí,' he said. 'It's a lovely spot for walking.'

'*Canuck na Shee*?' Sarah repeated, trying to form the strange Gaelic sounds.

'It means hill of the fairies,' he translated.

'Seriously?'

'I'm not codding you; "*Cnoc*" means hill and "*Sí*" is the Irish for fairies. Did you think it was something we just made up for the Yanks?' he said, winking at her. She was glad to see he was thawing a little.

After a slight dip in the road, the countryside opened out in front of them once again. The little river from the village reappeared, almost leading the way to a solitary cottage standing proud and dignified on its own little patch of land bordered by a whitewashed stone wall. He glanced furtively at Sarah to gauge her reaction as he pulled up at the little blue gate.

'Welcome to Butler's cottage. It's just been newly thatched and you know, despite what people might think, thatched houses are very warm,' he pointed out.

Sarah, however, did not need convincing. The cottage

was like something from a postcard. The single-storey home was painted white with a neatly trimmed thatched roof that boasted a beautifully scalloped design. They trod carefully up the frosty garden path that was made up of a jigsaw of flagstones and came to the matching light blue door. As he jiggled the key in the lock, Sarah noticed that the door seemed to be split into two sections.

'Oh yes, it's an authentic half door,' he explained, slipping into his role as tour guide. 'It was a great way to let air into the cottage, without any four-legged friends getting in.' On seeing Sarah's face he continued, 'You know they used to say that if you were stood leaning on the half door, you were passing time; but if you were stood leaning against an open doorway, you were wasting time!'

Marcus was right about the original features; it felt like stepping back in time.

'When was it built?'

'Oh, probably in the mid-1800s. My son bought it back in the nineties, but we still call it Butler's cottage. That's just how it is around here; the Butlers built this house and worked the farm for over a century, so it'll always be Butler's. It's pretty much open plan,' he continued, 'but it should be enough for you.'

The ceiling had been knocked through to the rafters, giving the place a light and airy feel. Sarah was relieved to see a small but modern country kitchen with a sunken porcelain sink and on the opposite wall a giant hearth with two cosy-looking armchairs upholstered in plaid. A toy-sized window with four little square panes looked out onto the back garden. The place was certainly working its charm.

'Now here's what we used to call the "back bedroom",' he continued, opening a door to the side of the hearth where Sarah could see a double bed dressed with a homely patchwork quilt.

'Can I afford this?' she asked, concerned that her budget might not stretch.

'I hope so,' he laughed, then saw the look on Sarah's face. 'Well, it's low season anyhow, so I'm sure we can hash out a deal,' he assured her. 'But of course, it depends on how long you want to stay…?' he said, trailing off.

'Oh, you know, maybe a week, or two. Just checking out the old family tree,' she said, cringing at the cliché.

'Right so, I'll leave you to it. My son dropped off a few essentials earlier on, tea and the like,' he said. Without much further ado, he was gone. The stillness he left in his wake was almost startling after the day's events.

'Hello, Butler's cottage', Sarah whispered to herself, as she kicked off her boots and turned to look at her new home.

She couldn't recall the last time she had done something so impulsive and purely for herself. She kept expecting the panic to set in, but as she took in her new surroundings, all she felt was joy. 'Maybe,' she thought, 'this is what following your heart feels like.'

Chapter Three

I t felt like the middle of the night when Sarah woke with
an awful familiar feeling. Her chest tightened and her
stomach felt sick with dread. It was a panic attack.

'Shit,' she said aloud to no one. There was only one way
to get through it and that was to get up and out into the
fresh air. The room felt cold, and while she didn't want to
leave the warmth of her bed, nature called. She pulled the
woollen blanket from the end of the bed around her
shoulders before letting her bare feet touch the cold floor.
Without turning on the light, she got up and walked
straight into the wardrobe, stubbing her toe.

'Shit, shit, shit!' It took a few moments to remember
where she was and to register why her surroundings were
so deathly silent. She was in a tiny village in the west of
Ireland, not her apartment in New York City where the
buzz of human life never stopped. It was stupid to think
she'd outrun it – left The Big Bad Thing in the US. How
would she deal with the panic attacks here? Despite Jack's

objections, she had begun jogging at night. Whenever the panic struck, she would blindly pull on her sneakers and take the elevator down to the ground floor. Bursting out onto the neon-lit streets, she would pound away the shakiness in her legs until she couldn't feel anything anymore and returned home wasted. It was the only thing that worked. The fact that her sports bottle was laced with vodka was a detail she kept to herself.

Reaching for the light switch, she looked at her watch and was shocked to see that it was just after eight in the evening. She must have slept all day. She had crept under the duvet almost as soon as Mr Sweeney's car was out of earshot that morning. 'Just to rest my eyes,' she had said to herself.

She tiptoed cautiously through the living room, wondering how on earth anyone could live with this kind of cold. Her whole body shivered as her skin touched the marble-cold of the toilet seat. Thankfully, there was toilet paper, even if it was a little damp. Her heart was still thumping and she knew she had to get running. She washed her hands then pulled at her case, which was sitting exactly where she had abandoned it that morning. She dressed as though she was being timed with a stopwatch. Pulling on two of everything was her best defence against the Irish weather, and so she fought her way into extra socks and knitwear before tumbling towards the door. She plunged her hand into her handbag and felt the smooth curves of the whisky bottle. As she lifted it out, she could see that there was barely a third of the bottle left. She hoped they sold liquor at the little store in the village. Digging her feet into her boots, she burst out into the evening air and realised that the place was pitch-dark. She couldn't even see the road from the cottage. Retracing her steps, she flicked the light switch on in the kitchen and raided the drawers for a flashlight, her breathing shallow and ragged. After scattering several kitchen utensils on the floor, she felt a palpable sense of relief when she located an industrial-size orange flashlight.

The air was cold and frosty, chasing away any residual drowsiness. There was the occasional bark from a dog in the distance, but apart from that, the only sound was the gentle gurgle of the river making its unseen journey through the fields. There was a moon up there somewhere, but it was concealed behind a heavy covering of clouds. Sarah shone the flashlight on the narrow strip of grass growing in the middle of the road. She couldn't jog here, but walking briskly was good enough to convince her fight-or-flight reflex that she was in flight.

Looking ahead, she could see an occasional light in the distance, perhaps from a house or a shed. She slugged hungrily from the bottle, letting the bitter whisky warm her insides. It flooded through her bloodstream, giving her that instant feeling of detachment and something close to relief. At that very moment, the flashlight began to fail, then flickered and died, along with any hope of making it to the village.

'Oh, crap,' she said aloud, tapping it against the palm of her hand. She turned around to see how far she had come from the cottage. It wasn't very far and it probably would have made more sense to turn back, but she had to keep moving. Her eyes were adjusting to the dark and besides, what was the worst that could happen? Just as she began to pick her way forward, she noticed something in the distance, a shape at the side of the road. She kept walking, affecting an air of quiet confidence that felt more like grim determination. It was so dark and the figure on the road was dark, too. In fact, it looked like someone wearing a hooded cloak. She tried not to think of every horror movie she had ever seen.

Her instincts told her to run, but she held her nerve. Besides, running in the dark wasn't a great option. It's probably nothing, just shadows, she told herself.

All hopes that she was seeing things were dashed as she drew closer. It was a black figure standing by a stone wall and it was very much alive and moving. She was holding her breath, perhaps even saying a short prayer, when she finally reached him, or her, or it. A large head with long ears and a creamy white nose came into view, braying for all its worth. The noise almost finished Sarah off, as she grabbed her chest and the briar behind her for support.

'Jesus H Christ!' she roared at the donkey who seemed equally put out by her presence. 'You almost gave me a heart attack, you know that!' she told him, relieved. A large glassy eye turned towards her and she stroked his furry neck. 'What are you doing out here?' she asked, quickly followed by 'Why am I talking to a donkey?' It was comforting, in some strange way. He made her feel less alone. Less silly for being here in the first place.

As if to say their meeting was over, the donkey slowly turned and shuffled along to only he knew where. 'Bye, then!' she called after him, her heartbeat finally restored to some normal rhythm. It felt oddly satisfying to be frightened by something real, instead of the fears inside her own head.

She leaned her weight against the wall behind her so she could catch her breath. Like a slow avalanche, the stones beneath her started to shift and crumble until she found herself flat on her behind in the field.

'Great! Just great,' she said, wondering what else could go wrong. A light flurry of snow began to fall and spiral around her. 'Happy Christmas,' she whispered to herself. The winter moon began to pull the clouds from her face and nestled them around her, like the tresses of a Pre-Raphaelite muse. The earth was suddenly illuminated and in the sodden grass beside her she spied a small, circular thing. A nest, cleverly disguised with dead leaves. Tentatively, she reached out and gently picked it up. An empty nest; beautifully intricate, made with such care and now cast aside. The effects of the whisky seemed to evaporate all at once. The air became still as she cradled the little home of twigs, moss and cobwebs in her hands. A symbol of everything she'd lost. Something within her threatened to break. Looking up, she saw the branches of a large tree reaching overhead. As she looked closer, the moonlight picked out a dark shadow on the rough and twisted bark. The night air was twitching with an energy that was intoxicating; unpredictable even. Her life in New York had been reduced to a set of rules and habits that she thought would keep her safe, or sane at least. Yet sometimes, holding on so tightly to a routine was like clinging to a life raft, awaiting rescue. There was never an end or a point when she could say, 'It's okay; I'm safe.' In Thornwood, there were no such rules.

The grass was long and wet underfoot as she got to her feet and made her way over to the tree. She could see it clearly now: a large hollow in the trunk. She had the idea of burying the nest inside the hollow. It seemed like the right thing to do. Yet at that moment, with the nest in one hand and the bottle of whisky in the other, she let her gut make the decision. If she had to bury something, let it be the drink. When the bottle hit the ground inside the tree, it made a loud clank, rather than the soft thud she had been expecting. It had hit something that wasn't wood. It sounded like tin, which could have been an empty can of beer, but the sound was deeper than that. Her curiosity soon got the better of her.

Five minutes later, Sarah was on her knees and up to her armpit in tree trunk. With her cheek pressed against the rough bark, she had fished out three polystyrene cups, an empty packet of cigarettes and two Coke cans. She could just feel the edges of a square tin box, but her fingertips struggled to lift it. It was wedged in and so she had to search for some rudimentary equipment to help her lever it out. Her nostrils were filled with the smell of damp earth and her fingers were almost numb at the tips. Feeling on the ground around her, she found part of a branch and broke off a long piece with a sharp end. A voice (which sounded suspiciously like Meghan's) kept telling her to give up, to go home and set a fire so she could stave off pneumonia. But her inquisitiveness forced her on. Who knew what she would find? Maybe it would be something trivial, but there was a chance it could be something … meaningful. Perhaps her imagination was running wild, but what if finding the nest was a sign? That she was meant to find whatever was hidden inside this gnarled old tree. Feeling the side of the box, she dug the stick into position and levered it as much as she could in the small space, praying it wouldn't break. There was a slight give and then the triumphant sound of the tin breaking free from its hold.

'Yes!' she said, congratulating her own tenacity. She was able to manoeuvre the box onto its side with her fingertips, so she could get a good grasp of it. It was a snug fit and she had to wiggle it up and down, back and forth, to get it out. Finally, she freed the box from the tree and held it firmly in her hands. She shook it lightly and sensed that there was something inside. Fighting every urge to open it there and then, she wedged it under her arm and started back for the cottage, with the moonlight guiding her way.

After a lengthy negotiation with the half door, she set her treasures down on the wooden dresser that was already heaving with cups and plates of varying colours and sizes. Once she had built a small but functioning fire with the logs that Mr Sweeney's son had left stacked in a woven basket by the hearth, she reached for the box. It was remarkably clean, apart from a general green tinge to its edges. The hollow in the tree had preserved it very well, but then again, Sarah had no idea how long it had been there. There was a tartan design on the front, but no writing or brand name. Sitting on the rug in front of the fire, she pulled hard on the lid and when it gave, her eyes took a moment to figure out what she was looking at. It appeared to be a piece of lace, but there was something red showing through. She carefully lifted it out and, as she did, the lace unravelled to reveal a torn and sorry-looking remnant of what might have been a beautiful garment made of golden thread. Wrapped inside was a book and, resting on top of that, a cream envelope with a navy trim. She opened that first and was amazed to find a timeworn ticket for a transatlantic journey from Queenstown to New York with the Cunard Line shipping company. She searched the document for a date. The year was 1911. She could hardly believe what she was seeing. As she turned it over and over in her hands, her mind reeled with questions, the foremost being: why hadn't the ticket been used? Laying the ticket on the rug beside her, she turned her attention to the red leather book. Would she find the answers inside? On opening the cover, she read the sweeping handwriting:

The Diary of Anna Butler

Anna's Diary

Saint Stephen's Day, 1910

The winter moon is keeping me awake tonight, but I don't mind because now I have somewhere to keep my thoughts. Christmas Day was such a treat (as was receiving this diary) and even though it was only yesterday, it seems like weeks must have passed in between. But I'm getting ahead of myself! It began in the usual way for me, in the parlour with Betsy. I'm not sure that Betsy concerns herself much with our feast days, but I wished her a very Merry Christmas all the same, as I warmed my hands well before milking her. This has been our morning ritual for years now and despite my excited carol singing, Betsy's earthy warmth and steady breath always brings a wonderful calm to my heart. I leaned my head against her taut, fat belly and almost fell asleep just like that, if it wasn't for the noise of her hooves shuffling against the parlour floor. I had hardly slept the night before, such was the excitement of decorating the house with holly and ivy and lighting the Christmas candle. At eighteen years of age, some might say I am getting too old for such carry on, but Mother and Father always make it special for us. It is my favourite time of year; the food, the visiting and the merriment. Everyone is in a gay mood and there is a sense of magic in the air. I patted Betsy lightly on her hindquarters to let her know that she had done a great job. As I lifted the bucket, I let a little drop of the milk splash on the ground. 'That's for the Good People,' I said, as is the custom, and I skipped briskly across the yard, back to the warmth of our cottage.

Our home sits so neatly in its surroundings that my father used to say it grew up out of the ground. The land slopes gently upwards at the rear of the cottage, providing a protective barrier from the north wind, and hedgerows line the laneway up to the main road, almost hiding our little home from view. The household was already stirring in preparation for the big day ahead. The fire was sparking and filling the room with the scent of pine cones, which we kept in a little pile by the hearth. Mother took the bucket from me and scooped the cream off the top with a ladle to make a deliciously rich pot of porridge, and I sat around the table with my brothers, Patrick, Thomas and young Billy. We all rushed to show each other what Father Christmas had brought us and I was proud as Punch to show everyone my new diary.

After putting on our best clothes for Mass, we all set out into the expectant darkness and began the three-mile walk for eight o'clock Mass. There was a full moon and so it was easy enough to see our way along the road. Billy, the youngest, kept all of our spirits high by singing every carol he knew in his head! And some that he didn't, but we all joined in, so we made a merry band of churchgoers. Father and Mother walked a little behind, arm in arm and quietly satisfied with their happy family.

'Joe,' I heard her whisper, 'you know you spent far too much on their presents this year,' to which he replied, 'Hush now, Kitty, wait till you see your gift, you'll be delighted that I spent half nothing!' She dug him in the ribs with her elbow, smiling despite herself, and that was that.

As our little troupe wound its way through the valley, lights began to appear out of the darkness, as the countryside awoke to Christmas morning and lit their candles in the windows. Like a necklace of twinkling pearls on the horizon, our neighbours' houses lit the way to the village and various stragglers joined us on our walk to the church. Neighbours, friends and relations gathered in the aisles, where we all marvelled at each other's finery and the church itself, which was decorated with bright green holly and bountiful berries hanging from every beam. The excitement of all being together on such a special day almost threatened to drown out Father Peter's Mass, but once the bells rang and the older people shuffled to their seats, we all lifted our voices to 'Hark The Herald Angels' and the chatter died down.

The sun was rising over Cnoc na Sí as we left the church, but the frost clung on to the grass like a magical sprinkling of fairy dust over the land. Once outside, the conversation began anew, with the men congregating on one side to talk about milk prices and which heifer had calved, and the women on the other. I broke away from the crowd and looked down the road towards Thornwood House. Of course, the Hawley family attended a different church, so there was no chance of spotting the twins or their father. I could just make out the pointy roofline of the house and the large chimneys that looked dark and uninviting in the shadow of the rising sun. I wondered what Christmas might be like in that grand house, and as we passed it on our way home, I strained my neck to see up the long drive and beyond the high poplar trees that shielded the entrance, but could see no sign of life. Two large ivy wreaths tied with red bows hung formally on the cast-iron gates, looking forlorn and somehow lacking in festive spirit. But the stillness of the winter air changed suddenly and we all turned at the sound of horses' hooves and cartwheels spiriting down the drive. At the last minute, I saw George Hawley in his carriage, dressed like a lord in a fine overcoat with leather gloves and trilby. My heart beat frantically at the sight of him, and even the neighbours we walked with shuffled and altered their manners as he approached.

'Season's greetings!' he cried, with a well-schooled accent, as one of his servants opened the gate.

'Good day to you, Sir,' came the dutiful reply. There is no real affection among the locals for the Hawley family, but as the largest landowners in the area, their standing is begrudgingly observed. Yet despite his Anglo-Irish heritage, which puts him beyond the reach of us ordinary folk, every girl with eyes in her head swoons over George Hawley. His thick blond hair combed into a perfect wave at his temples and his strong features has us all stealing glances, Protestant or not. I dawdled and tried to catch his eye, feeling sure he would remember me from last summer. He was shipped off to university in England for most of the year and probably didn't give Thornwood a second thought.

Alas, the carriage hurtled off down the road. He never saw me. I put my disappointment away, for there is no point in pining after something you can never have. We returned home and my mother and I resumed our preparations for the grand feast. The goose was cooking nicely with the fragrant scent of goose fat filling the house. We ate and drank and sang and played, but just as my day had began, it ended with Betsy in the milking parlour – my hand steady against her belly, her warm breath lulling me to sleep.

This morning, however, it was the clatter of drums and discordant voices that woke me from my peaceful slumber. I crept back into my unmade bed after milking Betsy, which is a rare treat in our house and only tolerated on special occasions. I had fallen into a deep and dreamless sleep and at first, the sounds made no sense. Yet as I pulled myself from the arms of sleep, understanding began to dawn on me.

'Up with the kettle and down with the pan, give us a penny to bury the wren!'

'Wren boys,' I shouted, as I thumped my foot hard on the floorboards to wake the boys who were asleep in the room below. I jumped up and pulled my woollen skirt over my nightdress and wrapped my shawl around my shoulders, stubbing my toe on the foot of the bed with my haste. Father, of course, was already up and had the kettle boiling on the hearth. The house, still decked with holly and ivy, smelled like a warm and cosy forest with a promise of left-over goose for lunch.

'We'd better give them their money, Anna, before they deafen us,' my father said, the devilment in his eyes belying his gruff voice.

I opened the door, and there stood a rowdy bunch from the village, dressed in the most outrageous attire. I hardly recognised them, despite the fact that I probably shared a classroom with half of them. Our school has only one room and one teacher, and so we all end up learning together, no matter our age. Their faces were painted black and concealed with the most unfashionable of hats, adorned with feathers and ribbons. Their outfits, hastily sewn together with pieces of brightly painted calico, made them all look like second-hand jesters. Two banged a bodhran with a stick and one even had an old fiddle, although he hadn't bothered to learn how to play in key. All in all, they were a riot of fun, noise and colour, and we couldn't have imagined Saint Stephen's morning without them.

'Where's the wren then?' my younger brother Billy called out from underneath my arm. His soft, boyish hair kept falling into his eyes and gave me an excuse to fuss over him and comb it back with my fingertips.

'Up there,' said one of the young men, pointing to another fella holding a stick with a small box swinging from the top.

'How do we know it's really in there?' Billy said, being his usual inquisitive self.

'You're right, Billy,' came my father's voice from behind us, 'how do we know you really caught the bird?'

'Oh, she's in there all right, Mister Butler,' declared the one holding the stick.

'And you wouldn't fib now, would you, Seamie Gallagher?' Father said, at which point Seamie pulled his hat down further over his face and we all laughed.

I felt sorry for them then, because I knew the box held only moss and a few leaves. But that wasn't the point. It was the tradition of the thing, and so I stepped towards the young boy holding the moneybox and dropped in a sixpence.

'Thanks, Anna,' he winked, and straightaway I knew it was Eoin, Nelly's son from the post office.

'Go on let ye now, and don't spend it wisely,' my father called to them, as they began their tuneless song once again.

I had hardly turned to close the door again, when my two older brothers, Patrick and Thomas, almost knocked me down.

'Hang on, lads, we'll join ye!' they called, as they pulled on two old sacks with holes cut for arms and belts tied around their middles. Their faces painted with boot polish, I hardly recognised them as they hopped around the front yard like two lunatics, joining the troupe of jesters. I laughed to myself watching them marching up the lane, off to collect money for the Mummers' Ball, a rather grand-sounding name for a round of drinks at the public house.

That was the first time I saw him, the American. You could tell, even by the way that he walked, that he wasn't a local. He cut a tall, lean figure in a tweed suit, with his trousers tucked into his socks. He carried a satchel over his shoulder and walked with his head erect, open to adventure. For some reason, he looked to me like a man chasing butterflies and all he was missing was a net. He was pushing his bike as he met the wren boys and they stopped in conversation that I could not hear. I saw my eldest brother Paddy pointing back to the house and the man nodded, shaking his hand. To my great surprise, he turned down our laneway and caught sight of me standing at the door, raising his hand with an enthusiastic wave. I should have run back into the house, fixed my unruly hair or put on my shoes, but I stood transfixed.

'Good morning, Miss!' he called out, struggling to guide his punctured bicycle through the potholed lane.

'Good morning,' I replied, 'and Happy Saint Stephen's Day.'

'Oh, yes indeed. I just met the Mummers,' he said, pointing back to the road where the wren boys were making slow progress. 'What a fascinating tradition,' he remarked, in a broad American accent. He seemed to linger over his vowels and no matter what he said, it sounded happy. Leaning the bike up against the gable of the cottage, he ungloved his hand and presented himself formally.

'How do you do, Miss, my name is Harold, Harold Griffin-Krauss.'

I had never heard such a mouthful, but I knew that the last name didn't sound American.

'Are you a German?' I asked, before taking his hand.

'No! Well, in a way, yes. My father was born in Germany, but I'm American. From California... I don't know if you've heard—'

'Of course I've heard of it,' I said a bit defensively. I love geography at school and in a house full of boys, I am always having to prove my intelligence.

He still stood there with his hand suspended in mid-air, and I realised how rude I was being.

'Anna Butler,' I blurted out finally, shaking his hand with gusto.

'Lovely to meet you, Miss Butler,' he said, holding my gaze in a way that wasn't arrogant, but interested. He wasn't like the other boys from around here. For starters, he wasn't a boy, but he wasn't really a man, either. He was well educated, that was obvious by his turn of phrase, but it was his ease of conversing with complete strangers that made him stand out. His smile was wide and in danger of invading his cheeks, but each time he did so he dropped his eyes. There was a shyness behind that smile of his; something that spoke to the shy creature lurking behind my own smile.

'You have a wonderful view,' he said, turning to look out over the fields and the hills beyond.

It was all I could do not to burst out laughing. No one ever has the time or the inclination to talk about 'views' in our village, but I nodded my head politely. He had thoughtful eyes; not blue exactly, but more of a grey colour. They seemed to hold a gentle curiosity, unlike when the schoolmaster came to visit, all airs and graces and looking down his nose at the place.

We stood for a moment like that, him looking out at the horizon and me free to stare at this mysterious stranger. Our shared silence was broken by my father's voice, shouting 'Who is it' from the kitchen. I could hardly think what to answer and so I just replied, 'An American'. This made Mr Krauss smile again and I giggled too, as we both stood on the threshold, waiting for my father to come.

Chapter Four

'I must apologise for my intrusion,' Mr Krauss addressed my father rather poetically, 'but I'm afraid I have not one but two punctures and the Mummers said you might be able to help me out.'

'We'll see what we can do for ya,' my father said, reaching past me to shake his hand while giving me a look. 'Well, what are you doing, keeping the man out in the cold? Will you not invite him in for a cup of tea while I'm repairing his wheels?'

'Oh, yes, of course. Come on in, Mr Krauss', I said a little self-consciously, tucking my hair behind my ears.

'I appreciate the offer, Miss Butler, but I'd like to help your father fix the bike first, if you don't mind?'

I was bowled over by his manners. Mother always says that you can tell a man's worth by his manners. Perhaps that was why her parents were so against her marriage to my father. Although she was never the one to bring it up, we've always been aware that Mother's people come from money. A city girl from Dublin, her father is a well-respected man who runs his own drapers. It was something of a scandal when she announced that she was marrying a farmer and moving to the West of Ireland, with no schooling to speak of.

With that, the two men disappeared around the back of the house and towards the shed. As I hurried back into the kitchen, my mother was just emerging from her bedroom, carrying her teacup and saucer to the sink. My father, being an early bird, always brings my mother her morning tea in bed in her favourite china cup. My mother, being more of a night owl, is always sure to have the teapot washed and laid out for him.

'Morning, Mother,' I blustered, kissing her cheek.

'And what has you all excited this morning, Anna?' she asked, taking in my dishevelled appearance.

'You missed the wren boys,' I said, suddenly remembering why I had got up in such a hurry. 'And there's an American here,' I added, rinsing out the teapot.

'An American?' my mother repeated, as though a visit from the archangel Gabriel would be more likely.

'His bike is punctured. Daddy's helping him repair it in the shed.'

'Oh. And what's he doing in Thornwood?'

'I don't know. Sure, I didn't speak to him, did I?' I said, a bit testily. 'He's coming in for his tea though, maybe you can ask him then?' I was bursting to find out what he was doing in Thornwood just as much as my mother, but I was content to let her do the grilling.

When the men came back from their work, shirtsleeves

rolled to their elbows, I cut several large slices of fruitcake. We have been feeding it the good brandy since November, so by now it is quite potent. The dark, rich cake revealed plump jewels of ruby cherries and amber raisins that tumbled onto the pretty china plates we saved for special occasions.

My father led him into the house, announcing, 'We have a scholar in the house, Kitty,' while Billy trailed behind them both.

I took in the tray of tea and cake from the pantry, reminding Billy to wash his hands and face on my way.

'Thank you, Mrs Butler, I appreciate your kind hospitality,' Mr Krauss thanked my mother politely, and sang my father's praises for mending his bike.

Sitting in the armchair by the fire in his stylish clothes and cultured accent, it was as if the president was visiting our home and we were all on our best behaviour. I've never met an American before and I'm not sure my parents have either. But we played down our fascination with his impromptu arrival on our doorstep as much as we could. I could see that he was enjoying my cake, the very same cake that my friend Tess had mixed three times in search of a husband.

'This is delicious,' he said, and the words were barely out of his mouth before my mother had plonked another thick slab of cake on his plate.

'And what brings you to Thornwood, Mr ... um?'

'It's Krauss, Griffin-Krauss. My mother is Irish actually,' he said.

'Is she really, from Clare?' my mother asked, fascinated.

'No, actually, she was from Sligo,' he said, munching the juicy cake. 'She died when I was very young.'

'Lord have mercy on the poor woman,' my mother said and we all blessed ourselves.

'So, what are you doing here then?' Father asked, earning himself a sharp look from my mother. 'What? I only mean that if he's looking for his relatives, he's landed a bit far south,' he said.

'I shouldn't imagine a scholar would make such a mistake,' my mother said, and as my parents argued the point, Mr Krauss looked at me with an amused shrug.

'A scholar of what, might I ask?' my mother continued, determined to have the full story.

'Anthropology – I began my studies at home in California, but I'm currently in Oxford.'

'Oxford?' my mother repeated, touching her cheek.

Billy took advantage of their conversation to snatch himself a very large piece of Christmas cake.

'In fact, I'm travelling through Ireland as part of my thesis,' he said, leaning forward on the chair. 'I'm a story collector, of sorts.'

'What kind of stories?' I asked.

'Oh, you know, local folklore, interviewing people of the area to see if the fairy faith is still alive.'

The room fell silent then and we all glanced at each other furtively. Mr Krauss, however, was not deterred.

'It was your poet Mr William Butler Yeats who first ignited my interest in the area. He paid a visit to my university in California and spoke so eloquently about the vast knowledge of the otherworld held by the Irish people, in particular. It seemed to me, as an anthropologist, no one had ever made an academic study of the fairy faith and that's why I'm here.'

He took a long gulp of tea after his little speech and let the words settle around our ears.

'You're studying … fairies?' my father said eventually.

'Well, more or less, I suppose I am. I have gathered quite a lot of evidence…' he said, opening his satchel and taking out several large black notebooks.

'Evidence?' my mother asked.

'Well, testimonies really. I've been to all of the Celtic countries now – in fact this is my last stop before I return to Oxford.'

We all shifted uneasily in our seats. My parents instinctively looked in my direction and it would have been obvious to the cat that we were making a poor attempt at subterfuge. My mother is quite a modern woman, being educated in the city. She doesn't bother with superstition and says it is something country folk rely on to make sense of the things they can't understand. That's what made my situation so tricky.

'What are the Celtic countries?' Billy asked, having satiated his sweet tooth enough to join the conversation.

'Ah, well, there's Scotland, Wales, Cornwall in the south of England, the Isle of Man and Brittany in northern France.'

'And you've travelled to these places, in search of fairies?' I said, unable to hold my tongue any longer.

'Well, the aim of my thesis isn't to find fairies as such,

but to find evidence that the belief in the fairy faith still exists among the Celtic people.'

We were all enthralled by him. What kind of a man, a well-educated man at that, would travel all the way from America to learn about *na Daoine Maithe*, The Good People, as we call them? It isn't something that people talk about easily, even amongst our own. As if reading my thoughts, he described his difficulties in procuring these testimonies.

'Some people are happy to discuss their experiences, but many are wary of a foreigner asking questions,' he explained. 'So, in each area I visit, I try to hire a local person to help me with my interviews.'

'Well, isn't that something?' my father said in admiration, as he filled his pipe with tobacco. It always amuses me to see his thick, calloused fingers struggling with the fiddly little pipe. His hands are like two shovels that can carry in enough turf for the whole evening or dig a field of potatoes. He always ends up with more tobacco in his lap than in the pipe. 'And have you found someone to help you here?' he probed.

'Well, I have only just arrived from Sligo, so I haven't found anyone yet. Perhaps you could suggest someone to me?' he said, placing his cup and saucer on the hearth.

'I could do it,' I blurted, catching myself by surprise. I knew my parents would never agree to such a thing, so it was mostly bravado on my part.

'You will do no such thing,' my father blustered, immediately confirming my assumption.

'Thank you, Anna, it's very kind of you to offer,' said Mr

Krauss, 'but I'm afraid I couldn't accept without your parents' blessing.'

'What exactly would be involved in being your assistant?' my mother enquired, stirring her tea and ignoring my father's gaping mouth.

'Oh, just visiting the houses in the village, making introductions and such. The real quality I'm looking for is trust; someone who gets on well with people and inspires confidence in them to share their personal experiences. And then there's the Gaelic, of course, that's something I haven't been able to master, and so I would need someone who can translate.'

My mother looked away, thinking. My father puffed his pipe and I had to sit on my hands so I wouldn't jump up and shout that I was the best person for the job. Pride is a deadly sin, after all.

'No daughter of mine is roaming the countryside with a strange man – no offence, Mr Krauss,' my father said. 'What would the neighbours think?'

'They'd think she was a clever young woman with a good job, Joe Butler,' my mother said. It was no secret that she had high hopes for me, which meant a life beyond the farm. Now that there were more silver hairs than black threading across her head, her hopes had become more assertive.

'Would there be payment?' my father asked.

'Don't sully the debate with talk of money, Joe,' my mother hissed.

'It wouldn't be much, but yes, I will compensate Anna for her time,' Mr Krauss replied.

'Oh, say yes, Mother, I can get my work done here before breakfast, spend the day assisting Mr Krauss and be home in time for supper,' I said.

'And what about your other job, the lace-making?' she said, but I knew the decision had already been made in my favour.

'I can still do my needlework in the evening,' I promised, although I would have promised the moon by then. I had travelled to the Sisters of Mercy in Kilrush when I finished school to learn how to crochet lace and I am able to make a good wage working from home. The Sisters get orders from Dublin and all across England for Irish lace, so there is never any shortage of work.

But life for an eighteen-year-old girl is quite uneventful in Thornwood. An opportunity like this was as rare as hens' teeth and I couldn't let it pass me by, not when it landed on my own doorstep. It was a sign.

'So you'll let me go?' I said, looking from one to the other.

'You'll look after my Anna now? No public houses and no coming home after dark?' my father said, although it was dark at four o'clock these days.

'You have my word, Mr Butler. It's an honour to have your daughter as my assistant and I'm sure she will be instrumental in making my thesis a success,' Mr Krauss said, rising to his feet and shaking all of our hands, even Billy's.

'Would you have any stories yourselves?' he added, buoyed up by the high spirits in the room.

'No, we have no such stories in our family, Mr Krauss,'

my mother said firmly, 'but I'm certain you will find the village of Thornwood fertile ground for your studies.'

He treated us all to more tales of his adventures in Ireland and abroad. It was a marvel to listen to him knitting his words together like a fine piece of lace, all delicate and intricate. I know many people who have not half his brains, but twice his boastfulness. Yet he was so humble, as if being a university scholar was only an afterthought and would count for nothing without the research. Still, my mind began to wander, as the real reason behind my eagerness to help Mr Krauss began to take shape. Maybe I'm being selfish, but it seems as though fate is intervening and I would be a fool not to heed it. Whether by divine intervention (because God knows I prayed for it enough) or pure chance, I believe that Mr Krauss has been sent to our door to help me find Milly.

Chapter Five

27th December 2010

"T was a Yank.'

'What?' Oran asked irritably, not lifting his eyes from the paper to look at his father.

'A Yank that rented the cottage,' Brian Sweeney said, pouring himself a mug of milky tea.

The old kitchen at the back of the house had hardly changed since Oran was a child, and neither had his father's routine. A big mug of tea, two thick slices of toast drowned in butter, and two hard-boiled eggs. The old range hummed away happily with heat and was never allowed to go out.

'I hope you asked him for a deposit this time,' Oran said, regretting the words as soon as they were spoken. He didn't mean to be spiteful, but living under the same roof as his father again had been, at best, trying.

'Well, of course I did, I'm not going to make that mistake

twice, am I?' his father replied, easing himself into his chair at the table with a groan. 'It wasn't a fella though, but a young woman.'

The last statement floated unheard between them, as Brian Sweeney tapped the side of an egg with a spoon. A few moments passed before Oran looked up from the newspaper article he was reading.

'A woman?'

'That's what I said,' Brian replied.

'On her own?'

'Well, unless she was hiding someone in that suitcase of hers, which I suppose is entirely possible these days.'

'God, ye sound like two old farmers!' said Hazel, suddenly appearing in the doorway, still in her pyjamas.

'I am a farmer!' said Brian with gusto.

'That's no excuse, Granddad,' she said, kissing him lightly on the cheek. 'You're being sexist.' This last comment caused a now familiar look to pass between father and son. A look that said they were both out of their depth.

Oran couldn't help thinking how much she resembled her mother in the mornings, that sleepy look in her eyes and her strawberry blond hair rolled into a small bush at the back of her head. Sometimes, he just had to look away and distract himself with other things.

'So, what can I get you for breakfast?' Oran said, getting up and searching through a cupboard above the range for sugary cereals.

'I can make my own, Dad,' came the withering reply.

'Anyway, I wasn't being sexist,' Oran said, sitting back down to his paper. 'It's just strange that someone would travel all that way, with nowhere to stay over Christmas. Man or woman.'

'Maybe she's a Humanist. They don't celebrate Christmas,' Hazel pointed out, while expertly scrambling some eggs for herself on the stove.

'All right, I give up, you win!' he said, frustrated and proud in equal measure.

Gradually, they all became aware of a pervading sour smell in the kitchen and shouted in unison at the little dog asleep in his basket by the back door.

'Aw Max!' The brown and white setter raised his sleepy head and looked about him, mystified as to the cause of the commotion.

'Have you been feeding him tuna again?' Oran accused his father as he rushed to unlock the door. 'You know it gives him … wind!'

Hazel erupted with laughter and the two men shook their heads. Communication between three generations wasn't always easy, but they had their moments.

Sarah had mice. Or rather, Sarah hoped she had mice and not their larger cousins. She woke to the sound of scratching in the eaves and, rather than spend an undignified afternoon searching for further evidence, she decided to head straight for the village shop in search of a solution. Picking up her bag and keys, she saw the diary sitting on the dresser and decided to bring it with her. She had become strangely attached to it, as though it were some sort of talisman.

It was a peculiar feeling, locking the door of the cottage and setting off down an Irish country road in the middle of winter. It was only one or two in the afternoon, but it seemed later as the clouds hung low in the sky and drained the landscape of its colour. It was uncanny how the weather could transform the countryside from a thing of beauty into something to be endured.

A few people were chatting outside the church as Sarah came into the village and they waved at her as if she were one of the locals. She found herself waving back and calling a Christmas greeting to boot. The closed sign on the door of the shop took the wind out of her sails, not least because she had hoped to pick up a bottle of wine along with her mousetrap. Glancing up the road, she could see lights twinkling in the windows of Mr Sweeney's house and before she could change her mind, she knocked on the door.

'Sorry to bother you again,' Sarah began, but before she could continue her planned monologue, Mr Sweeney had invited her inside.

'Oh, well, I won't stay,' she assured him, but he wasn't listening. He was leading her to the kitchen at the back of the house, which emanated a wave of welcome heat. The house was a mixture of old and new; mostly new fittings with old furniture. A battered old table took up the length of one wall, at which was seated a young girl.

'Make the woman a cup of tea, Hazel,' said the man, earning himself a silent but threatening look.

'No, really, I don't—'

'Sit down there now and don't be complicating things

with airs and graces,' he said in a way that seemed welcoming and reproachful all at once.

'I just, well, the thing is, I think I have mice.'

'Well, there's no need to go bragging about it, everyone will want them!' Mr Sweeney replied straight-faced.

'Granddad!' Hazel groaned.

'I'm only coddin' ya. I should have a few spare traps in the drawer here,' he said, getting up to search the largest of them all.

'Sugar and milk?' came a tired voice from the other side of the room.

'Yes, please.'

The girl was tall and fair; like herself at that age. All limbs and attitude.

'I'm Sarah, by the way,' she said, accepting the bright yellow mug of tea.

'This is my granddaughter Hazel,' Mr Sweeney said, coming back to the table with two wooden mousetraps. 'Now don't use cheese, they prefer a bit of chocolate.'

'O-kay,' Sarah replied.

'Here's a bit of Cadbury's, they can't resist that—'

'It's inhumane,' Hazel interrupted. This statement was followed by a heavy silence that Sarah instinctively rushed to fill.

'Actually, I found this diary, too,' she said, taking it out of her bag. Mr Sweeney reached over to have a look at it, but for some reason her fingers wouldn't relax their grasp. He pulled it a second time and dislodged it.

'It looks very old.'

'Well, yeah, it's a hundred years old, actually. I just

thought you might know something about the Butler family.'

Mr Sweeney leafed through the pages rather carelessly and Sarah had to distract herself so she wouldn't grab it back.

'Are you enjoying your Christmas break?' she asked Hazel, blowing on her tea.

'Yeah, it's okay.'

'I don't know what the school system is here, but I'm thinking you must be in high school?'

'Secondary school, I just started in September,' she said, pulling her long legs up under her as she sat at the table.

There didn't seem to be much point continuing in this vein. The girl was naturally uninterested in small talk, so Sarah decided instead to fill them in about her 'meeting' with the donkey.

'Well, I'm glad you think it's funny,' Sarah said, as Hazel sniggered at the hapless city girl. 'I was terrified!'

'Ah, I'll have to tell Christy to keep that animal in at night, he's forever wandering,' Mr Sweeney said. 'What possessed you to walk the highways and byways at that time of night, anyway?'

'Oh, you know, jetlag,' Sarah said vaguely. 'Besides, you forget how dark it gets in the countryside.'

'So how far did you make it, in the dark?' the young girl asked, twirling her long hair between her fingers.

'Not very far. I saw the entrance to some kind of country manor on my way here today, so I definitely didn't make it as far as that.'

'You mean the haunted house?'

Sarah looked to Mr Sweeney for clarification and he obliged.

'Thornwood House. It's a derelict old building now, but it used to be the local lord's house. And you shouldn't be filling people's heads with silly ghost stories,' he said, turning to Hazel.

'Everybody knows, Granddad, Katie Flynn's brother went up there at Halloween with his friends, and he said—'

'I don't care what Katie Flynn's brother did,' he said, cutting her off.

'Right, well, I suppose I should be getting back and leave you two...' Sarah said, draining her mug. 'Thanks for the traps and sorry again for intruding.' She stood hovering over Mr Sweeney's shoulder, waiting for him to hand over the diary.

'It says here the first entry is in 1910.'

'Yes, and a mysterious American has arrived at the cottage, Harold something-Krauss. I think she likes him, or liked him,' Sarah said, feeling as though she were betraying Anna's secrets.

'Sounds like a bit of a romance novel,' he scoffed. 'Isn't it a funny coincidence all the same?'

'What is?'

'Well, I'm not saying you're mysterious, but you're an American staying at the cottage, exactly one hundred years later!'

Sarah felt like a complete idiot that she hadn't already drawn the same comparison. Self-awareness continued to elude her and the obvious still presented itself like a surprise. Mr Sweeney finally handed the book back, restoring her sense of calm.

'Hey, it's snowing!' Hazel squealed with joy, momentarily revealing the childlike spirit still alive within her. 'I'll walk you as far as the church,' she said, pulling on her coat and gloves.

As they strolled down the street with a light snow shower dancing about them, Hazel proceeded to give Sarah the grand tour of Thornwood.

'And that's the newsagents,' she said, completing her description of a small street that consisted of a pub, a post office and a church. 'So, what made you want to come here, anyway?' she asked directly, sticking her tongue out to catch the snowflakes as they fell.

Sarah wasn't sure how to explain her reasons to a teenage girl. She wasn't sure she could explain them to herself. 'Oh you know, sometimes you just have to get away.'

'To find yourself?' Hazel asked precociously.

'Something like that, yeah.' It was Hazel's knowing look that made her smile. At that age, you felt as though you knew it all, the depths of life's despair and its ecstasy. When really it was all just like a movie playing out before your eyes. You couldn't possibly understand how scary it was to be a grown-up.

'You'd love Boston, we get a lot of snow over there – up to your knees sometimes.'

'Oh, cool! It doesn't last very long here, you know, because of the jet stream. So, are you into paranormal stuff?'

Hazel asked, as though it were the most obvious segue in their conversation.

'Um, I'm not sure. I suppose I believe that there's more to this life than just "here today, gone tomorrow".'

'Hmmm. Do you believe in the afterlife?'

'Wow, Hazel, you're straight to the point!'

The girl just shrugged her shoulders, as though she couldn't see the point in being otherwise.

'I'd like to believe there's something out there, some meaning. But wanting to believe and actually believing are two different things.'

'I suppose. My father thinks the whole supernatural thing is a load of old rubbish,' she said, digging her hands into her pockets.

'Well, enough people believed in that fairy tree to move the motorway, right? I read about it in the paper.'

'Hmm.' She seemed quite pleased with Sarah's argument.

'But don't worry,' Sarah said, raising her hands in submission, 'I'm not here looking for leprechauns!'

They had reached the church and Hazel turned for home.

'Maybe I could pop over and visit sometime?' she asked out of the blue.

'I … I'd love that,' said Sarah. 'Anytime you like.'

By the time Sarah got back to the cottage, the snow had already been relegated to the grassy verges, while the road was slick and wet. She kicked off her shoes at the door and set about lighting a fire in the stove. The sky was turning a dark shade of lavender and it felt like the night was coming on again, even though it was only four o'clock in the afternoon. She boiled the kettle and filled a hot water bottle and made a small cup of tea to warm her. It was the perfect time to sit, reflect and 'be with her pain' as the therapist had said. But all she wanted to do was wrap herself in a woolly blanket, open Anna's diary and lose herself in the life of a girl who lived here a century before.

Chapter Six

Anna's Diary

2nd January 1911

'Now, Anna, you don't need me to tell you that we expect you to be on your best behaviour around Mr Krauss,' my mother said, choosing to tell me anyway. I sat in front of the warm fire as she brushed my damp hair. I had spent all evening scrubbing and cleaning and setting out my best outfit. The men were out helping the Lenihans, who had a cow calving.

'Don't think I agreed to this lightly; there are many who would say 'tisn't proper. But I know my daughter and I've made my own enquiries about Mr Krauss. We've received a letter of good character from Doctor Douglas Hyde, a respectable Roscommon man and President of the Gaelic League. His word is good enough for me and your father has satisfied himself that this young man's intentions are honourable.'

'Mother, I'm not marrying the man!' I protested, and got a hard tug on my hair in return.

'You're a smart girl, Anna, most of the time,' she said sternly, 'so I want you to make the most of this opportunity.'

'Sure, I'll only be chatting to our neighbours – the same as what I do every day,' I said.

'It's not them I'm talking about. Mr Krauss is a very intelligent man and you could learn a lot from him. You never know what will come out of it,' she said, combing my hair and humming an old tune to herself.

I wasn't sure I liked the sound of that. It sounded as though she wanted me to move beyond Thornwood; to go out into the big bad world. I felt like a fledgling being nudged by its mother to fly, but I wasn't so sure I wanted to or even knew how.

Thornwood is my kingdom and our cottage my castle. The story of my childhood is etched all over this familiar landscape. Living this close to nature, I feel as though I am part of it; as much as the river flowing through it or the ever-changing clouds passing overhead. We alter together with each season, transforming, yet always staying true to our nature. I can read the weather coming in across the hills like I can read my own moods. Leaving Thornwood would be like leaving a part of myself.

We began our research on New Year's Day. Mr Krauss is only to be staying for a few weeks, so there was no time to lose. Of course I rose before dawn to milk Betsy and let the geese out, not forgetting to make a fresh cake of soda bread with extra fruit. That is the beauty of Christmas: there are always extra supplies for anyone with a sweet tooth. There was a hard frost on the ground, so I wore two pairs of woollen socks inside my boots and the gloves my aunt had sent me from Dublin. I had knitted a warm and fashionable hat from dark green wool, the colour of moss by a lakeside. As I sat at the kitchen table, having a quiet cup of tea before the rest of the household stirred, I tried to calm the butterflies that flitted around my stomach. Naturally, I was excited about my new position as Mr Krauss's assistant, but it was the chance of seeing Milly that really made my heart leap like it had the legs of a frog. I spoke not a word of my hopes to Mother or Father – it wouldn't do to go dragging up the past again.

When the knock came on the door, I started, then composed myself with a deep breath and rose to open the door.

'I hope I'm not too early,' Mr Krauss said, in that broad, expressive accent of his.

'Of course not, Mr Krauss, I've been up for hours,' I said brightly, shutting the door behind me and taking my mother's bicycle from the side of the house. It was gleaming like new.

'Christmas present?' he said, tilting his head toward the bike.

'Oh no, it's my mother's, but she doesn't use it much. She doesn't know how to ride it,' I replied.

'I see, and is she learning now?' he asked.

'No, she just likes to walk with it to the shops,' I said and we both smiled awkwardly.

Our dog, Jet, who has become quite lackadaisical in his duties of late, took to barking at us as we walked out the lane.

'It's no good barking at a stranger when he's on his way out, Jet,' I called back at him and he wagged his tail in response. He is a black mass of wiry hair and, despite his shortcomings around the farm, is a treasured member of the family.

'So, what shall we call each other?' he asked. 'Mr Krauss makes me think my father is standing behind me, and I know Mr Griffin-Krauss is a mouthful... So how about Harold?'

'I'm not sure it'd be proper. You are older than me, after all,' I said, hopping on the bike.

'Now you're making me feel like an old man when I'm only twenty-four,' he said good-naturedly.

'Oh, I thought you were older – or rather, what I mean is...'

'That's settled, then. Anna and Harold it is,' he said, pedalling his own bicycle happily along the road to the village.

It was a dull day, heavy with mist and dew that made the spiderwebs look like diamond necklaces. We chatted sporadically on our journey, avoiding any awkwardness by continually referring to the weather. Mr Krauss, I mean Harold, asked lots of questions about the general history of the area. I thought it would be wise to take him into the village first and introduce him to the important people in the community, like Nelly O'Halloran from the post office, Father Peter the priest, and the schoolmaster Mr Finnegan. However, it was Thornwood House that caught his attention before we even reached the village and he brought his bike to a halt with a loud squeak of the brakes.

'Now I met someone on the train here who mentioned this place to me,' he said, his eyes bright and eager to uncover some new tale, or an old one at that. 'Was there a fairy fort here?'

'No, not a fort, but a tree. It's quite sad actually,' I began, wiping my nose with a handkerchief. 'My mother never told me the story outright, but I overheard her discussing it with our neighbour Gracie. Adults never think their children are listening when they whisper, but that's the exact time we are listening!' I said, laughing at the memory.

'Looks like I chose my assistant well,' Harold said, urging me to go on.

'Lady Hawley took ill after her children were born and well, they had to keep her away from them. I'm not certain why, but there are two versions of the story.'

'There often are.' Harold nodded sagely.

'Well, there are those that say she took a jump from the top window, there', I said pointing. 'No one will walk past here on Halloween night, for fear they will see her ghost at the window.'

'She killed herself?'

I crossed myself instinctively, neither confirming nor denying what he had said.

'There is another story, that which the locals believe,' I continued, lowering my voice to a whisper, although we were quite alone. 'They say that when Lord Hawley came to Thornwood, he cut down an ancient hawthorn tree that grew on the grounds. People said the family was cursed after that, although you wouldn't think it to look at them now. They are the wealthiest landowners for miles, with the best of everything.'

'So, people think that Lady Hawley's death was some kind of revenge by the fairies?' Harold said, taking a notebook out of his satchel and licking the end of his pencil. He was still standing with his bicycle balanced between his legs and it struck me that he could probably take notes standing on one leg whilst balancing on a ball, such was his focus.

'Well, I can't say for sure what happened, but the seeress foretold that no one would ever be happy living in that house,' I said, telling the story as truthfully as I could.

'The seeress?' he asked, and I cursed myself for mentioning her. It was too soon to go telling him about her. Just then, I heard the clip-clopping of a horse trotting down the avenue towards us and as I held my hand above my eyes to block the glare of the sun breaking through the clouds, I could see the outline of George Hawley, Lord Hawley's son. I flushed instantly, ashamed to be gossiping about the death of his poor mother. I hadn't expected to see any of the occupants stirring so early in the morning, as their annual New Year's Eve party often runs into the following day. Sure enough, Master George looked flushed and wild-eyed, as though he hadn't slept a wink.

'Can I help you?' he said, talking down to us from atop his mare. His dark blond hair fell into his eyes in the most agreeable way and his handling of the horse gave him a powerful air of authority. He was a dazzling spectacle and I found it almost impossible to meet his gaze. Eventually, I found my voice, although it was somewhat hoarse.

'Master Hawley, begging your pardon, but I was just showing Mr Krauss around the village,' I said rather shakily.

'Pleased to make your acquaintance,' Harold said, offering his hand to Master Hawley.

'Likewise, Mr Krauss. What brings you to our little village?' he asked, as the horse swished her tail and nibbled at the hedgerow.

'He's making an anthropological study,' I butted in, barely getting my tongue around the syllables. Both men looked at me, surprised by my outspokenness, but I couldn't have Master Hawley thinking we were searching for fairies. He would lose all respect for Harold before he had even begun. Although it was his opinion of me that concerned me the most.

'You – I've seen you before. Emma, isn't it?' Master Hawley asked, pointing his whip at me.

It was near enough to my name that I almost didn't want to correct him. The mere fact that he had recognised me made me blush, I'm embarrassed to admit.

'It's Anna,' Harold replied on my behalf. 'Miss Butler has kindly agreed to be my assistant on my anthropological study of the area,' he said, smiling at me with a look that gave me great reassurance.

'Has she now,' Master Hawley said, narrowing his gaze. 'Well, I hope she will be of use to you,' he added, while a servant opened the gates and he kicked the mare to walk on. 'We shall cross paths again, no doubt,' he called behind him and saluted us without turning around.

Harold mumbled something under his breath and I didn't ask him to repeat himself.

We cycled on towards the town in silence, past the church and over the little bridge, with the brown river water gushing below. I was lost in my thoughts of last summer and the delightful day we spent at Thornwood.

Every May, when the bridal hedges of whitethorn bloom, we celebrate a great Thornwood tradition. The Hawley family open their grounds to the public on May Day for all kinds of sports on the river and merriment on the land. The well-to-do with their sunshades and pretty dresses mix with the local villagers for a day of fun and gaiety. Tents appear all along the embankment with sweet vendors selling sugar sticks and sweet pipes, fruit and drinks, and music echoing all around.

There is dancing and song and all kinds of games to test your strength and agility, like throwing rings and the greasy pole. The rowing club from Thornwood won the senior eights last year and my brother Paddy was part of the crew. My friend Tess almost screamed herself hoarse shouting for Paddy. Everyone knew she had a soft spot for him, but it wasn't clear if her feelings were reciprocated. Paddy is cute like that. But how will anyone ever know that you have a fancy for them if you don't tell them, or at least give them a sign? When George Hawley's boat moored up, I took a fit of daring and tossed my handkerchief towards him. Despite his disappointment at losing to the local team, he picked it up and as he clutched it in his large hand, he gave me a great big smile and a wink for good measure. It may not have meant so much to him, but it was everything to me.

'Your father insisted, no public houses,' Harold said, as I leaned my bike against O'Malley's pub. We had spent the morning meeting and greeting at the post office and the grocers, and while everyone was cordial and took Harold's inquiries seriously, we had yet to meet a representative of the male species. Other than George, that is, but he didn't count, as he couldn't possibly have had any stories that would interest Harold. At this hour, most of the farmers were at the creamery or busy on the land. I felt as though it was my job to show Thornwood village and its people in their best light, but catching the best talkers at the right time would take far better planning on my part. There is a forge at the end of the village where we have new shoes made for the donkey and Aengus, our horse, as well as iron bands for the timber wheels on the cart. But the blacksmith is both deaf and mute and while most requests can be made using sign language, I wasn't sure if he was the best candidate to get things going. There was one sure spot where the chattiest of all our residents could be found.

'If you want to meet the schoolmaster, the doctor or the priest, O'Malley's is the only place to do it,' I said plainly. 'That's where they have their dinner, washed down with a pint of porter.'

'Well, I shall have to speak with them alone then,' he said, leaning his bike beside mine. 'Not to worry,' he added, seeing the disappointment on my face, 'the public house is rarely the place for sharing fairy stories. You won't miss a thing.'

It wasn't much of a start. Our first proper meeting and I couldn't join in. I listened from the doorway and heard Doctor Lynch introduce himself and the master. They were both falling over themselves to flatter the new visitor and were suitably impressed on hearing that Harold had endeared himself to the founder of the Gaelic League, Douglas Hyde. The master Finnegan of course was sweet-talked by the notion that W. B. Yeats had inspired Harold's interest in the fairy world. However, they both put a distance between themselves and the 'superstitions' Harold was studying. I could tell by their tone they were humouring him; an American, and a scholar at that, collecting fairy stories. He might as well have been collecting dandelions for all the importance they gave it.

Perhaps Harold was right; I wasn't missing much. I wandered up towards the church, where a group of women were chatting. I saw my good friend Tess with her mother and decided to share my news with her.

Tess Fox and I have known each other since we were babes, and we went to Kilrush together to learn the lace-making. We are fortunate; most girls our age have to leave home to find work, or enter service. But with the demand for Irish lace being what it is, we can make a tidy sum working at home. I could hardly wait to tell her about our American visitor and my new, if somewhat temporarily elevated, position.

'And why did he pick you?' she said, in a tone that I tried not to interpret as jealousy.

'It happened by chance really,' I admitted truthfully. 'His bike got a puncture outside our house and Father helped him to repair it. The boys were out with the Mummers, so I just chanced my arm and Mother agreed.'

'Hmm, I see,' she said, begrudgingly. 'I suppose you always had a touch of the second sight anyway.'

'Shhh! I told you that in confidence, Tess. Besides it was only the one time,' I said, looking all around me in case anyone had heard. It was all so long ago now; I was beginning to doubt whether it had actually happened. My memories of that time seem to play hide-and-seek with me and remain always slightly beyond my reach.

'Well, surely you're going to tell the Yank?' she said, bringing my thoughts back to the present.

'Tell him what?'

'About Milly, of course.' She said this under her breath. This is how everyone says her name now, like a whisper. As though saying it out loud might bring bad luck. But most people don't say it at all.

'I … I will, in my own time.'

'Is he a looker?' she asked in a whisper, so her mother and her pals wouldn't hear.

'Tess!' I said, smacking her on the arm. But this only seemed to encourage her.

'You are keen on him, aren't you?'

'I am not! He's far too old for one thing,' I said, though that wasn't entirely true. I admire him, more than anything, but I know he doesn't make my skin tingle or my breath quicken. Not like Master Hawley. But I couldn't tell Tess that. There would be no end of torment.

'We'll be visiting with ye tonight,' she said, having already lost interest in my petty concerns. Tess has altered significantly in her ways since her body began to bloom. Her big bosoms seem to have blossomed out of nowhere and she has become quite aware that she could have her pick of the boys. 'Will the Yank be there?' she asked, as if it didn't matter to her one way or the other.

'I don't think so,' I replied honestly. I wasn't even sure where he was staying or whether he would want to spend the evening with us. In our village, there is no such thing as an invitation; people flit freely from neighbour to neighbour like swallows in the summertime. Most evenings, we make our way through the fields or across the bog to each other's houses to play cards or music and sometimes even to dance.

'Oh, look, is that him there? Talking to Miss Hawley?' Tess pointed over my shoulder towards O'Malley's. Sure enough, Harold had stepped outside with Doctor Lynch, who was introducing him to Olivia Hawley – a vision in fur. She has piercing blue eyes like her twin brother and a laugh that could shatter glass. I stood frozen to the spot, unable to decide whether I should go and join them or stay at a distance, watching from the outside.

'Did you hear there was a big ruckus up at Thornwood House last night? One of the maids – I think she's from Cork – was found wandering around the grounds half naked.'

'You're having me on?' I said, stunned.

'No, I am not. My aunt's cousin had it this morning from the gardener that works up there. Apparently, she was making all sorts of accusations against Master George, saying that he was responsible for her state of undress.'

'Never! Master George is a gentleman.'

'Well, the story is that she must have got herself pregnant and spied a golden opportunity to earn herself some money by blaming Master George.'

'That's terrible!' I exclaimed. 'Are you sure it's true?'

'As true as I'm standing here,' Tess said firmly.

I couldn't fathom it. Why would a young woman who worked for the family want to ruin the Hawleys' reputation as well as her own? It didn't make any sense.

'You simply must come to the house for luncheon on Sunday,' I could hear Miss Olivia say, in her sing-song voice that travelled across the street. Thornwood House, unlike the rest of the village, required an invitation to enter.

Harold turned his head and spotted me, waiting dutifully outside the church. He waved at me to come and join him and I can honestly say, I felt a strong rush of sinful pride as I strolled over to him. All the ladies from the village watched me and even Olivia Hawley was forced to acknowledge my existence for once.

'Miss Hawley, may I introduce Anna Butler, my assistant. She's helping me with my research while I'm in Thornwood,' Harold said, completely ignoring the social structure of our village.

'Miss Butler,' Olivia nodded and it was all I could do not to curtsy in the face of her grandeur. Instead, I just bobbed my head in greeting.

'We would love to lunch with you on Sunday,' Harold said, catching us both by surprise.

'We?' she echoed.

'Yes, Miss Butler and I.'

But Miss Olivia didn't miss a beat.

'No matter if you cannot attend, Miss Butler. I'm sure you have previous engagements.'

It was a very clear warning shot. They are of a different class and it is above my station to attend the big house for lunch or any other kind of meal.

'On the contrary, I will be quite free on Sunday,' I replied, in my haughtiest accent.

'Very well, we'll see you both then,' she said, keeping her composure and offering her hand to Harold.

Chapter Seven

There are two roads out of the village and if you cycle far enough down either one, you end up in the same place. We chose the longer route, but not before we had made our first proper stop at Cathal O'Shaughnessy's cottage. The smoke curled lazily from the chimney above a neglected thatch roof. At ninety-eight, Cathal is the oldest man in the village and is, in my humble opinion, the ideal candidate to begin Mr Krauss's studies. Not only because there was a greater chance of him passing away before we got around to seeing him, but also because he has been keeping a watchful eye over Thornwood for longer than anyone else.

We had spent the previous half hour outside the church, going over Harold's meticulous method for the gathering of evidence. He took out some of the notebooks he had used while researching the areas around Benbulben in Sligo with the poet W. B. Yeats. He is certainly one for detail. Every eyewitness account was noted with careful accuracy and even the physical appearance of each person has not escaped his observant eye.

'Above all, our witnesses must be of good character. I will not use their evidence unless they can be vouched for as reliable sources.'

That rules out Maggie Walsh, I thought to myself, the seeress who lived behind *Cnoc na Sí*. Besides, I have been warned by my mother on more than one occasion to keep well away from the woman.

'Now, as you can see, I have divided my evidence into three main classifications: Fairy Abductions; Changelings; and Appearances of Fairies. Then I have sub-divided these into, one, 'Legendary stories' two, 'First-hand accounts'; and three, 'Second-hand accounts'.

'That sounds very... sophisticated,' I said, marvelling at how he was taking something so magical and unseen and transforming it into an academic study.

'I suppose I am approaching this with a scientist's brain,' he confessed, as though it was something to apologise for. 'But my heart is in the right place,' he said, smiling at me.

I led the way to Cathal O'Shaughnessy's back door. I leaned in over the half door and called out to alert him of our presence. When I heard no greeting in return, I reached in and lifted the latch. He was there all right, sat on a *súgán* in the chimney corner, smoking a pipe with his gaze lost in the glow of the peat, dreaming of days gone by. Harold, God bless him, with his city manners still intact, was reluctant to disturb the old man.

'We can't just walk in, can we?' he blustered.

'Of course we can, I come with Mother once a week to help tidy the house and bring him provisions,' I said.

Harold was still standing by the entrance, with a look of admiration on his face.

'That's very generous of you. Are you related to this man?'

'No, but sure, he's our neighbour and he's old.' I really didn't see why I needed to explain the obvious to Harold, but he is an outsider after all and perhaps people behave differently in California. I set about thickly buttering bread and laying it on a plate before setting a kettle of water over the fire for our tea. It wasn't long before Cathal stirred from his trance, and welcomed us with a great big smile, revealing a mouth empty of teeth. His face was well used, like an old leather shoe that had seen many roads.

'*Cé hé sin?*' Cathal asked for the umpteenth time at a volume that would wake the dead. He was dressed in his uniform of brown trousers, waistcoat and cap, none of which have seen the inside of a washtub for a long time. Poor Harold, in comparison, looked the picture of sartorial elegance, despite being half-choked by the peat smoke billowing out of the fireplace. His eyes were watering and turning red as he blinked hard. I opened the small window, but as there was no wind to draw the smoke out, it hardly made a difference.

'He's an American, Cathal; he's come to talk about *na Daoine Maithe*', I explained, sitting back at the table. We conversed entirely *as Gaeilge*, for Cathal speaks only Irish.

'Oh well, tell him –' he paused to take a great big slurp of tea from his cup '– that no one can introduce you to

83

The Good People. They'll either make themselves known to you or they won't. You can spend all night shivering your bones up on Cnoc na Sí and never see a single thing other than your own breath. Or you might be walking along the road, minding your own business, when they'll jump into your path causing all sorts of mischief. It's up to them.'

'And have you ever seen them yourself, Mr O'Shaughnessy?' Harold asked after taking some notes.

'Indeed I did, when I was a young buck. The time is getting short for such things now. You won't see them now like you did when I was a boy.'

I relayed this information with no small measure of smugness. I was already proving my worth as a guide and feeling very satisfied with Cathal's eagerness to share his time-worn memories.

'And what did they look like?' I translated.

'Oh, sure, can't they take any shape they like, the little feckers?' Cathal replied with a hoot. 'They can be as pretty as you please, all long and slender with big eyes and blooms in their hair to draw you in. That's when they want something from you. But if you ask me, their true nature is very different. They're not like us; I can tell you that for nothing. They don't think like us, nor do they feel the way we do. It could be why they're so drawn to the human world, interfering and trying to capture what they cannot have. Don't go messing with them fairy folk, tell him that now, Annie!'

I did as he bade me, but his warnings had no effect on Harold. He simply noted down the words I relayed to him and asked if Cathal had any other experiences, or stories he might have heard about the fairies.

'There used to be a house on the other side of the village,' Cathal began, 'where the land turns barren and stony. The man that lived there had a sick child, but of what complaint I cannot now remember, nor is it of any importance,' he said, spitting a gob-full into the fire. 'One of the gables of the house was built partly over a fort or rath, as you may call it. It was said to be haunted by the fairies, and considered dangerous and unlucky to pass.'

I began to explain to Harold what a fairy fort looks like: a mound with large stones creating a circle. We were always forbidden to enter such places as children and have never questioned why doing so would be foolish in the extreme. Harold simply held up his notebook and showed me a drawing he had sketched roughly with his pencil; the exact shape of a fairy ring. I nodded at him, realising that he must have heard all about the fairy forts in his research, and returned my attention to Cathal.

'At all events, the season was midsummer; and one evening about dusk, during the illness of the child, the noise of a handsaw was heard upon the fort. This was considered rather strange, and, after a little time, a few of the locals assembled and went to see who it could be that was sawing in such a place, or what they could be sawing at so late an hour. On going to examine, however, they could discover no trace of either saw or sawyer. In fact, with the exception of themselves, there was no one, either natural or supernatural, visible. They then returned to the house, and had scarcely sat down, when it was heard again within ten yards of them. Another examination of the premises took place, but with equal success. On the third occasion, they heard the sawing, to which was now added hammering and the driving of nails within the fort. The man's neighbour, being a brave soul, went down into the hollow to investigate and with a heavy heart, he solved the enigma.

"''Tis the fairies," said he. "I see them, and busy crathurs they are."

'"But what are they sawing?" asked the man.

'"They are makin' a child's coffin," he replied; "they already have their body, an' they're now nailin' the lid together."

'Well, the man near fainted, but what strength he had left in his legs, he ran back to the house to check on the wee child.'

Before translating the story for Harold, I couldn't help myself and asked the old man if the coffin was for the sick child.

'The child died that very night. The man left the house then and it has since crumbled back into the earth. It should never have been built so close to the fort,' he said, shaking his head ruefully. 'It could only end in misfortune.'

I tried to conceal my own disquiet while retelling the story to Harold in English, but I'm not sure I managed to do a great job of that. I could hear the trembling in my voice and on more than one occasion he asked me to speak up, for my voice had fallen to a whisper. I couldn't believe that all this time, while my mother and I have cleaned and conversed with Cathal over the years, he had never shared his eerie tale. Then again, we are all bound by an unspoken rule not to mention these things, as if more misfortune will be heaped upon us. I realised then that this would be the consequence of Harold's visit to our village: he was going to ask the questions that no one else would. Who knows what knowledge the people of Thornwood quietly hold inside their hearts?

Once our tea was supped and our bellies satisfied, we took our leave of Cathal and set off down the road again on our bicycles. My thoughts were still with the supernatural carpenter making the child's coffin and I hardly noticed Johnny Kilbride cutting across the field with a basket of turf on his back.

'Who's that?' Harold asked, almost throwing me off the bike with fright.

'Who?' I screeched, trying to drag my thoughts back into the present.

'That man over there with the cap.'

'Oh, that's Johnny Kilbride. He's not a local but he does some labouring on any of the farms that might need him.' I was already dismissing him as an outsider, but as I would learn, Harold wasn't one for boundaries.

'Perhaps he might have a story for us?'

We left our bicycles on the verge and waited for Johnny to make his unhurried way over to us. He was a lanky fella and always looked in need of a good feed. Once I had made the introductions and Johnny had ensconced himself against the old stone wall, he began to tell his tale in Irish. I know he has perfect English, but he said that when it comes to The Good People, he prefers to tell his tale in his native tongue.

'When I was a young man, I was cutting turf back the road with my father. It was getting late in the evening and as the sky turned a rosy colour, I thought I could hear music. I asked my father if he could hear anything, but he couldn't and so we kept on cutting. Then, from out of nowhere, a very tall man dressed in fine clothes approached us and said, "You have finished cutting turf for the evening. Go home now and don't turn back." My father and I turned to each other and when we looked back, the man's face had changed. His teeth had become sharp and his features wizened, as though with age. He was nearly a foot shorter and it was then I understood that he was ageing before our very eyes; his hair was falling out and everything. Well, I can tell you, Anna, we dropped our spades and ran like the clappers from him, never looking back.'

I translated the story for Harold who noted it down carefully. I almost felt like adding a little bit onto it, for the story had ended so abruptly.

'Did anything else happen?' I asked, impudently. But Johnny just gave a faraway look and he kept his *whisht* while Harold took his notes. I realised then that Harold must have become accustomed to hearing these strange half-stories that didn't really prove anything, one way or the other. But perhaps proof wasn't what he was after.

Then out of nowhere (or perhaps to give the Yank his money's worth) Johnny saw fit to impart another fairy encounter he had.

'Well, there was that strange woman who told me my mother would die,' he said, unsure if this would be of interest.

'Perfect!' I replied, a little too enthusiastically. 'And sorry for your loss, Johnny,' I added a little more solemnly.

'Oh, I was in my late twenties, I'd say,' he began, rubbing his chin. 'I was fishing for trout in the river alone, with me trousers rolled up and the cool water trickling over me feet, when I heard a whistle. I looked around and saw one of the gentry standing behind me. Well, I clean fell over in the water and got soaked up to me oxters with fright! She was a vision, with golden hair all the way down to her … well, down her back. She beckoned me to sit beside her for she had something to tell me. "Your mother will die in twelve months – do not let her die un-anointed." It was only as she began to explain that I should call the priest and make the arrangements that I realised her lips were not moving. And yet, I could hear her voice, like a soft whisper in my head. Anyway, my mother died, exactly when she said she would, and we were all so obliged to the gentry that we had the preparations made.'

'Well, this is really something,' Harold said, noting it down as I translated. In my opinion, Johnny wasn't much of a storyteller and, as he went on his way, I couldn't help but wonder if Harold felt short-changed in coming to Thornwood.

'We didn't get as many stories as I'd hoped,' I said, like a fisherman disappointed with his catch.

'Oh, it's not the quantity that matters Anna; I have two first-hand accounts of fairy sightings and a second-hand account. I would say that is an excellent return for our first day's work. It shows that the fairy faith is alive and well all along the western coast of Ireland. What's more, all of these short snippets will back up the previous accounts I have already taken. No, I am quite satisfied with our findings,' he said, beaming with satisfaction.

As Harold insisted on walking me home (we had given up on cycling at that stage as there was no rush on us) I thought it only right to be equally concerned about his welfare.

'Where are you staying, if you don't mind my asking?' I said.

'I've arranged to stay at the lodge in the next village,' he said, assuring me that once he fortified himself with a bite of food, he would be equal to the journey.

We passed by Doherty's house, Fox's and O'Conghaile's, and finally turned the corner at Gallagher's where my own house came into view.

'Look!' he cried. 'A murmuration over your house.'

I looked at the house, terrified of what sight I would see, but there was only the nightly dance of the starlings, swooping and soaring their shifting shapes before the setting sun.

'Do you mean the birds?' I asked, and when he confirmed the answer, I had to ask him to write this strange new word down for me. 'You have a name for everything.'

'It doesn't make it any more magnificent,' he replied. 'As Shakespeare said, "A rose by any other name would smell as sweet".'

'*Romeo and Juliet*,' I said, instantly recognising the lines from my favourite play.

'Did you learn that at school?' he asked, as we turned down the lane for home.

'We did in our hats!' I laughed. ''Twas my mother who read it to me,' I said, with no small amount of pride. Anything that was lacking in our country school education, my mother made up for. Joe Butler isn't much for books, but allows my mother this little indulgence only after our work on the farm is finished for the day. He believes in the poetry of the plough and the soil, the sun and the rain. But my mother would argue that to lose one's intellect is akin to letting seeds wither and die in the dark ground, and she routinely wins the argument.

Chapter Eight

28th December 2010

S arah woke as the sky filled with the vivid red strokes of a winter sunrise, the book lying open on her lap. A few moments passed before she realised she had slept right through the night. She felt well rested and altogether ravenous. In fact, for the first time since she'd arrived, she really felt as though she were on vacation. She snuggled back under the warmth of the quilt, but it wasn't long before she was feeling guilty about Jack and wondering if he was doing okay. It had taken about a year to realise that the relationship was over, and even then they were bound together by work and the lack of a decree nisi. She had no appetite for divorce; after all, they had become good friends and neither of them wanted to cause any more trauma than they had already suffered.

She knew she couldn't put off calling her parents for much longer. Meghan would have given them her jaundiced summary of the situation – Sarah got drunk and flew to Ireland. Sarah couldn't argue with the facts, but facts only tell part of the story when taken out of context. Her parents were very fond of Jack and thought she had landed on her feet when she met a New York gallery owner. There seemed to be a shared perception that she was punching above her weight, which gave her a misplaced sense of achievement and a suitcase full of insecurities. It soon became clear that Jack was the type of person who fell in love too easily, but recovered just as quickly. It left her feeling a little disoriented – while she was still enjoying the fall, he had already moved on to the next stage. He was making all the right noises, but everything felt at a distance, as though he was keeping her at arm's length. Or else he just didn't love her anymore. She looked back on those days now, when all she had to fret about was losing the spark, and felt ridiculously foolish. She had still been naïve enough to believe that misfortune happened to other people.

The temperature in the cottage had risen slightly since she'd moved in, so there wasn't such a shock to the system when she got out of bed and pulled her chunky woollen cardigan around her. Walking out into the living area, she smiled smugly to herself, still smitten with the cottage. Then she remembered the mice and forced herself to check the traps she had set in the tiny attic space above the mezzanine. Shutting one eye, she shone the flashlight into the attic and saw that the trap was still empty. Not only that, but the chocolate had vanished, too. No matter how long she stared at the empty trap, Sarah couldn't work out what had happened, but resolved to reset them.

Realising that there was nothing much to eat in the house (apart from the chocolate that the mice seemed to be enjoying with impunity), she figured it was time to venture outside. Among the last few things she had taken from the apartment in New York were her sketchpads and pencils. She hadn't sketched in a long time, but being here, it felt like the perfect opportunity. Sarah wasn't much of a photographer, but whenever she visited a new place, she liked to capture it on the page. She stuffed the materials into her bag, put on her walking boots and coat and started off down the road.

The air was still and quiet, save for the tiny birds that seemed to live in the hedgerows alongside the narrow road. They whistled and swooped and then disappeared back into the bushes, as though checking out their new neighbour. The land was so green, just like the picture postcards of Ireland on sale in the gift shop at Newark Airport. The river gurgled past her and as she turned at the bend in the road, she spotted a rather grand entrance to the woods, with two large stone pillars either side of a dirt track. They must have held a gate at some point, Sarah thought. The ground was a carpet of indistinguishable leaves in various stages of decay. It was soft and sticky underfoot, cushioning the sound of her footsteps. It felt as though she could disappear into the woods, without a trace. The tranquillity of the forest always drew her in. She would take her sketchpad and a collection of pencils and begin the almost hypnotic task of rendering the intricate lines on a piece of bark. There was something spiritual about trees that seemed to bring about an inner calm.

Looking skywards, the taller limbs criss-crossed overhead to create a wonderfully natural canopy as she walked further and further uphill and deeper into the woods. She recognised many ash, beech and oak trees. Everywhere she looked was full of inspiration for her sketchpad. Stumbling into a grove of hazel trees, she noticed a bed of snowdrops nodding their little heads in the breeze. Thinking how pretty they would look in a vase in the cottage, she bent down to pick a few and was so distracted by the task that she didn't notice the man in a khaki uniform coming towards her. It was only when his dog began to bark that she looked up.

'Oh, hi there,' she called, startled by their presence. Without showing it, she suddenly felt quite vulnerable, all alone with a stranger in the woods. Any fairy tale worth its salt would have warned against it.

'Max, heel!' the man commanded and the dog obeyed with a practised flourish. He was a small dog, white with brown spots, who was highly alert and looked to Sarah as though he should be searching for truffles.

'What are you doing?' he asked, pointing to the flowers in Sarah's hand.

'I'm, eh … sorry, who are you?'

'I'm the conservation officer here in East Clare,' he replied with an authority that his height and build affirmed.

'Oh, right, well, I was just picking some flowers, officer.' She said the last bit in mock flirtation, thinking that he would see the funny side. He did not.

'I'd rather you didn't.' He spoke as though the words were being choked out of him.

'Are they a protected species or something?' she asked sincerely, but she could see by his face that he took her sincerity for mockery. 'It's just that I'm not from around here. I'm on vacation, from the States.'

'I'd never have guessed,' he said, under his breath.

His eyes, an unusual mix of green and brown, reflected the scattering of light through the canopy and held such an intense look that it was hard to keep eye contact. His hair was shaved close to his head and the stubble on his jawline gave him a rugged appeal. With the uniform, he almost looked like someone from the military, but it was the yappy dog that blew his cover. Only a softie could put up with a dog like that and Sarah knew it.

'Well, the damage is done now,' she said, shrugging. 'But I won't pick any more snowdrops, if that helps?'

'Just not *these* snowdrops.'

They both stood awkwardly, looking at Max the dog for rescue. Right on cue, he gave a loud bark then sat back, looking quite pleased with himself.

'Look, I didn't mean … I must sound like—' he began, but his mobile phone rang and he said he had to take it. Sarah swapped the snowdrops from one hand to the other, wishing she could magic them back into the ground. She could hear him discussing the intricacies of a Land Rover's engine and saw her chance to escape the situation. He seemed so distracted with the call that as soon as he turned his back on her, she walked quietly and quickly out of the woods. Even the dog had given up his guard duties, opting instead to sniff out a rabbit hole.

Sarah headed for the village shop to pick up some groceries and a very large bottle of wine. She felt as though she had just walked on someone's grave, or was it someone walking over hers? Either way, she had the shivers. She replayed the odd encounter in her mind and couldn't figure out if he had overreacted or if there was something she was missing. She felt a bit silly, running off like that, but she would never have to see him again so it didn't really matter.

At a brisk pace, the walk took about fifteen minutes, and she felt invigorated after it. The local shop was essentially one long room, tightly packed with such a broad spectrum of goods that it was hard to tell if it was a grocer, a chemist or a veterinary supplies store. A young girl was serving behind the counter and, for once, Sarah's American accent did not prompt the usual interrogation.

'It's cold out there, huh?' Sarah said, blowing her warm breath on her hands.

'It's the damp,' the girl said, 'you get used to it.' Somehow, her tone seemed to imply that Sarah wasn't up to the task.

Taking her supplies, Sarah almost collided with Marcus at the door. 'Hello, how's it going? All well at Butler's?' he asked, giving her arm a squeeze.

'Hi, yes, it's fine. The cottage is just so quaint. In fact, why don't you stop by tomorrow?' Sarah said, surprising herself with her newfound spontaneity.

'Oh, that sounds lovely, but I have lots to prepare for the New Year's Eve party, don't you know.'

'God, I almost forgot about New Year's Eve.'

'We're having a bit of a hooley at the hotel. It's not exactly Times Square, but you're more than welcome to come along,' he said.

'Oh, I'm not sure.' Sarah didn't really feel like celebrating.

'It'd be a great way to meet some of the locals,' he added, winking.

'I've just met one and it doesn't augur well.'

'Oh?'

'Yes, I've been told off by the local park ranger for picking flowers,' she said, showing him the crumpled bouquet she had squished into her pocket.

'Ah yes, Oran.' He gave a knowing nod.

'I thought I was uptight, but he takes it to a whole new level.' She felt petulant after their meeting and now began to wonder if Marcus could see the two bottles of wine through the plastic bag.

'Don't let that put you off. Oran, well, he's a good lad really but I suppose he can be a bit sensitive about things. Which is understandable, of course.'

Sarah had a horrible inkling that Marcus was going to try his hand at matchmaking, so she cut him off as politely as she could and made her way back to Butler's.

Chapter Nine

1st January 2011

For the first time since she could remember, Sarah had spent New Year's Eve alone. She had nursed herself to sleep with both bottles of cheap, headache-inducing wine, so when a knock came at the door, she wasn't sure if it was real or inside her head. 'Go away,' she slurred into the pillow. But the knocking persisted, so she sat up slowly and waited for the room to stop spinning before standing up.

Pulling at the front door, she somehow loosened the latch that held the two sections together and ended up opening only the bottom half of the door.

'Sorry,' she said, bending down to see who was there. 'I can't get the hang of this latch!' She could see two skinny legs and sparkly sneakers. 'Is that you, Hazel?'

A bark came in reply, heralding the dog's presence in the front garden.

'Hi, Sarah,' the girl replied, her amusement apparent in

her voice. 'You have to close the door again and give the lock a good hard whoosh when you open it.'

With brute force, Sarah managed to open the entire door on the second go.

'Well, this is a … surprise,' she said, trying to muster an enthusiasm she didn't feel. If her welcome was lacking in warmth, her guests took no notice. The dog had already invited himself in and made a beeline for the rug in front of the stove.

'Max!' Hazel shouted, but he seemed determined to flaunt his talent of selective hearing.

'Hang on, did you just call him Max?'

'These are for you, from Dad,' Hazel said, ignoring her question and handing her a small bouquet of carnations and baby's breath.

'Oh?'

'His exact words were "Bring these down to the Yank and tell her I'm sorry about the snowdrops."'

'Oh.' Sarah took the flowers and brought them to the sink. 'You mean, your dad is the conservation guy?'

'Yep,' she said, looking about the place and touching things with a hint of nostalgia beyond her years. 'Or Sergeant Major, as we call him,' she snorted. 'He's a … a little bit OCD about things,' she explained, with a bizarrely American twang to her accent.

'Tell me about it,' Sarah agreed, filling a jug with water for the flowers. 'Sorry, I probably shouldn't have said that. He was just doing his job,' she said, placing the jug of flowers on the table. 'I was just about to make a pot of tea if you'd like some?'

Hazel nodded and unzipped her coat. She pulled out one of the chairs at the table and looked perfectly at home. With her finger, she began tracing invisible swirls on the table and they both remained silent, listening to the kettle hiss and bubble.

'He planted those for my mother,' Hazel said, quite out of nowhere.

'I'm sorry?'

'The snowdrops, they were my mother's favourite. He planted them there, after she died.'

Sarah stood like a statue holding two cups between her fingers.

She couldn't find any words.

'He said it would be nice to have somewhere else to go, to remember her. In the grove by the hazel trees. That's where she told Dad that she was pregnant with me, hence the name,' she said.

'Ah, of course. It's a beautiful name.'

Sarah forced herself into action and carried the cups to the table. Sitting on the chair opposite Hazel, she looked her in the eyes and said, 'I am so sorry.'

'Yeah, well. It was a while ago, so...'

Sarah knew this was code for 'please don't make me talk about this'.

As if on cue, the kettle began to whistle and Sarah got up to prepare the tea.

'So, are you the half-door-whisperer around here? I still can't master it,' she joked, pouring and stirring the tea.

'Yeah, there's a bit of a knack to it. This used to be our

home, before – you know. Then we moved back with Granddad.'

'I see, I didn't know that. Well, anytime you want to come over and visit, you just feel free,' Sarah said, sitting back down beside her. 'I mean, as long as your father agrees,' she added, trying to channel her sister's 'perfect mom' routine.

'Oh, where did you get the wren's nest?'

Sarah froze. She probably wasn't meant to take that home, either. The tips of her ears reddened with guilt and she suddenly felt like her younger self, back in high school.

'I didn't know what kind of nest it was,' she replied vaguely.

'Dad taught me. The way you can tell is that they look like a teacup. They're so tiny,' she said, scrunching up her nose.

'I don't think I've ever seen a wren.'

'Some people say they're bad luck, that a wren betrayed Saint Stephen and that's why the mummers bury the wren on Saint Stephen's day.'

Now it makes sense, Sarah thought, remembering Anna's diary.

'But other people see the wren as a sign of spring, that change is coming.'

'I like that,' Sarah said, as she opened a packet of chocolate chip cookies and spread them onto a plate. 'Did your father teach you that too?'

'Eh, no. He doesn't believe in … that kind of stuff.'

Sarah hoped that finding the nest was a good sign. It had already led her to the diary.

'Can I have a look at this?' Hazel asked, biscuit in one hand and Anna's diary in the other.

Sarah had left it open on the table the night before.

'Of course. It is pretty cool, actually; she's helping an American guy look for fairies!' Sarah said, her voice sounding slightly hysterical.

'Here in Thornwood?' Hazel said, dropping her cookie back on the plate and taking the diary in both hands.

'Uh, well, yes. Although I think this guy travelled all over Ireland and Britain, too.'

Sarah felt an odd sense of panic; like she was back in kindergarten and another girl had taken her toy to play with. She hovered over Hazel as she flicked the pages back and forth, checking her fingertips for melted chocolate.

'We went to the march, you know, to protest against the hawthorn tree being cut down,' Hazel said, wrapping her adolescent hands around the teacup. Sarah took the opportunity to push the diary out of harm's way.

'I begged and begged Dad to let me go, but he said the only way he would was if he came with me. I painted a big placard saying "Save Our Fairies" and it worked!'

She was such a charming young girl, skittering on the verge of womanhood, and yet in certain lights she still held a wonderful childlike quality. It caught Sarah by surprise when she flitted so easily between these two conflicting states.

'So you see, he's not all bad,' she concluded, swallowing a healthy mouthful of tea.

'I'm sure he isn't,' Sarah agreed.

They sat for a while, talking about Hazel's favourite

books (which all seemed to contain a supernatural theme) and life with two men who never remembered to put the toilet seat down.

When they had eaten the first layer of biscuits and drunk their tea, Sarah was about to suggest walking them both home, when Hazel reached into her rucksack and extracted an old book.

'I thought you might be interested in this,' she said. Her expectant face tugged at Sarah's heart and curiosity. The book looked antique, bound in cloth boards of a rich forest green. There were bright gilt designs on the cover and spine, but it was only on closer inspection that she saw the author's name.

'Harold Griffin-Krauss?' she shouted in amazement. 'You have his book? How is this even possible?'

Hazel tilted her head to the side, as a satisfied grin crept across her face.

'I knew you'd be psyched. When you mentioned the diary yesterday and the American, I knew it was him,' she said.

'May I?' Sarah asked, reaching for the book.

'Sure, go ahead.'

It was a bit surreal, having read Anna's diary and her humble descriptions of this young man, now to see his published work. Sarah had questioned the likelihood of an American student, which was essentially what he was, taking a jaunt to Ireland to 'study' fairies. But lifting the cover of the hefty book and seeing that it had been published by Oxford University Press made the whole thing more real.

'Will I make some more tea?' Hazel asked, interrupting her train of thought.

'Um, no. I mean yes, just one please. Sugar.'

Hazel smiled contentedly to herself as she brought the cups to the table. She was pleased to have found a kindred spirit.

'So, where did you get this?' Sarah asked.

'I ordered it online.'

Sarah was slightly disappointed that Hazel's explanation wasn't more elaborate. She wanted to hear an anecdote about how she'd stumbled upon a darling little second-hand bookshop and just spotted it sitting in a bargain basket, waiting to be picked up. 'I found it on Amazon' didn't have quite the same ring to it.

'And did you know that he had stayed here in the village when you got it?'

'There wasn't much about Thornwood in the book, apart from a few stories from the locals that he recorded. Other than that, he didn't say a whole lot about it.'

Sarah was baffled. He had obviously spent quite a bit of time here and made some strong connections, but perhaps his thesis was purely academic and he didn't want to muddy the waters with personal accounts. Hazel slurped her tea loudly and dunked biscuits for alarmingly long periods of time, just rescuing them before they sank to the soggy depths of her cup. Sarah, meanwhile, explored the book with her hands, as though reading Braille. The cover design was an intricate array of symbols embossed in gold. A circle within a pentagon, divided into six sections. Each section contained a symbol, only one of which Sarah recognised. 'Well, that's a shamrock, right?'

Hazel nodded, enjoying the game.

'Okay, I don't have a clue about the rest! Although the dragon, that one I know … it's on the tip of my tongue,' she said, scrunching up her face in thought.

'Wales,' shouted Hazel, unable to keep it in.

'The Welsh dragon, of course. Now what are those three legs in the middle?' Sarah asked, turning the book as though that would help.

'That's the Manx symbol for the Isle of Man. This thistle here is the Scottish emblem.'

'Of course, I should have known that one. I think I saw it in *Braveheart*!'

'That one there, that looks like a cross? That's from the Brittany flag,' Hazel continued.

'And the grapes? Somewhere in France?'

'They're not grapes,' said Hazel patiently, stifling a giggle. 'They're gold coins and represent the Duchy of Cornwall.'

'I'm impressed, Hazel, you really know your stuff.'

'Well, I've had this book for years, it's almost like a friend,' she said, shrugging it off lightly.

The spine of the book was emblazoned with the title *The Fairy Compendium* and below that was an image of what looked like Stonehenge, although Hazel pointed out that this was in fact Carnac in France.

'So, these are the six Celtic countries then?' Sarah said, and Hazel nodded sagely.

'Do you think I could keep this for a while? I'd love to

read it.' Sarah realised that Hazel had bided her time before showing her the book, sizing her up and waiting until she was sure she could trust her.

'Um, yeah, I suppose so.'

'I promise I will take good care of it.'

As Hazel prepared to leave, Sarah casually asked after her grandfather.

'He's grand,' she said and then with a cheeky grin added, 'My dad's grand, too!'

Sarah made a slightly pathetic attempt at both ignoring and denying Hazel's insinuation, but the girl was not to be fooled.

'Just tell him I said thanks for the flowers.'

'I will and thanks for the tea and biscuits,' she added, expertly lifting the latch on the half door, causing Max to raise his head a little reluctantly. Once it became clear that his mistress was leaving, he galvanised his limbs into action and sprinted for the door.

'You're welcome and, like I said, come by anytime.'

'Oh, eh – just don't tell my dad about the fairy thing,' she said, her fair brows knitting together. 'He doesn't really like me talking to people about that kind of stuff anymore. Anyway, enjoy the book!' She waved and skipped off down the road with Max at her heels.

Closing the half door, which she still struggled to do, Sarah couldn't deflect the schoolgirl thoughts that ran through her mind. Oran was attractive, despite his bristly behaviour. But now that Hazel had explained about the snowdrops and their mother's passing, she understood it. The vain attempt to hold onto something that was long gone. Still, he had certainly kept his distance since that day in the woods, so chances were he wasn't interested in her. Besides, she wasn't really in a position to start something with another man, especially one who was still grieving for his wife.

The rays of afternoon sunlight warmed the room and the dust motes created a slow-motion aerial display by the window. Her hangover had lifted with Hazel's visit, but she was still tired and so she decided to light a fire and nestle in front of it with Harold's book. There was such impressive craftsmanship in the older bindings, embossed with gold letters, and with covers that weren't fussy or distracting. *The Fairy Compendium* by Harold Griffin-Kraus spoke of a gravitas seldom granted to its subject matter. The first page revealed that it was published in 1912. 'Just before the war,' Sarah whispered to herself, recalling her European history. Scanning the quaint introduction, it was immediately clear that the author was extremely articulate, even verbose, with a profound respect for the Celtic people. Following his studies of Celtic folklore in Europe, he had decided to make an anthropological study of the fairy faith in Ireland and had turned his findings into a book. Not the typical pursuit for a graduate from Stanford University. Looking through the contents, it became apparent that he was treating these 'findings' as scientific research and was backed up by other well-respected men such as the poet Yeats and Dr Douglas Hyde, a former Irish president.

Finding the diary and now this – it seemed to Sarah something more than a coincidence. The newspaper article about the fairy tree had sparked a series of events that all seemed to be connected, like a chain, even though she couldn't figure out how they were connected to her. She wasn't sure if she could ever believe in the existence of fairies, but she was a firm believer in synchronicity. She had experienced it in her artwork. A truly creative life demanded a kind of blind faith in signs, hints or nudges towards a certain direction, from which things would inevitably flow organically. She had never questioned it and never shared her process with another living soul – as though talking about it would jinx it. But that was a long time ago; she wasn't even sure she could do it anymore. The grief that consumed her mind and her heart had taken away her appetite for creating anything.

The book was far more intriguing than its austere cover suggested and Sarah settled herself in for a good read. His writing was like pure poetry.

Above Erin, hovers a halo of romance, strangeness and of mysticism. Feel isolation, rest, wander, listen to the ocean winds, linger, lost in the mists. When there are dark days and stormy nights, sit beside a blazing fire of fragrant peat in a peasant's straw-thatched cottage listening to tales of Ireland's golden age – Gods, heroes, ghosts and fairy folk. Then you will know Ireland and why its people believe in fairies.

Chapter Ten

Anna's Diary

3rd January 1911

I write by candlelight and have much more to recount of the events of yesterday with Mr Krauss.

The boys were home and so the house was all a racket when we stepped inside. The spuds were laid in the middle of the table, their skins coming loose and revealing the white floury goodness underneath. I could already taste the butter melting on them, such was my appetite after the long day. My mother was cutting slices off a bacon joint that her brother-in-law had given to us when they killed their pig. Each family shares their bacon and sausages with their neighbours and that way there is always a bit of ham on the go. The boys displayed no airs or graces in front of our visitor and tore into the food. At twenty years of age, Paddy is the eldest now, and he could eat enough for ten lads. The only difference between him and Tommy is that all the growing seems to go into his legs, whereas Tommy's seems to concentrate around his gut. Father gave Harold pride of place at the table and Billy was sure to offer his services as a plate cleaner, should Harold's appetite not be up to scratch.

After dinner, I helped Mother with the dishes while the men began playing cards. I could hear the boys asking all about America and all of the things they have that we don't, but the talk inevitably led to the state of affairs here at home. Paddy is the most politically minded in the family, and he follows the progress of the Home Rule Bill through parliament with a keen interest.

'We have the right to govern our own affairs here at home,' Paddy argued, as Billy handed out the cards for pontoon. 'And as for the Land League, there are still far too many tenants badly treated by their English landlords. Are you a member of *Clan na nGael* in America?' he asked Mr Krauss.

'I can't say I've ever heard of it, but then again I am from the West Coast and there aren't a significant number of Irish there,' Harold replied diplomatically. 'What do they do?'

'They send money to the Irish Republican Brotherhood,' Tommy answered and that was when my father pounded the table.

'There'll be no politics in this house,' he bellowed, as he is known to do when anyone begins talking about independence. We are rich in the sense that we own our own land – it has been passed down from father to son – and my father does not want to be drawn on complicated issues that he feels powerless to change. He throws himself into working the land and doesn't concern himself with the politics of the day. My mother, on the other hand, is very sympathetic to the Brotherhood, but she has not endured all these years of marriage without learning a few tactical manoeuvres of her own and has always found a reason to install herself in another room when talk turns to politics.

As the darkness of the evening closed in around the house, I made sure to light all of the lamps and stacked an extra pile of turf by the hearth. The neighbours arrived in ones and twos, until half our village were warming their rears before the fire.

The Gallaghers are our closest neighbours. Gerard Gallagher took over the farm when his father died and married a beautiful young woman from Lisdoonvarna with flowing dark hair that we all envy. Everyone thinks that she is too good for Gerard and his fussy mother Eileen, who lives in the house with them, but Rosie seems content in her choice. And ever since the birth of her baby boy in the spring, who has also been blessed with a thatch of jet-black hair, she is like a doting mother hen. The Fox's live just across the bog from us, the largest family in the parish, and we trample such a deep path across to each other that we hardly need a lamp at night to find our way. There are four boys and five girls, the youngest of whom is Tess, my best friend. Old Nora Dooley usually drops in of an evening also, to warm herself by our fire and save her own turf.

The younger ones continued playing cards at the table while the women took out their knitting needles and sat in a row on the settle, clicking rhythmically like little clockwork toys. I made a large pot of tea, and handed around plates loaded with leftover Christmas cake.

I took my usual spot beside my friend Tess and we whispered and giggled behind our knitting, sharing silly pieces of gossip about who was courting who. Poor Harold must have felt like a prize heifer in a parade ring, with the men eyeing up his form and the women throwing furtive glances at his smart clothes. When he did speak to greet the visitors, his accent only served to alienate him further. It was Paddy who saved the day in the end, with that easy charm of his, when he announced: 'Come and meet our friend, Harry, he's raising money for the Irish Volunteers out in America!' He put his arm around Harold's shoulders as he spoke. The room went quiet for a moment and my father glared at Paddy, but wasn't it Mrs Gallagher herself who was the first one up to shake his hand. After that, there was almost a queue to shake the Yank's hand with a chorus of 'God Bless Yous' and 'we knew America wouldn't forget her own'. Harold gave me sort of a helpless look, like a groom who has picked the wrong bride, but I just shrugged my shoulders and nodded at him to go along with it. It is better if people think you are on their side, especially in our village.

With the tea drunk, the gathering began to relax and people sat themselves on whatever stool or wooden box they could find. Harold, being the guest of honour, was given pride of place in Father's armchair and despite many protests, was encouraged to take a sup of poitín. As we all huddled around the fire, we each began telling bits of old stories about banshees and singing old songs. The peace was disturbed when a hard knock came at the door. Tommy jumped up from his seat and let the visitor in.

'God bless all in this house,' came the greeting from the schoolmaster, Mr Finnegan.

'You're welcome, Mr Finnegan,' my father said, shaking his hand vigorously.

It isn't often the master comes visiting, so we all straightened our backs a little at his arrival. He has lost all the hair on the crown of his head, but what is left on the sides has grown long enough that he could scrape it over to meet the other side. My mother says he is the kind of man who could have an argument with his own toenails, but there is no badness in him, only pride.

'Mr Krauss, it's fortunate you're here. I had occasion to hear the most disturbing news following our meeting today.'

The men shook hands and drinks were replenished.

'There is a dark and twisted man locked in a jail cell this very night,' he said and we all held our breaths. 'Would you believe, his defence is that the whole sorry affair is the work of The Good People!'

The schoolmaster looked unusually flustered. He was a man who enjoyed the sound of his own voice and normally took pleasure in finding a captive audience. Yet somehow the telling of the story already seemed to tug at his conscience.

'Take the child into his bed,' my mother instructed me, with her lap full of socks for mending.

I carried Billy into the boys' room and told him to change his clothes and that I would be back shortly to settle him. I returned to the room, where everyone sat expectantly, but stood quietly in the doorway, neither in nor out.

'Perhaps it isn't a tale for this house tonight, but it'll be in the papers soon enough and then at every crossroads.'

'Spit it out man!' said Tadhg Fox, Tess's father.

Mr Finnegan swallowed his drink in one quick gulp and gestured to my father for another.

'I've had word from Ennis; a man was arrested today and is due to face the Justice in the morning. The master of the school over there sent word to me...' Mr Finnegan paused to hold his glass out for a refill. 'He saw the man himself and said he had a wild look about him. It all began when his wife took ill. She was delivering eggs, when it was said she accidentally walked upon the site of a fairy ring. Well, from that day on, she fell very ill and was bed-ridden for days. The doctor was sent for, and the priest, but no one knew what ailed her. Weeks passed and still she failed. Her husband was at his wits' end and so he called on a *bean leighis*.'

I saw Paddy explaining to Harold that this meant a medicine woman. At this point in the tale, I was fairly glad to be stood by my own hearth. It would test anyone's nerve to cross the countryside in the darkness of night after a story about fairy rings and sickness.

'When the priest called again to see if she was any improved, he found the man restraining his wife in her bed and forcing milk and herbs down her throat. The husband was shouting at her, "Are you my wife, Mary, in the name of God?"'

'Whatever came over the man?' Mrs Gallagher asked, clutching her shawl close around her chest.

'It seems the man had become very afraid that she had been struck down so suddenly. He began to doubt if she was his wife at all, or had been taken by Them and turned into a witch.'

'The Good People,' said old Nora Dooley, blessing herself.

'He was testing her then, to see if she was really his wife or … well, someone else in her stead. If she did not answer him three times that yes, she was his wife, then he had his answer. Well, the sorry tale ended when the woman would not answer him a third time. A neighbour witnessed him throwing her to the ground and mounting her, with a knee on her chest and a hand on her throat. When she would not answer him, he grabbed a hot stick from the fire and held it close to her mouth. Finally, he stripped her to her slip, doused her in lamp oil and set her alight.'

I covered my mouth with both of my hands, stifling a shriek that might upset Billy. I could hear the gasps from the gathering in the room as Mr Finnegan continued.

'"I am not going to keep an old witch in place of my wife, so I must get back my wife. It is not Mary I am burning," he was heard saying, as he watched her body burning on the hearth, "This is not my wife."'

'The Lord bless us and save us,' Tess's mother said. 'He was a mad man!'

'He had convinced himself that she was a witch; that she would fly up the chimney and his real wife would return.'

'And did she?' asked Nora. 'Did the witch return to her

own?' Some of the women blessed themselves and the men shook their heads.

'Of course she didn't, you daft woman!' Mr Finnegan spat. 'He murdered his wife, plain and simple.'

It is a rare thing when our visitors lose the use of their tongues. What was there to say? We all have our little superstitions, but to set someone alight because of them, well, that is another matter entirely. Yet it was almost as if there was a tear in the room. I watched the faces of the young and old gathered around our hearth and could see a tug between heart and mind, the old ways and the new, like two worlds coming asunder. It didn't feel safe not to believe in The Good People, not to respect them, but how could anyone justify what this man had done?

'Will he hang?' asked my mother.

Mr Finnegan just shook his head in a sorrowful way that didn't answer her question. People found their voices again, asking why no one had come to her aid, so I slipped back in to say goodnight to Billy. I settled him onto the soft mattress, stroking his hair lightly. He snuggled down into the warm blanket and his features lost all trace of the young man he was growing into. He was like a gentle babe, needing only a calming voice and a soothing touch. I began to sing him his favourite lullaby in soft whispers:

'Seoithín seo thó, mo stór é mo leana,
Mo stóirín ina leaba ina chodladh gan brón.'

Billy's eyelids were already growing heavy as I hummed the rest of the song. I rose ever so quietly to my feet and tiptoed towards the door, humming all the while – and walked straight into Harold, standing at the threshold.

'Jesus, Mary and Joseph!' I hissed with fright. He caught my arm to steady me and apologised for startling me.

'I was just leaving,' he whispered. 'I wanted to say goodbye and thank you for all of your help today.'

I brushed it off, unaccustomed as I am to receiving praise for simply doing what is expected of me. His eyes were glossy with *poitín* and in his hushed tones he lost that air of professionalism he tried to carry around with him.

'Might I ask you, what was that tune you were singing to Billy?'

'Oh, it's just an old lullaby my mother used to sing to me, and her mother before her,' I said.

'I do wish I could understand your language,' he said with that eager smile of his. 'Can you tell me what it means?'

I hesitated for a moment. He might think me foolish after Mr Finnegan's chilling report. Still, it was just an old lullaby, what harm could it do?

'It's a song about the fairies, waiting on the roof of the house to steal the child,' I said.

'And that brought him comfort?' he said in disbelief.

'No, you misunderstand,' I said, with a patient smile, 'the song goes like this:

'Hushabye, my child, asleep without any care,
On the roof of the house there are bright fairies,
playing and drinking under the gentle rays of the
spring moon;

here they come, to call my child out,
wishing to draw him into the fairy mound.
My child, my heart, sleep soundly and well;
may good luck and happiness forever be yours;
I'm here at your side praying blessings upon you;
Hushaby, hush, you're not going with them.'

Harold stood leaning against the doorjamb, as if mesmerised by the words.

'I would love if you could write it down for me – this translation of course,' he said. 'I would very much like to include it in my study.'

He had such an easy manner about him. For a man with all his learning and obvious wealth, he wears it lightly and if anything, seems at pains to fit in.

'Will you be writing that story about the man who killed his wife in your book?' I asked.

'Undoubtedly. I'm afraid it is not the first time I have heard such stories.'

He stood there for a moment, turning the brim of his hat with his fingertips, as though he were turning a mill. I wasn't sure what to say. The story had left me with a swirling nervousness in the pit of my stomach.

'You know, if you're having second thoughts about helping me to collect these stories—'

'Indeed, I am not!' I said, interrupting. 'I'm not frightened, if that's what you think.'

'No, that's not a mistake I'm likely to make,' he replied, running his hand through his hair, trying to hide a smile. 'Right, I'd best be off before I lose my nerve. It's pretty dark out there and my eyesight hasn't improved, even after half a bottle of moonshine!' he said with a sharp laugh.

We smiled awkwardly at each other and I walked him to the door. I waved him off as he cycled his bike down the lane. The little light on his bike danced through the blackness and I whispered a blessing that he would arrive safely at his lodgings.

Chapter Eleven

I used to be very good at keeping secrets. It wasn't that I lacked the desire to share, but as the grown-ups said, I'd lost the talk. It was after Milly. The boys at school taunted me for being dumb, but I didn't let them bother me. After Milly, nothing could make me feel angry, or sad, or anything really.

On this particular day, it was the height of spring and the bluebells arched above the primroses, colouring the roadsides with yellow and blue. I was thirteen and had escaped the household chores for the afternoon. My grandfather had sent me a beautiful new book from Dublin. It was called *A Little Princess*, by Frances Hodgson Burnett. He was always sending us gifts, but especially books. My father would roll his eyes when he saw the packages arriving, for the only thing he has learned about books is that they waste time and get in the way of all the work that has to be done. If he ever caught one of the boys reading a book at the table, he would ask if they had cleaned out the cowshed or stacked the turf or any number of back-breaking jobs. So we all took to reading in hidden places: back then, Paddy behind the shed, Billy and Tommy on top of the hillocks and Milly and I up in the old oak tree.

Milly taught me to climb up safely, testing the strength of the branches before committing myself. The trunk sprouted four giant arms, but there was one branch in particular that curved in the middle and was the most comfortable to sit on. It was beautiful in springtime, with its fresh new leaves breaking free from the dark wood that had been bare all winter. I had a great view of our farm and the surrounding fields. The lambs were head-butting their mother's udders for milk and then jumping around the place, doing their best to imitate a frog. I kept my book in the hollow, a secret place, halfway up the trunk, that looked like a gaping mouth into the otherworld. It opened into the centre of the tree and formed the perfect hiding place, deep enough to keep them dry and safe from the elements. Milly and I would stop at the tree on the way home from school and read a few chapters, before Father had us back out helping with one thing or another. I was sitting in the crook of the tree, with my back leaning against the trunk and my legs swinging in the breeze. I was just getting to the part where Sara's father dies, and if that wasn't bad enough, his entire fortune was gone. I wasn't sure how long I had been sitting there, but I suddenly became aware of voices. They weren't shouting exactly, but they were arguing.

'You do it!' one insisted.

'No, you have to do it. You found it,' the other replied.

Their accents sounded completely foreign in this

landscape. Even the birds seemed to halt in their singing at the sound. I leaned as far as I dared and saw the two Hawley twins standing at the side of the road, just beyond our dry stone wall. They were staring down at something and were dressed in their Sunday best on a Tuesday.

'You have to do it,' said Olivia.

'Why?' asked George, clearly unhappy at being bossed about by a girl.

'Are you too scared? Georgie Porgie is a big fat scaredy-cat!'

She continued taunting him with all sorts of unflattering rhymes. I almost lost my grip on the branch, as I strained to see what was the focus of their argument. I straddled the branch and inched out a little farther, like an insect clinging to a blade of grass. My eyes widened as the little brown ball of fur, nestled in the grass verge, came into focus. It was a tiny baby hare, frozen to the spot with fear. His ears were tucked neatly onto his back and he defended himself the only way he knew how: by keeping perfectly still and hoping that his attackers would not be able to see him. But somehow George had spotted him and now I could see the terror in his little face.

'I did the chicks in the nest, now it's your turn,' Olivia said, handing him a stone from the wall.

My mouth fell open as I saw him take the stone from her. Olivia was watching George, not the tiny animal, and seemed to relish his turmoil. He held the stone over his head for such a long time that I felt sure this was a silly dare that neither of them would go through with. Yet I still willed the baby hare to run; to find the strength in his back legs that would propel him out of this horrid situation.

George's arms began to tremble with the weight of the stone over his head. He was gritting his teeth and it looked as though he was about to cry. The sun caught his blond curls, which contrasted with his sister's dark features. Time had stood still for so long, but I could see now that George was also trapped, as sure as the helpless animal. Olivia knew he wouldn't dare show weakness in front of her.

'I'm going to tell Daddy you're a big fat cry baby!'

The sentence was hardly out of her mouth, when he threw the stone with all of his might. The only sound was a choked whimper, which I suddenly realised had come from deep in my own throat.

A wave of nausea came over me then and I had to clamp my eyes shut tight, so as not to fall from my perch.

'Satisfied?' he shouted at her. By the time I opened my eyes he was already walking home. Olivia, however, bent down and lifted the stone to make sure the skull was good and smashed. A wicked smile stretched across her whole face and as she rose to follow him, she raised her eyes to where I was sitting. Like the hare, I pressed myself into the branch, hoping to become invisible. She stepped closer, giving me a terrifying glare, then stuck her tongue out at me.

Soon after that day, my speech returned. It was too late for the little hare, but I vowed I would never feel so helpless again and for that, I needed my voice.

Chapter Twelve

Anna's Diary

4th January 1911

There was a hard frost this morning that captured the trees and the bushes surrounding the house in a sparkling trance. I wrapped my shawl tightly around my shoulders and tried to outrun the morning chill as I stepped across the yard to milk Betsy. I hung my lantern on a hook on the wall and patted my little brown cow in greeting. Betsy was a creature of habit and liked everything to be done at the same time and in the same way every day. Any deviation could throw her and she was often prone to kicking if things weren't done just so. I took my little three-legged stool and filled the silence with the reassuring sound of milk hitting the tin bucket in a regular rhythm.

Every other week, we use the milk for butter. We pour it

into large pans overnight and let the cream separate from the buttermilk. Then we skim it off the top and put it straight into the wooden churn. My mother and I take it in turns, churning the cream, and anyone who comes into the house has to give it a few turns as well. There is a saying that long churning makes bad butter, so the faster the cream is churned, the better.

Harold arrived just as I was feeding the scraps to the old sow in the yard. She was Paddy's pig and he normally looked after her, but he was over at Fox's, which I was sure would make Tess happy. 'Good morning to you, Anna,' he called, skidding on a patch of frost in the laneway.

'Good morning Mister— I mean Harold,' I said, catching myself just in time. 'I'll just grab my overcoat and hat.' Rushing into the house again, I realised that while I am always skipping back and forth and thinking of the next thing, Harold gives the impression of having all the time in the world. Perhaps it is an American thing, but where Harold is concerned, there always seems time to ponder every mystery or wonder at each new flower along the roadside. Everything is a discovery for him and none seems to hold more value than another.

'Now, where are you taking me today?' he asked, as we set off down the road, pedalling our bikes.

'John O'Conghaile's house. He's a healer,' I said, rather satisfied with myself.

'Is that so?' Harold asked, with a rather doubtful tone.

'John is the seventh son of a seventh son,' I explained, 'and that gives him certain abilities. When I was younger, I had a touch of ringworm in my hand. My father took me straight over to John and—'

'Forgive me, Anna, but you mean to say he didn't take you to see Doctor Lynch?' Harold interrupted.

'God no, sure we couldn't afford that! Besides, John looked at my hand and knew what it was immediately. He used a small piece of straw and wrote an invisible script on the palm of my hand. Then he spoke some words that I cannot recall now and that was it. Two more visits and the ringworm had healed. We paid him with a basket of eggs and butter.'

'That's extraordinary,' Harold said. 'You certainly wouldn't get that in California!'

'That's how it is. We all go to John for the healing. But if he can't help you, he'll tell you up front. My auntie Bríd couldn't conceive a child and went to see John for help. He put his hands on her stomach and told her straight that she wouldn't ever hold her own baby in her arms.'

'Well then, what are we waiting for?' he asked, tying his scarf into a tight knot around his neck. 'Lead the way, Anna.'

As we set off, I tried not to let my newfound sense of self importance go to my head. Everyone knows that pride is a sin, but I couldn't hide the joy it gave me when Harold, a scholar, followed my lead.

As we rounded the bend in the road, we freewheeled past Fox's cottage, where a queue of men were lining up outside their hay shed. They resembled a herd of cattle waiting for a farmer to open the gate.

'What's going on here?' Harold asked.

'The barber's here,' I replied, waving at my brothers in the middle of the queue.

'Sorry?'

'Declan the barber. He comes over from the next village once a month to cut hair,' I said.

Harold shook his head and smiled to himself.

'He sets up there in the red barn with a chair and trims all the men's hair, one after the other. Like shearing sheep!' I said, laughing along with him.

'I'm not sure I'll ever get used to how things work around here,' he said, 'but I know that I'll miss these peculiarities when I leave.'

'How do you mean? Do you find us strange?' I asked.

'Not strange, Anna, no. I think it's marvellous, the self-sufficiency of it all,' he said, his eyes glazing over as though he were seeing far more than Fox's shed. 'I envy you,' he said finally and I thought that even if I swore to my parents that he had said such a thing, they would never believe me.

John O'Conghaile's cottage is like a little apothecary. The rafters are strung with all sorts of dried herbs and flowers, giving the place a lovely scent of nature preserved. His abode is neat and well cared for, if a little plain. In fact he was sweeping out the dust when we arrived. As it turned out, he didn't like to talk about his healings, as he has a strict rule about keeping people's confidences. Fairies, on the other hand – he couldn't say enough about them and he had a story for nearly every one of Harold's categories!

I was glad that he and Harold seemed to get along from the off. John spoke in a mixture of English and Irish, so I was happy to be the go-between when needed. He shared

Harold's interest in the origins of the fairy people and turned out to be quite philosophical on the matter. There was a common belief that they were descended from the *Tuatha de Dannan*, but John held another view.

'I believe they fell from heaven, but they didn't go to hell. You see, there's no malice in them,' he began, as his fingers meticulously rolled tobacco leaves between paper.

'Fallen angels?' Harold said, as he began scratching the words into his notebook.

'You could call them that. If you study their nature, you'll see their way of being good to the good and evil to the evil, having every charm but conscience or consistency. They're harmless really, but so quickly offended that you must not speak much about them at all, and when you do, address them as "the gentry", or else *na Daoine Maithe*.'

Harold held up his hand for a moment and said that he would have to write the Irish words down 'phonetically', while I smiled and held my head high, eager to look as though I knew what he meant.

'On the other hand, they're so easily pleased that even if you leave a little milk for them on the windowsill overnight, they will do their best to keep misfortune away from you,' John explained.

'Have you ever seen a fairy, John? How would you describe them?' Harold asked.

'I have indeed, although it's not something I'd be telling people,' John said. 'Everything about them is capricious, even their size. They seem to take what size or shape pleases them. And isn't it well for them, they don't spend their days toiling like the rest of us, but feasting and fighting and wooing young girleens,' he said with a wink, making me blush.

'My father's people were from Belclare in Galway and he told me about a great hill there called Knockma. It is said that is where the King of the Connaught Fairies, Finvarra, is buried. There is believed to be an entrance to an underground world beneath the hill. Anyway, on this particular occasion, there was an almighty battle between the fairies of Connaught and Munster. Had anyone else been near they would merely have felt a playful wind whirling everything into the air as it passed. Or perhaps they would have heard a buzzing of bees. Be sure that if you ever witness the leaves whirling or the air fizzing with noise, you are in the presence of the fairies and you would do well to tip your hat and say, "God bless them".'

Harold wrote furiously, as the tales poured from John's mouth. Engrossed as they were, I allowed myself the opportunity to look at Harold from underneath my eyelashes. I studied his hands, which were smooth and callous-free. His fingers were long and slender and his nails were cleaner than my own! There were short, dark hairs that grew slightly longer at the cuff of his jacket and for one unguarded moment, I wondered what his arms would look like if he rolled up his shirtsleeves. My cheeks grew red again and I felt sure that both men must have noticed, for when I looked up, they were both looking expectantly at me.

'Tea?' I asked, instinctively, and thankfully they both nodded. I hooked the kettle onto the crane over the middle of the fire and stirred the turf underneath with the poker. As I busied myself with the cups, John continued.

'My sister-in-law's mother was a midwife in the region. She was requested by a strange man on horseback to go with him to exercise her profession, and she went with him to a grand mansion she had never seen before. When the baby was born, every woman in the place where the event happened put her finger in a basin of water and rubbed her eyes and so the nurse put her finger in and rubbed it on one of her eyes. She went home and thought no more about it. But one day she was at the fair and saw some of the same women who were in the castle when the baby was born. "How is the baby?" she asked. "Well," said one of the women, "tell me, what eye do you see us with?" "With the left eye," answered the nurse. Then the fairy woman blew her breath against the nurse's left eye, and said, "You'll never see me again." The nurse was always blind in her left eye after that.'

My skin prickled as I poured the tea. I had no idea that my neighbours had such a close affinity with the other world. Was it something we all experienced, yet kept close to our breasts for fear of betraying The Good People and suffering the consequences? And what of Harold? Would his story collecting release the secrets and cause untold chaos?

After much convivial chat, we said our goodbyes and Harold thanked John for his time. On leaving the house, however, we could not see our bicycles.

'I'm sure we left them by the gate, did we not?' he asked, turning about like a dog chasing his tail.

'We did,' I confirmed.

'You don't think someone would have stolen them, do you?'

'Stolen? God, no. Not around here.'

'Maybe it was the gentry,' he said, with a smile. I smiled, too. But then, as if we had both arrived at the same conclusion, we stopped smiling.

I looked back towards the house, and saw our bikes neatly propped against John's shed.

'There they are.' I pointed, though without conviction. Were they our bikes?

'Ah, of course,' he said, walking over and wheeling them out the lane. 'Now I remember. You know us old-timers have memories like Swiss cheese!'

I wasn't sure what Swiss cheese was, but I knew how it felt to doubt your own memories.

Chapter Thirteen

3rd January 2011

In her heart of hearts, Sarah knew her problems couldn't have been magicked away so easily, and, true to form, she woke up in the middle of the night again, sheets drenched and her heart racing. There was lashing rain outside. The thatch roof broke the fall of the raindrops, but the glass panes in the window left her in no doubt that it was not a night for walking. She pulled a cardigan around her shoulders and switched on the light. She suddenly felt utterly alone. The cottage, which had once seemed so endearing and romantic when softly lit, now looked stark and empty. What was she even doing here?

Walking into the living room didn't improve matters. It was filled with the scent of last night's ashes turned cold and a trace of damp. It was now January, and for the first time since she landed in Ireland, she wished she were at home. The bottle of wine she had been trying her best not to think about whispered to her from the kitchen cupboard. Despite a half-hearted attempt at ignoring the familiar pull and telling herself she could just as easily do without it, she poured a large glass of red wine and gulped down half of it at the kitchen counter. Her heart was still racing, so she swallowed another mouthful and refilled the glass. Moving to the kitchen table, she stroked *The Fairy Compendium* with her fingertips, but she didn't have the patience to sit and read. She went searching among her things and found her sketchpad and pencil.

'Right,' she said aloud, setting herself up at the table. She took on the voice of her old art teacher and pretended she was back in Boston. 'No one gets out until they have committed this room to paper.' Using the pencil as her guide, she began to measure the doorframe and calculated the angles of the skirting board and the ceiling. She used a soft pencil to create outlines and shapes, moving onto a harder lead for the shading and definition. She remembered learning in art class that the right side of the brain was like the artist's eye. Unlike the left side, it didn't deal in logic or language, but simply interpreted form, perspective and spatial awareness. The wine was making her loose and light. She could feel herself slipping into that 'right-side' mode of thinking, which wasn't like thinking at all. Her father was the same. Hours would pass by and her mother would call angrily for him to come in for his supper, as though he were a child. But that was the beauty of losing yourself in a task such as this; you reverted to that childlike state that only concerned itself with the here and now. How does this line match up to that curve? Where does this shape meet the edge of that one? These were questions she could answer.

Without her really registering it, the candle had burned down and the sun had come up. It was as though she had spent an entire season rendering the cottage on her sketchpad, for it seemed that spring had arrived in Thornwood. Her anxiety was a distant memory and she noticed that the glass of wine was still half full. Sarah couldn't remember the last time she had given herself the space and time to sketch like that. She propped the drawing up against the vase on the table and stepped back to look at her work. Something glowed inside her, a spark of self-satisfaction. The pipes were clanging overhead, full of gloriously hot water. After two cold showers and one scalding hot, she had finally figured out what 'the immersion' was and why it was so important to remember to switch it on and off. With renewed vitality, she made her routine inspection of the mousetraps before leaving the cottage. It was becoming increasingly clear that she was now feeding the mice, as every night she loaded the traps with chocolate and every morning not a trace remained. She smiled to herself and slipped her sketchpad into her backpack, determined to make the most of her newfound muse.

She found the perfect spot to sketch a landscape view of the town. The church spire, the pretty street lamps, all nestled into a background of trees and clouds and sky. The dark rooftop of Thornwood House peered out from behind a forest on the right, and even on this sunny day there was something forlorn about it. She brought a blanket from the cottage and sat herself down on the side of a sloping meadow. She wished she had thought to pick up some watercolours – the view was crying out for it – but she would have to make do with charcoal. She had barely begun marking down some basic outlines when a voice broke her concentration.

'That's very good,' Oran said, leaning over her. 'Sorry, you probably hate people doing that – looking at your drawing before it's finished.'

'No, it's fine, I don't mind,' she said, which was completely untrue. 'What are you doing up here?'

'Oh, just some … checking on things.'

She tilted her head, showing that she wasn't buying that excuse for one second. He was clearly trying to make amends.

'It's a good spot here, you have a good view of the village,' he said, looking out at the horizon.

Sarah began to pack her pencils and charcoal away, prompting Oran to apologise again for the intrusion.

'Not at all, I was finished anyway. It might be sunny but it's still darn cold around here, even with all these layers!' She had taken to wearing at least two layers of everything, from socks to gloves, when sketching outdoors.

'Listen, I shouldn't have gone off at you like that the other day in the woods. I mean, you weren't to know…'

'It's okay, Hazel explained everything. I'm sorry for your loss,' she said, holding his gaze.

'It'll be seven years next month,' he said, his eyes becoming vacant.

Sarah, of all people, felt she should have known what to say, but no words would come.

'Sorry, anyway, I just wanted to say that,' he said, rubbing the back of his neck. 'I'll leave you to it.'

That should have been the end of it, but somehow Sarah didn't want him to walk away.

'Actually, I was kind of hoping you could do me a favour.'

'Well, I suppose I owe you now,' he said with a broad smile. It was a thing he kept hidden away, so when it appeared it was all the more pleasing.

'Uh, yeah. I guess you do. I was kinda hoping to get a closer look at the old house: Thornwood House. I know it's all gated shut, but I thought a man with your connections…' She left the sentence hanging. She was all but flicking her hair at this guy and decided to make a concerted effort to stop this unintentional flirting.

'It's private land, you know.' He rubbed the stubble on his chin. 'That's way outside my jurisdiction,' he added, with a rueful shake of his head.

Sarah threw her eyes up to heaven and shook out the blanket before folding it and putting it away in her backpack.

'But, seeing as it's yourself, I suppose I could—'

'Oh, quit yammering and carry this,' she said, cutting him off.

They walked at a leisurely pace up the road and came to the entrance gates to Thornwood House. He was like a different person, without that cloak of grief that he wore. Was he trying to keep the painful memories in or keep happiness out? Sarah wondered if that was how *she* seemed to the world, then shooed the thought away.

A giant padlock secured a rusty old chain that wrapped itself around the gates like a snake. Oran took the padlock in his hand, as though checking its weight, then turned to Sarah and said, rather needlessly, 'It's locked.'

'I can see that,' she said, with a hint of a smile.

'Are you any good at climbing walls?'

'Funny you should ask, I came first in the Massachusetts state wall-climbing competition three years in a row.'

'Sarcasm – it's the lowest form of wit, you know,' he replied, with another one of those disarming smiles.

He led her to the side of the entrance and up a narrow pathway, edging the woods, where a seven-foot-high wall ran the perimeter of the estate.

'It's either this or take a boat down the river,' said Oran, cupping his hands for her to place her foot.

Sarah looked doubtfully at the soles of her boots.

'They're a bit dirty,' she said.

'Is this your way of backing out? I mean, if you don't think you can—'

She smacked her muddy boot into his hands.

'How heavy are you?' asked Oran, just as she was about to throw all of her weight onto her right leg.

She turned around and could see a devilish grin on his face. He was very different indeed.

She made it to the top of the wall, which was capped so she could sit comfortably. She offered him her hand, but instead he took a running jump at the wall, missing on the first occasion but saving his pride on the second.

'Right, well, now you've got us up here, how are you going to get us down?' she asked, looking at the rather steep drop. She felt like they were two teenagers, escaping the eyes of the world.

'I'll go first.'

He dropped and tumbled like a soldier on a training mission, which made Sarah bite her lip momentarily so she wouldn't laugh out loud. He looked back up with a satisfied grin on his face, like a boy showing off a new trick he'd learned.

'So just slide down and I'll catch you,' he advised, moving as close to the wall as the gnarled old fuchsia bushes would allow. He stretched out his arms and for that moment, Sarah felt something familiar inside. She felt happy. So happy in fact, that she didn't really focus on the drop. Next thing she knew, her legs were in a vice grip, while her upper body was slouching over Oran's shoulder, leaving her rear end beside his cheek.

'Sorry, I'm sorry,' she said, flustered, but as he tried to right her, his hand grabbed her bum and he apologised in such a formal tone that it finally made Sarah lose her grip on him and herself. She tumbled to the ground, with Oran's arms still holding on tightly to her knees, so it was like he was holding a wheelbarrow. She couldn't contain the laughter and rolled back on the grass in uncontrollable convulsions. He fell back on his rear, laughing. They stayed just like that, in the moment and chuckling like two breathless kids.

'Sorry,' he said, 'I thought I had you.' He was sitting

with his hands on his knees, like they were around a campfire.

'You did, you did. Good catch,' she said. 'Just let me get my breath back. God, I haven't laughed like that in years.'

The only sounds were their laboured breathing and a chorus of birds flitting in and out of the bushes. Sarah turned to see what she had actually fallen into and the sight of it silenced her giddiness. Despite decades of neglect, the structure of the gardens was still visible. The long, winding drive was lined with ancient trees, stretching out their limbs into what looked like perfect circles. Beyond that was the dark line of the river, caught by spontaneous sparkles of sunlight here and there and disappearing again under the shadows of trees. But nature was reclaiming her ground and tightening her grip with rapacious ivy that obscured statues and weaker plants. The grass had, over the years, been colonised by swathes of fierce-looking nettles, and Sarah silently thanked providence that they had not fallen into a patch. Hedges that had outgrown their original shapes still created borders throughout the grounds and led the eye, eventually up to the house.

'It's amazing here,' she said.

Oran heaved himself up and then rather gallantly offered her his hand, which she took for the briefest of moments to steady herself.

'Shall we?' he asked, gesturing for her to walk towards the driveway.

'So, do you come here often?' asked Sarah, as they walked up the gravel drive.

'You mean was this the local hotspot for teenage

romance? I may have brought a few young ladies here for a tour in my time. I had my first kiss over there,' he said, pointing to a stone portico with columns and a domed roof.

'Very sophisticated,' Sarah nodded. 'My first kiss was at the back of a McDonald's!'

All the talk about kissing suddenly made her feel self-conscious. She didn't want him to think she was looking for a holiday romance. Was she? No, absolutely not. She appreciated him as a person, that was all. And just because he looked at her in a certain way sometimes, with his eyes glinting in the light just so, that shouldn't cause anyone to jump to conclusions. He was probably seeing someone anyway, she thought to herself, trying and failing to put the subject to bed. Or anywhere else!

'It's a very unusual style of house, isn't it? It doesn't exactly scream Ireland to me,' she said, trying to focus on the architecture and noting the pretty tower in the middle of the hodgepodge of roofs, topped with chimneys and pointy little windows. As they approached the house, Sarah could see that the windows had been boarded up with unattractive plywood. It gave the place an eerie feel, as though something so bad had occurred there that even the eyes of the house had been nailed shut. No wonder people thought the place was haunted, she thought to herself.

'I found out a few bits about the house from my grandfather. He used to do a bit of work with the horses after the war. I remember him saying it was a strange place to be; so full of beauty and yet there was always a sadness about the place.'

Sarah knew exactly what he meant, although she was sure she wasn't seeing Thornwood in its best light.

'It was designed by an English architect and built around 1880. Apparently, there was all sorts of trouble during construction and in the end they had to hire outside people to finish it. It's Scottish Baronial apparently,' he said, pointing out the unusual architecture. 'They were inspired by old French castles.'

'Right, yes, that's it. There's something very gothic or medieval-looking about it,' Sarah agreed as they came to the front of the house. 'It's so imposing now, even in this state, but back then it must have been beautiful.'

'Yes, there are black and white photos of it somewhere. I remember seeing something in the paper when it went up for sale.'

'Will anyone ever buy it? I mean, surely it would cost a fortune to renovate,' Sarah said, peering through a gap in the plywood blocking the front door.

'I reckon they'll just leave it here till it falls down,' Oran said with a sigh that said he didn't approve.

'Still, it doesn't seem right, does it? That one family had all this wealth and the rest of the village were just poor farmers?'

'Of course it wasn't right, but that's how it was back then. That's how it still is, really, if you think about it.'

'Hey, I can see inside here! Come look.'

Sarah could see a grand wooden staircase sweeping down to a large hall. It was dark inside, but she could see carvings on the banister and wood panelling on the walls. Faded old wallpaper was peeling and curling everywhere she looked. Dust covered the floor, which had once been a mosaic of tiles, but it was too hard to make out their colour.

'Some place, huh?' she said, letting Oran step into her spot at the door.

'I've never looked in here before; it's a bit creepy. What's that in the corner, by the stairs?'

'What is it?' Sarah strained her neck to see.

'Here, have a look,' he said, letting her in front. He leaned in behind her, with his mouth up to her ear. 'See there, it's like there's something moving.'

'I don't see it,' she said, her heart starting to thump loudly in her ears.

'It's just over.... Boo!' Oran shouted, grabbing her shoulders and frightening the living daylights out of her.

'You asshole!' she shouted in capitals, but when the shock dissipated, she was able to join in his juvenile laughter. 'I'm gonna get you back for that,' she promised.

'I've no doubt,' he replied, still grinning.

Chapter Fourteen

Anna's Diary

5th January 1911

Harold left word that he was bound for Roscommon today. Dr Hyde had requested to speak to him on some matter of 'fairy business', he had said with a conspiratorial wink. The sun shone brightly this morning, raising the temperature to such a degree that it almost felt like spring. After the animals were fed and the men disappeared into the fields to repair the walls and dig out the drains, I took myself off down the road, with the excuse of delivering milk to the Gallaghers'. Their cow had gone dry and that is the way of things in our village; everyone helps each other. Whatever one lacks, the other provides. I didn't tarry, and uncharacteristically turned down the offer of tea and brown bread with melted butter. My destination was Cnoc na Sí and I had a half hour of walking through woodland ahead of me.

The pathway through the woods turned off just before the gates of Thornwood House. It edged the boundary of their land and, as the pathway rose, I could see the immaculate grounds, all manicured and shaped to the Hawleys' preference. All of our land is used either for tillage or for keeping animals. We work in harmony with nature, rather than trying to tame it with rounded hedges and pristine flower beds. Thornwood is pretty indeed, but not real.

I hadn't dared to tell my mother about the invitation to lunch there with Harold. I know all too well how she feels about the Hawleys. And the talk in the town of Master George is hardly flattering. '*Tá grádh gach cailín i mbrollach a léine*,' they would say. He has the love of every girl in his breast pocket, and it's many the kiss he gets and gives, for h

e is very handsome. He is fond of gambling, too, and if there is a fair, or a race, or a gathering within ten miles of him, you are dead certain to find him there. The Hawley family members never seem to spend any time working, but never run out of money, either. They employ at least ten house staff and, as my brother Paddy says, they live off the backs of their hard-working tenants. You can't help but be impressed by them, though, their fine clothes and their sophisticated air.

The dead leaves on the ground were wet and slippery, so I had to watch my footing as I made my way towards the summit of the hill. I have been coming here for years, but time has never dampened the hope that I will see Milly again. Old Maggie Walsh, the woman they call a witch, lives in an old hovel on the other side of the hill. She told me once that she saw Milly on a few occasions, dancing in the moonlight with Them. She said she was a 'seeress' and that she saw the gentry as clear as she could see me. I've never told anyone of Maggie's revelations. She isn't the kind of person you can trust. Everyone knows she is half mad but no one can remember why. I dithered over whether I should take Harold to meet her. I feel sure she will blab about Milly and I want to tell him in my own time. I have to be sure of him first. I will bide my time and listen well. Surely, with all of the stories he has collected, there will be one that can tell me what I should do. I will never give up.

As I stepped out from the dappled cover of the trees that stretched their long limbs over my head, the sun's rays dazzled my eyes. Cnoc na Sí held a singular beauty that never fails to impress me, regardless of the season. You can look out over the entire village of Thornwood, from the church spire to the grey stone walls dividing the farms into little patchwork fields. The birdsong almost seems sweeter on the hill and even in the dead of winter the withered old grasses and weeds create beautiful shapes and structures, which in a certain light look like miniature worlds, concealing magical inhabitants.

For all the countless times I have visited, I have never seen a thing beyond the ordinary. The belief is that if you walk around the hill seven times on a moonlit night, you will find the entrance. But I can never make my way up at night and so I can't say if it is true or not. In summer, I sometimes take a piece of fruit with me and lay out a blanket to have a picnic, thinking that if I wait long enough, surely, I will see something or uncover some clue. Occasionally, a branch will move and my heart pauses for a second, only to find that it is an inquisitive robin. But these kinds of disappointments will never put a halt to my visits. Just the opposite; being there makes me feel closer to Milly and that alone is a blessing.

I was following my usual route around the rocks that led to a cleft in the hill, when a grey mare startled me. She seemed to appear from nowhere and for an instant I thought that I was finally in the presence of the gentry. I fell backwards, landing awkwardly on my ankle, and when I looked up, I saw the profile of Miss Olivia Hawley, giving her horse a hard kick in the belly and disappearing back through the trees. She must have seen me, I thought, but before I had time to right myself, I felt a strong arm behind me lifting me up.

'Are you quite all right?' came the cultured voice, as he lifted my body easily and sat me on top of one of the flat rocks. 'It's Anna, isn't it?' George Hawley asked.

'I, um...' Hearing him say my name rendered me momentarily speechless. The sun shone brightly behind him, turning his hair golden. His hand was still holding my arm, steadying me.

'Olivia mustn't have spotted you there,' he said, looking back at his horse, which had lowered his head to investigate my hand. 'You're lucky she didn't rear up,' he added.

For a moment, I wasn't sure if he was talking about the mare or his sister.

'Horses like me,' I said, my words sounding so plain in comparison.

'I can see that,' he said, as he reached into his pocket and pulled out a hip flask. 'Here. Take a sip of this, it will settle your nerves.'

It was whisky, which seemed a bit unnecessary, when all I really needed was a strong cup of tea with some sugar. I declined politely and tried to regain my composure.

'What are you doing up here anyway, Anna?' he asked.

It felt like he was trying on my name for size. His eyes were almost turquoise in their brightness and were so full of life and vitality that it was hard to concentrate on such a simple thing as answering a question.

'I was just walking, that's all.'

'On your own?' he asked, finally letting go of my arm and trusting me to keep myself upright. 'Where is your American friend?'

'Harold's visiting a colleague in Roscommon today,' I said. I used the word 'colleague' just as Harold had, and it felt very grand indeed, as though I myself had colleagues throughout the parish.

'I see. Well, perhaps you will allow me to accompany you home?' he asked, as if this was the most natural thing in the world.

'Not at all, Master Hawley, I wouldn't dream of imposing on you,' I said all-of-a-rush. As I went to stand up, the pain that shot through my foot almost toppled me again. His arms reached out to hold me once again and despite my best efforts to ignore the sensation, my heart thumped hard against my ribcage, like that of a small bird held in your hands. He looked down at me with a penetrating stare that made me want to run and stay in equal measure. But I couldn't run.

'You're clearly injured; I will take you back to the house and get the doctor to have a look at you.' I wasn't in much of a position to argue. I couldn't walk and so I nodded my agreement. At this, he deftly swung me onto the horse's back, so I was sitting side-saddle. I know how to ride a horse, even without a bridle, but there was something very ladylike about the way I was propped on Master Hawley's horse.

'I'm sure I don't need a doctor, Master Hawley,' I protested, 'I've probably just sprained something.'

'I think we ought to let the doctor make the diagnosis,' he said sarcastically. 'You, my dear, are a damsel in distress and it would be a dereliction of my duties as a gentleman if I did not rescue you from your current predicament.' He clicked his tongue and led the horse by the reins back to the forest path.

All I could do was think about my mother's face when she saw me arriving home sitting atop of Master Hawley's horse and him walking ahead of us. I couldn't speak, for my thoughts were reeling about in my brain. It wasn't right for me to be having notions about a man like him and it wasn't proper either.

'And do stop calling me Master Hawley. My name is George,' he said, in that Anglo-Irish accent of his. 'Now, Anna, tell me why you were up here alone when there are grown men in this village who won't pass this way for fear of vexing the fairies?'

I couldn't answer. My mouth was dry and I fumbled blindly for words.

'I can only deduce that you don't believe in these ... superstitions,' he said, spitting out the word.

'No, of course I don't believe them,' I said, my cheeks burning with shame and guilt. I convinced myself it was safer if he didn't know what I was up to, but in truth, I was embarrassed by my beliefs and his disdain for them. We are worlds apart, but for that moment at least, if we had to share one, it was easier for me to slip into his.

'And I'd imagine that a girl as pretty and bright as yourself must have a beau?' he enquired casually.

His conversation glittered and every word held infinite possibilities. My heart began thumping again and I thought how I had never felt this way with any of the boys in the village. As we came to the main road, the horse turned right instead of left and I had to speak up.

'My home is the other way, Master— I mean George,' I said.

'Yes, but Thornwood is closer,' he said, leading the horse and ignoring my objections.

I felt like I was in some outlandish dream, being led up the long drive to Thornwood House. I had only ever seen the grounds during the May festivities on the river, along with half the county. But now I felt like the personal guest of the Master and it was thrilling. The horse lifted his head and picked up his pace to a gentle trot, sensing the comfort of hay and a warm stable ahead of him.

'Woah there,' George said, patting the horse and speaking to him in a soft voice. Turning to see if I was still safely aboard, he gave me a ravishing smile and said, 'Nearly there now.'

I began to wonder if George was really so different from us. Yes, he speaks beautifully and wears fine clothes, but maybe he doesn't mind if a girl comes from money or not; unlike his sister Olivia, who only mixes with her own kind. He seems like the perfect gentleman, and while, yes, his confidence could be mistaken for arrogance, his genuine concern was admirable. While I had felt a bit nervous at the thought of being brought to Thornwood – a half lame farmer's daughter with leaves in her hair and mud on her boots – my curiosity and vanity were abating my fears. How many other girls in my position would ever see the inside of this great house? Except for those in service, who would set their fires and scrub their floors. Tess Fox will be fit to be tied when I tell her!

The stable boy came to lead the horse around the back of the house and of course I assumed that would be my entrance to the building also. But to my complete shock and exhilaration, George reached out his arms and waited for me to slip myself off the saddle. When I stared blankly back at him, he laughed comically.

'I like to think that I'm a hospitable man, but I can't have you walking into the house on old Seaborne here.' He gestured towards the chestnut mare. 'You'll have to dismount at some point, and you can't hop all the way up those steps,' he said, gaining an inordinate amount of fun out of my good etiquette. 'So that leaves us with only the one option. I'll have to carry you,' he added, stretching out his arms once more.

Looking down at his blond head and his smartly cut riding suit, I ran through the options one by one, trying to find one that wouldn't involve me throwing myself into the arms of the local lord's son.

'There's no other way, I'm afraid,' he said, coughing slightly. 'But we can stand out here in the cold as long as you wish.'

I pushed my bottom off the saddle and slid down into his arms. I'm sure that Seaborne's hooves made a noise as he clip-clopped back with the stable hand and that the birds still whistled their callings through the air, yet I heard nothing. My arm grasped his shoulders and he carried me like a baby lamb up the stone steps to the large wooden doors, which seemed to open merely at his presence.

'Welcome to Thornwood House,' he whispered so close to my ear that I felt his breath on my cheek. He smelled like leather and sandalwood – not like my brothers, who always smell of grass and sweat. I had never felt so deliciously happy and nervous at the same time. The feeling started in my ears and shot out through my toes.

'Good morning, Master George,' came the greeting from a butler dressed in fine livery. 'May I help you with your … guest?'

'No, thank you, Malachy,' he said, carrying me through a grand hallway with walls pannelled in dark wood and arches carved in meticulous detail. Large paintings hung on the walls, of men dressed in uniforms and ladies in exquisite dresses. 'Do bring some tea to the library and something sweet for the young lady,' he added, whisking me past a grand staircase and into another opulent room, full of furniture that looked seldom used. The walls were lined with dark mahogany shelves that held all of the books in Ireland, or so it seemed to me. It was a world away from our home, where the dresser and its tower of china are our only show of wealth.

He placed me gently on a long settle with armrests, covered in a pale-yellow fabric. Having never been in a library before, I had not imagined that such places exist. The room held a collection of books that it would take me three lifetimes to read. George moved about at ease in his own surroundings, while I felt like an imposter.

The tea arrived and no sooner was it set out than George ordered the butler to fetch the doctor to look at my ankle. I was afraid to touch anything, but George urged me to drink and to taste one of the heavenly scones dripping with cream. In all of my years, I never imagined I would experience such grandeur. He fetched a cushion to rest my foot upon, but I screeched my objection.

'I can't put my boots on your lovely cushion!' I cried.

'Well, we'll have to remove them then,' he said. Crouching beside me, he reached to take my foot at the exact moment I bowed my head to do the same. Our heads butted, and we laughed like silly children, but a shrill voice from the doorway broke the spell.

'What a darling little tableau,' Olivia said, throwing her words as though they were daggers. She was taking off her riding gloves, loosening one finger at a time. 'And who do we have here?' she asked, peering at me, as though her brother had brought a wounded fox into the house.

I made to answer, but George spoke on my behalf.

'This, dear sister, is Anna, from the village', he said, clearly having forgotten my surname.

'Anna from the village,' she repeated, as though it were a farce. 'And what is Anna from the village doing in our library?'

'She twisted her ankle up on the hill, so I brought her back here to await the doctor,' he said, getting to his feet and leaving me to undo my shoelaces.

'How … charitable of you,' she remarked and under her breath said, 'Make sure Father doesn't see her.'

'Well, it was the very least I could do, seeing as it was your horse that caused the accident. What sort of a scoundrel would leave a young lady stranded?'

'My horse?' she asked, her fingers touching her chest with mock surprise. I knew then that she had seen me and had knocked me over on purpose. 'Heavens, I shall have to keep a closer eye for little girls hiding in the bushes next time I ride.' Her shrill laugh pierced the air and yet again, I felt unable to challenge her.

She remained in the doorway, neither here nor there, and with a puss on her face that would sour milk. George went to her then and rather oddly, placed one hand lightly on her waist as he whispered in her ear. Now it was my turn to feel like the intruder, as though I was disturbing a strange and unnatural intimacy between brother and sister. I looked away and when I turned around again, Olivia was gone.

'Never mind my sister.' He took a crystal glass from the sideboard and poured himself a drink. 'She's not very good with strangers,' he said, by way of explanation.

'You must be very close,' I said, even though I hadn't meant to say anything of the sort.

'Twins,' he replied, and I smiled as though I understood the implication.

'My name is Anna Butler, by the way,' I said, wincing as I tried to lift my leg onto the cushion.

'Of course it is,' he said, taking a mouthful of his drink. 'Here, allow me...' He rushed forward to lift my foot and place it gently on the cushion. 'I knew that,' he gave me a mischievous grin that made my heart pound again. 'You have a very pretty smile.'

This, naturally, made my smile even wider and I blushed openly. I was relieved when I heard the butler announcing the arrival of Dr Lynch, for I couldn't have spent another moment alone with George and his easy manner. I did not trust myself to be anything more than a foolish young girl.

'You're lucky I was in the area,' Dr Lynch bellowed from the hallway. 'Now where's the patient?' he asked, as George got up to show him in.

Following a perfunctory examination, he confirmed what I already knew. Nothing was broken, but I had definitely sprained my ankle.

'You'll have to keep it elevated for a week at least and use a cold compress for the swelling,' he said, offering to take me home in his carriage.

In all the drama, I had completely forgotten that the doctor would need paying. My father would hit the roof when he found out.

It was a far less romantic exit from the house, as the doctor insisted that he and George each take one of my arms, and I leaned on them like crutches. They lifted me into the carriage without much ceremony, but while the doctor returned to the house for his bag, George took my hand in his.

'I hope you will forgive us for all of the trouble we've caused you,' he said softly.

'Of course,' I said, 'there's nothing to forgive.'

'You are kind. And I am glad you don't bear us any malice, for if my sister's horse had not crossed your path, we might never have met,' he said, 'and that would be unforgivable.'

My cheeks burned at his flattery, spoiling my attempts to appear unmoved. In the distance, I could hear the doctor bidding the butler a good day. Our time together was almost at an end. Still holding my hand, he raised it to his lips and kissed my wrist, just above my glove, so tenderly that I thought I would faint.

The doctor hopped into the carriage and brought the heavenly morning back to earth with an ungracious thump. As the horse spirited us down the drive, it took all of my willpower to not look back. I smiled to myself when I thought how Olivia's plan had backfired; she might have acted out of spite, but her actions had brought me closer to George and that was all that mattered.

Even though our little cottage lay but a quarter of an hour from Thornwood House, I felt as though I had been in another world. Yet, as we left the big house in our wake, I couldn't help but think about the maid from Cork that Tess had told me about. The rumours had died down quite quickly for a small village like ours, but this was probably more to do with the fact that she had left Thornwood that very day. Having spent the afternoon with Master George, I knew that he couldn't have a bad bone in his body. The poor girl must have been desperate to accuse him of such terrible things, God help her. When the doctor pulled up in our farmyard, I began to see my home with new eyes. Despite the fact that the walls had been whitewashed for Christmas and the place was generally tidy during the wintertime, it still looked drab and lacked the elegance of Thornwood House. My stomach burned with shame at my own treachery.

My mother rushed out to meet us, apprehensive on seeing the doctor's carriage.

'What's happened?' she asked, the words sliding sideways from her tight mouth.

'It's all right, Mother,' I assured her quietly, but Dr Lynch let the entire yard know that I had sprained my ankle. He helped me down from the carriage and I couldn't help but feel a pang of regret that it was no longer Master George carrying me.

He sat me down on the settle beside the fire and Billy brought over a little stool to rest my foot upon. My mother reached for the old tin box at the top of the dresser and asked the doctor if she could repay him in instalments.

'No need, Mrs Butler, the bill has been settled by Master George up at Thornwood House,' he said, and I looked out of the window as my mother's eyes burned a hole in my back.

'Now, she'll need to keep the weight off it for the next few days and I've told young Anna to use a cold compress.

That should keep down the swelling,' he advised, as he swished out of the door and on to his next patient.

When the dust had settled and Dr Lynch's carriage was just a distant sound down the road, my mother set a basket of clothes on the floor and put the flatiron on the hearth. She worked away quietly, expertly stretching the clothes on the table, but I knew she was simply biding her time. When the silence had almost become unbearable, she finally looked up at me and spoke.

'Now, perhaps you'll tell me what you were doing over at Thornwood House?' she asked calmly.

'I wasn't at Thornwood – well, not at first anyway,' I said, defensively. 'I was up at Cnoc na Sí,' I told her, and at that, her face softened somewhat. She knew how often I visited that place, and why. 'The Hawley twins were riding in the woods and I slipped when Miss Olivia's horse came upon me,' I explained, curling a loose thread from the blanket around my legs. 'Master George carried me back on his horse and it was he who sent for the doctor. I told him I was fine.' Everything felt so void of colour now that I was back home, and again I berated myself for having notions of grandeur after spending less than half an hour in the big house.

'I see,' she said, testing the heat of the iron by splashing drops of water on its surface. They immediately hissed and evaporated into steam.

I have never before had a grown-up, woman-to-woman conversation with my mother. We have very little spare time or privacy living on a farm. There is always something to be done, some job to tend to. Luxuries such as private conversations are in short supply. 'You know, the Hawleys are very different to us, Anna,' she said, jabbing at a shirt with the iron and forcing the wrinkles out.

'I know that,' I said, a little impatiently. 'They're Protestant, English and rich.'

'It's not that,' she said. 'Well, it's not just that. They come from a very different world. The landed gentry have an obligation to marry well. It's not merely for the education that they send their young ones to school in England. It is their duty to make a good match and increase their estates,' she explained.

I had never heard my mother speak about such things. She has very little interest in the goings on at Thornwood House (unlike the rest of the village, who are, despite themselves, fascinated by them).

'Please don't fret, Mother, he merely offered me a cup of tea, not his hand in marriage,' I joked rather flippantly.

'Don't be so cheeky to your mother,' she scolded, her tone taking me by surprise. 'You're making light of this now, but I know his type, Anna. Men like him have a talent for breaking hearts,' she said in a way that made me wonder if she was still talking about Master George. 'He is full of charm and flattery, but in the end, he will stick to his own kind. I'm warning you: get any foolish thoughts of that young man out of your head.'

I said nothing in response. It was no surprise to me that my mother could read my thoughts like the parish noticeboard, but her accuracy stunned me. Worse still, her words burst through my bubble of contentment like sharp needles. I have never felt so enamoured of any boy in my life and here she was, ruining it.

'I'm telling you this for your own good, Anna,' she said finally, gathering up the clothes and taking them into her own room to sort.

Chapter Fifteen

3rd January 2011

'I took a few art classes at school myself, you know,' Oran said, returning from his walk around the perimeter of the house and gazing over her shoulder at the rudimentary outline of the building she had sketched.

The morning had yawned and stretched itself into a capacious afternoon, with a blue sky that held endless promise.

'Would you like to…?' Sarah asked, offering him the sketchpad and pencil.

'Well, I wouldn't like to steal your thunder or anything,' he said, but took the sketchpad nonetheless.

Oran was nothing like Jack, she thought to herself, as she watched him taking careful measurements with the pencil held in his outstretched hand, eyes squinting against the sun. Oran was more like the boyfriends she used to bring home to her parents in Boston. Easy-going jokers, who always seemed to please her father but never her mother. Frank Harper liked good honest guys who could help you unload a trailer of wood or fix your boiler. Regular guys, who enjoyed a beer at the end of the day and a good game of baseball on TV.

When she'd brought Jack home, her mother was overjoyed.

'He's a keeper, Sarah,' she said and made lasagne from scratch to celebrate his arrival into their lives. One of Sarah's college tutors was exhibiting in his gallery in the East Village. That was how they had met. It was quite romantic really. The entire gallery was in darkness, save for singular spotlights, which shone down on discs of glazed ceramic in a beautiful turquoise. They were like petals of sea, floating on the ground. Sarah was engrossed in the atmosphere of the exhibition, shuffling along through the darkness, when she bumped into a broad chest, spilling her drink in the process. She apologised and tried to move out of the person's way, but as he attempted the same manoeuvre, they only ended up getting closer.

'I hope you're good-looking,' came a seductive voice from the blackness, which made Sarah laugh. 'Normally I would ask a girl to buy me dinner before groping me in the dark,' he added, causing her to giggle again like a schoolgirl. In the end, she turned in the opposite direction and found her way back out to the reception, which fortunately was well lit. After getting herself another glass of cheap wine, she spotted her tutor and went over to congratulate her.

'Sarah, you must meet Jack Zaparelli, the gallery owner,'

said the woman. On hearing his voice, she knew it was him. The wine stain on his shirt confirmed it.

'Hi, I'm sorry, I think I bumped into you back there,' Sarah said, shaking his hand. He was tall, dark and unafraid to make his intentions known. Your typical Italian, with olive skin and a smile to make your knees wobble.

Taking her hand and kissing the inside of her wrist he simply said, 'I knew you were good-looking,' and that was that. A lot of the time, Sarah couldn't believe she had landed someone so handsome and charismatic. He was successful, discerning, and turned schmoozing clients into something of an art form. While he complimented her work, and discussed how she could make her style more commercial, it was clear to Sarah (even though she didn't want to admit it) that he didn't consider her to be among the elite, and she wouldn't embarrass either of them by mentioning it. And that was how it happened; Sarah began working in the gallery as Jack's assistant and spent less and less time creating. She found herself arranging exhibits for other artists and selling their work. She didn't mind; it was great to have a job in the arts – something her mother was wont to remind her of at every opportunity. She moved into his apartment and, rather too quickly, became assimilated into his life. Jack was the protagonist and Sarah was just a secondary character. She became 'Jack's Sarah', even before the proprietorial band was slipped on her finger. But then she got pregnant and everything changed.

'Finished,' Oran announced, pulling Sarah out of her reverie. She had almost forgotten what they were doing there. He went to hand her the sketchpad, then changed his mind and took it back for a final flurry of vigorous strokes and scratches with the pencil which was, by now, blunt.

'Almost forgot to sign it,' he said, pulling back from it slightly and squinting. Sarah was eager to see his work. It had been a long time since she had worked with someone like this. Probably college.

'Well, what do you think?' he asked, expectantly.

Her mouth curled into a smirk.

'Oran, you've been drawing for twenty minutes.'

'I know, I think I have repetitive strain injury,' he said, twisting his wrist.

'It's a square block with two stick people standing beside it!' Looking at him, she could see his pleasure in having made her laugh again.

'It's cubism,' he explained, mock-offended.

'Oh, I see, of course, how silly of me.' She looked straight at him then, putting her hand up to shield her eyes from the sun. 'You're not what you seem, are you?'

'I don't know about that,' he said, laughing off the remark. 'I know I made a terrible first impression, so you know, I wanted to give you the chance to see my real talents,' he added, pointing to the drawing.

'It's certainly … something,' she said with a nod. Then an invitation slipped out before she had a chance to think it through. 'I think we've earned ourselves a coffee. Fancy joining me at Butler's cottage for a cup?'

The pause after she spoke was all she needed to know. Oran got up rather too quickly and the atmosphere changed.

'But I've taken up enough of your time as it is,' she added hurriedly.

'Thanks, I just, I eh…'

'It's fine, you don't have to say anything.' Sarah felt embarrassed, as though she'd tried to kiss him and he'd knocked her back.

'No, it's just that I try my best to avoid the cottage, if I can. I supply the fuel and that, but I let my father take care of the rentals, since Hazel and I moved out.'

He turned his back to Sarah and looked up towards the house, as though carrying out an in-depth chartered survey of the building.

'Sorry, I didn't think—'

'Don't be sorry, why should you? I know it's irrational. It's just a house. Just four walls.'

It sounded as though these were words Oran had heard many times from well-meaning mouths.

'Maybe, but it's full of memories.' Full of ghosts, she had almost said, but recovered just in time.

'That's for sure,' he agreed, turning towards her. 'Hazel was born there.'

'In the cottage?'

'Yep, right on the living-room floor. A water birth. Cathy wanted everything to be natural.'

'Wow.'

'That's one way of putting it. I think she changed her mind at one point, but it was too late by then, we just had to push through.'

'We?'

Oran smiled at that, a lopsided grin that revealed a

dimple in his left cheek. Not that she was paying much attention to that sort of thing.

'It was surreal, but she was right in the end, as she usually was. She didn't want doctors and hospitals.'

'Yeah, I get that,' Sarah said, clearing her throat. Now she was the one who was uncomfortable. She couldn't tell Oran about The Big Bad Thing. They'd only just met and it seemed like he had enough on his plate.

'Hazel is a great kid,' she said brightly, covering over the cracks. 'Sometimes I think she knows more than I do!'

'Ah, you noticed that?' Oran smiled like a proud parent who cannot claim any real credit. 'She takes after her mother; a total bookworm. I used to worry that she wasn't playing with kids her own age, but Cathy—' he stopped abruptly.

'She does seem to act beyond her years,' Sarah agreed. She remembered Hazel's warning not to tell her father about *The Fairy Compendium* and, like a bad poker player, she looked at the ground and scratched her ear.

'She's always looking for meaning where there is none. A few years ago she watched a film about the Cottingley Fairies. You know, those two little girls who claimed to have taken photographs of fairies somewhere in England?'

'Can't say I'm familiar,' Sarah said, wishing he would change the subject.

'You've heard of Arthur Conan Doyle?'

'Of course, Sherlock Holmes,' she said, packing away her things.

'Well, he was convinced the photographs were real. Anyway, that's neither here nor there, but the point is Hazel became obsessed with the supernatural. Of course living beside Cnoc na Sí didn't help.'

'Ah yes, the hill of the fairies.'

'She would spend hours out on that hill, searching for fairies with her digital camera. And when she wasn't there, she was in the library reading every book she could get her hands on about "The Good People" and the old beliefs. At first, I just thought it was a "girl" thing...' he said, as they began walking down the drive, away from the house.

'Yes, because all girls believe in fairies,' Sarah said wryly.

'But after Cathy—'

Sarah saw this as her chance to change the subject.

'How large are the grounds here, anyway?'

'It's about a hundred-acre holding, so you should get home by nightfall,' he replied with an irresistible grin as they reached a lower part of the wall that they both climbed over with much less drama than earlier. 'But seriously, if you need anything while you're here, just call up to the house. We'll look after you, Sarah.'

She wasn't often stuck for words, but hearing him say her name like that in his low, gravelly voice made her skin prickle with heat. But she wasn't going to read anything into it.

Sarah's mood was buoyant when she returned to Butler's cottage. She couldn't recall the last time she'd just had fun and let herself go. Being around Oran made her feel young and free again. The last few years had left her feeling so old before her time and it was reinvigorating to spend time with someone who could just see her for herself and not her scars. She was starting to see herself, too, without the dreadful story that seemed to be defining her entire life.

She made a cheese sandwich and absent-mindedly opened Harold's book at the table. It occurred to her that no one seemed to question Harold's motives when he'd arrived in Thornwood. They simply took him at his word and never queried why an educated man such as himself was devoting not only his life but also his professional career to fairies. Even back then, it must have been a peculiar thing to do. Then again, the working classes probably wouldn't have batted an eyelid at the frivolous jaunts of the upper classes, who had the time and, more importantly, the money to chase whatever dream took their fancy.

For the first time since she'd arrived, Sarah plugged in her phone. She hadn't wanted to see any messages from home. There were texts from her sister and a few missed calls from her mother that she resolved to return later, but not just yet. The Wi-Fi was patchy, but just strong enough for her purposes. Being disconnected from her old life, even online, felt deliciously delinquent, like dodging school, and she wasn't in a hurry to go back. She typed the name Harold Griffin-Krauss into the search engine and waited patiently for the pages to load. There wasn't a huge amount of personal information, just the date of his birth and death. Sarah was happy to read that he reached the grand old age of eighty-nine. He had only ever published one book, *The*

Fairy Compendium. However, he had written many essays on his anthropological studies, which had taken him from Australia to India and lots of exotic places in between. There was one paper, however, that must have been his final thesis, entitled *The Story Collector*.

My mother used to tell me stories when I was very small, but I could only recall fragments of songs, echoes and whispers. She died when I was eight years old and in time, her stories were lost to my infantile brain. All of that folklore, the beliefs and culture had died with my mother. It became my obsession to safeguard people's stories, especially those whose cultures are disappearing. Oral traditions are dying out with the people who speak them. It is my vocation to remember these individuals and save their knowledge by recording it.

Griffin-Krauss was instrumental in gathering Aboriginal mythology in Australia in the 1930s, the website claimed, documenting the concept of 'everywhen', a time and place inhabited by ancestral figures of heroic proportions and supernatural abilities, which later became popularised as 'dream-time'. An elder told him:

'Our story is in the land … it is written in those sacred places. My children will look after those places … that is the law.'

It struck Sarah as such an uncanny thing – here was an Aboriginal elder on the other side of the world saying practically the same things as the folks in Anna's diary. Similarly, the people of County Clare were still protecting their fairy tree, a sacred place guarded for centuries. Each generation passed along an ancient knowledge and a solemn respect for the land. Tracing these beliefs back hundreds, possibly thousands, of years, made them all the more believable in Sarah's eyes. Were we really sharing this earth with other ancestral or spiritual beings? Progress was divorcing society from such beliefs and yet Harold was determined to save these stories. He knew how important they were, even if the modern world turned its back on them, pronouncing itself too clever or too sophisticated for such fairy stories.

His final words were the most poignant of all.

'If we lose our stories,' he wrote, 'we lose ourselves.'

She took out her sketchpad and laughed again when she saw Oran's drawing. She then took a look at her own sketch of Thornwood House, trying to imagine what stories lay hidden behind such an intimidating edifice. Even in its current dilapidated state, there was something haunting about it. Sarah had roughly sketched in some of the mature trees around the house, but something in the background was catching her eye. There was a dark patch, what could have been a smudge, at the base of one of the trees. She held the sketchbook up to the light of the small window and realised on closer inspection that the smudge had eyes. Defying all belief, there was a creature peeking out from behind the tree trunk. A creature she hadn't drawn.

Chapter Sixteen

Anna's Diary

11th January 1911

When Harold returned from Roscommon, he was full of enthusiasm for another day of story collecting. My mother welcomed him into the house like a long-lost cousin and I could hear her chiding him for bringing a gift.

'You shouldn't have, these must have cost a fortune!'

'It's only a box of chocolates, Mrs Butler, and besides, I wanted to thank you for your kind hospitality the other evening,' he replied, entering the room behind her.

I attempted to stand on my good leg to greet him, but on seeing my bandaged foot, he removed his hat and gloves immediately, as though he would have to perform an impromptu medical operation.

'It's fine, just a sprain. But I'm afraid I won't be able to accompany you today,' I told him, genuinely disappointed.

'Don't fret about that now. You must keep your foot elevated,' he said, bringing a stool over to the settle for me. He explained at length the importance of compressing the sprain and making sure that the bandage wasn't too tight. In fact, he sounded more like a doctor than the doctor himself.

My mother looked on in quiet amusement.

'Has no one offered the poor man a cup of tea?' my father asked, as he burst through the door, bringing the cold air with him.

'Thank you, Mr Butler. As it happens, I am due at Thornwood House today for luncheon. I was rather hoping Anna would be able to accompany me, but under the circumstances…' Harold said, pointing his hat at my foot.

'Anna won't be visiting Thornwood House anytime soon,' my mother said, rather tersely, and I glared at her in return.

Harold and my father exchanged a brief look of confusion, and then silently agreed not to question the root of this current disagreement.

We have kept my jaunt to Thornwood House with Master George a secret from my father. It is bad enough that I am now lame and missing out on my new position with Harold; I don't want to add to my father's disapproval by telling him that I have spent an afternoon with George Hawley.

'Well, I'd best be off,' Harold said, breaking the uncomfortable silence. 'I get the impression that Miss Olivia does not like to be kept waiting,' he said wryly. 'Perhaps I can call in on you tomorrow?'

I went to answer, but my mother spoke first.

'That would be most kind of you, Mister Krauss.' Mother was using her 'posh' accent again and with that she bustled him out of the door.

'What's gotten into you, Kitty?' my father asked, lifting the lid on the large black pot of potatoes boiling over the fire.

'Sit down there and stop your gabbing, if you want your lunch,' she threatened mildly and there was no further discussion.

I was fuming about Olivia Hawley. Her spiteful plan was now clear to me. She hadn't wanted me to accompany Harold for luncheon and made sure that I wouldn't be able to. It gave me chills when I thought how determined she was to get her own way, no matter who got hurt.

The boys came in for their lunch and the only sound was the clattering of cutlery against plates. Father had been given a trout, my favourite, by one of the neighbours. But my face obviously betrayed the conflicting emotions brewing under the surface.

'You look like you lost a pound and found a penny,' my brother Tommy said.

I pushed my food around the plate and gave him a watery smile.

'Is your foot sore?' Billy asked.

'A little bit, yes,' I said, ruffling his hair.

The truth was, I couldn't stop thinking about George. Every time someone came through the door, I had the foolish thought that it might be him. I felt like a caged animal, being stuck in the house with my injury. I couldn't exactly have called to see him, any more than he could call to see me, but I wished with all of my heart that I could get to Cnoc na Sí, for I felt sure he would find me there. I almost agreed to accompany Harold to luncheon, but Mother had swiftly snatched that idea from me.

When Paddy had finished his lunch, he lifted me up, put my arm around his shoulders and led me outside to the barn.

'I've been working on something for you,' he said.

'What is it?' I asked, hopping alongside him.

'You'll see.'

He leaned me against the windowsill at the back of the house and went off into the shed. When he emerged, he was carrying a long piece of ash, sanded and shaped into a crutch, with a piece of material nailed on top as padding.

'I've tested it out myself,' he said, putting it under his arm and leaning all of his weight on it. 'It's plenty strong,' he assured me as he gave it to me to try.

I put it under my left arm and walked round in a circle like a óne-legged chicken, but as I got used to it, I became more adventurous and did a tour of the whole cottage.

'It's fantastic, Paddy!' I cried, giving him a hug and almost toppling both of us in the process.

Paddy has always been skilled with wood and makes hurleys for all the local boys. I wasn't surprised by his cleverness, but I was touched that he had taken the time to make a crutch for me. In fact, he hadn't just given me a crutch; he had given me back my freedom.

It wasn't long before I was up and about again, resuming my visits with Harold. My recovery was hastened by the sheer boredom of being stuck indoors and my longing to see Master George. I kept my eyes peeled for him along the road and grilled Harold on his luncheon with them.

'So who was there?' I asked casually, as we cycled over to Lenihan's. My foot was still strapped, but I found cycling easier than walking.

'Miss Olivia and Master George. Lord Hawley was detained elsewhere,' he replied.

'Is it true they have their food sent down from the Shelbourne Hotel in Dublin on the evening mail train? Tess's mother said it arrives in wooden crates packed with hay to keep the food warm,' I explained.

'I really couldn't say, Anna.'

I frowned slightly as I searched for more questions that wouldn't arouse suspicion.

'Did you eat well?'

'Very well, thank you,' he said, as we passed by the graveyard with its crooked headstones like loose teeth.

'Did you ever wonder at what point those below began to outnumber those above?'

I looked at Harold, agape. Only he would ponder such gloomy ideas. He reminded me of little Billy, the way his thoughts would snag on passing notions, like wool on a thorn bush.

'What a cheery thought,' I replied, not bothering to conceal my sarcasm, such was our growing familiarity with one another. I was beginning to think he didn't want to share any news from Thornwood House, which only made me more curious.

'Was the conversation lively? Did Master George ask after … your work?'

'If he did, it was purely out of politeness.'

It was the first time since I had met him that he sounded uncharitable. He caught my eye and immediately his face flushed and he attempted a smile.

'You must ignore me, Anna. Luncheon with the Hawleys was rather an ordeal, if I'm honest.'

'An ordeal? Lunching in the most beautiful house in the land!'

'I would rather have a great big pot of potatoes swimming in butter and served in your mother's kitchen,' he said, a smile returning to his face. 'They are so very isolated up there, the two of them, living in that big house and completely cut off from the rest of village society. I'm not sure it has been beneficial to their mental states.'

Harold was turning my view of the Hawleys on its head. They were supposed to be separate from us. They associate mostly with other well-heeled landowners in the county.

'They must have had a very lonely childhood,' he continued. 'As I understand it, they were both sent to boarding schools in England. Olivia confided in me that she felt neither Irish nor English, yet she is despised for being both.'

'I suppose I never really thought of it like that,' I said. They are the wealthy family living in the big house and want for nothing. How could anyone feel sorry for them?

At this stage, we had reached Lenihan's farm and Harold helped to steady my bicycle as I gingerly stepped off on my good foot. Similar to our own house, it was whitewashed and gleaming in the winter sun, but with one decorative addition that I always admired – a weathervane with a large cockerel telling you which way the wind was blowing. My father used to say that if a farmer needed a cockerel to know the direction of the wind, he needed his head testing, but I thought it made the house look very genteel.

Harold leaned our steeds against the wall, which was covered in a beautiful tangle of goldheart ivy. I rested against it for a moment, taking the weight off my ankle and catching my breath.

'So, you didn't like them then, the Hawleys?' I asked, even though I wasn't sure if he would tell me.

'You're not going to give me any peace, are you?' he said, busying himself with his satchel.

I just shrugged in reply.

'There's just something I can't quite put my finger on, a barrier between them and everyone else. For a brother and sister, they have an unusual … rapport. I suppose it's only to be expected, following the death of their mother, and from what I can gather, their father hasn't inconvenienced himself with their rearing.'

'Who reared them, then?' In my world, if your parents don't bring you up, you are an orphan.

'A long and varied list of nannies by the sounds of it. Their antics made sure that the staff never stayed for very long.'

'Ah sure, all children are full of mischief,' I said, suddenly feeling the need to defend George. I thought of the day on the road and the baby hare and the way they had goaded each other. I wanted to believe George to be the innocent party and merely acting under the influence of his wicked sister.

'That's true. Pay no heed to me, Anna. Perhaps it was the house itself that left me cold,' he said. 'There is certainly an atmosphere there. Tell me again the story of the fairy tree at Thornwood House,' he asked.

To my great inconvenience, we had to cut our conversation short, as Mary Lenihan came out to greet us with her little dogs, deafening the lot of us with their welcome.

Chapter Seventeen

Mary Lenihan welcomed us into the house, along with her two small but feisty terriers. They couldn't decide whether to bite us or lick us, but in the end, when the old woman showed me to a seat beside the fire, they both curled up on my lap. Out of a family of fourteen, Mary and her two brothers, Ned and Jimmy, have never married. In a small community like ours, marriage is a numbers game and, as with musical chairs, many find themselves without a partner once the music has stopped. They live here together in the old family home, where the passing of time is marked only by the lines on their faces. Everything in the cottage is exactly as it would have been in their parents' time and the routines are carried out in the same, precise manner. I can't tell their ages, but it is clear that they have all seen off their seventieth year quite some time ago. The main peculiarity of this sibling arrangement is that the two brothers don't speak to each other. They fell out many years ago – in fact it was so long ago that I doubt anyone can remember the reason. Nevertheless, the feud has come too far to be given up so easily and so Ned and Jimmy live out their lives quietly ignoring each other, for a cause that is lost to history. All communication has to go through Mary, who has resigned herself to her position as the go-between.

They have very little, but what they do have is shared with whoever comes by, and Ned, the youngest of the three, made the tea and cut the seed cake, placing the slices on delicate china plates, serving it up to us as though we were at a very fine tea house.

'Mister Krauss has come to collect stories about *na Daoine Maithe*,' I explained, after they had all sat down and supped their tea. 'He has been all over Ireland and even England and France, collecting stories – from the priest to the beggar,' I added, proving that social status was not a prerequisite for a belief in the fairy world.

'And what does he want to know for?' Jimmy asked.

'Will ya tell that fella not to be interrupting the young girleen!' Ned said to Mary, prompting Mary to repeat the same sentence at a higher volume back to Jimmy.

I suddenly felt that this could become a very long day indeed.

'Well, if you'll permit me, Anna,' Harold said in his polite American accent, 'I'm studying anthropology at Oxford University and I'm really very interested in the beliefs of the Celtic people.'

'What's he sayin'?' Jimmy asked; his expression was that

of a man trying to work out the distance between here and the moon.

'He's writing a book about it,' I said, trying to put an end to the explanations.

'Well, it's more of a thesis really…' Harold said, but I gave him a sharp look and he abandoned the explanation.

'Right, let's get started,' I said, clapping my hands together.

Harold opened his notebook and held his pen poised for the next story.

'Well, there's the old beliefs,' Mary began hesitantly, unsure of what was expected of her. 'Like, you'd always call out a warning before throwing out a bucket of dishwater, in case there is a fairy nearby,' she said, a self-conscious smile forming at the corners of her lips. 'And the *piseogs* of course.'

I explained to Harold that piseogs are a kind of superstition and in order to ward off bad luck, you have to undertake certain rituals.

'Every May Eve, we tie a red ribbon around the necks of the milking cows, to protect them.' Mary said this with a half smile, as if she knew it would sound ridiculous to a foreigner, but that was the way things have always been done and, to her mind, always would be.

'I'll tell you a story about those little demons,' Jimmy interrupted, looking fierce and shaken.

'Jimmy, there's no need to rake all that up again,' Mary said, reaching over and putting her hand on his arm, restraining him.

Harold and I looked at one another for an explanation.

Ned shot Jimmy a stern look and it was clear that there was fresh tension between them.

'You don't have to tell me anything you don't want to,' Harold said, hoping to calm their nerves. 'But please be aware that I will treat your evidence with the strictest confidence.'

Mary and Ned exchanged a worried look, but Jimmy shifted in his chair and leaned his arms on his knees, looking at the floor for inspiration.

''Twas me wedding night,' he began, his voice filling the space and holding us all in a trance. 'Everyone from the village was here, in this very house, dancing and eating their fill. 'Twas the happiest day of my life when Rosaleen Garrett agreed to marry me.'

'This was all such a long time ago,' Mary said again, but Jimmy wouldn't be swayed.

'We danced and danced as the fiddler played every tune in his head, and Rosaleen came inside to freshen her face with some water from the bowl,' he said, pointing to the earthenware jug and bowl still on the sideboard. 'She was gone for a long time, and when I came in to look for her, I found her collapsed on the bench there, clutching her breast.' His voice broke and he pulled a greying old handkerchief from his waistcoat and blew his nose hard. 'Her heart had stopped.'

'I am so sorry for your loss, Mister Lenihan,' Harold said softly.

Jimmy just nodded his head silently.

'But that wasn't the end of it,' he continued, rocking his chair forward and back. 'She appeared to me, so she did, a week later and she told me that she wasn't dead at all, but that she was put from me for a time. She told me that she was not badly off, where she was, but that she wanted to return. She said that if I was to help her come home, I was to stand by the gap at the side of the house and catch her as she went by.'

'Where did she appear to you?' Harold asked.

'I was lying in my bed, in the dead of night, when she came to me,' he said. 'Still in her wedding dress.'

The little dogs in my lap gave me great comfort, as the warmth of their bodies warded off any chills that Jimmy's story stirred. Ned disturbed the room by scraping his chair back and blustering out the door in a huff. Mary was visibly torn as to which brother she should comfort, but couldn't leave the house when there was company.

'She told me that she lived nearby and could see me, even though I couldn't see her,' Jimmy continued, his chapped lips making every word seem a hardship. 'I came to the place on Saint John's night, when there were bonfires all around, and I waited to see her. I sat in my spot for hours, cursing myself for believing such nonsense. But then, I saw some strangers passing by. They were unnaturally tall, like they were walking on stilts, and wore the strangest clothes. As sure as I'm sitting here, didn't I see my wife approaching behind them. As she passed through the gap, I tried to grab her, but I found myself frozen to the spot,' he declared, tears forming around his wrinkled eyes. 'I was struck down with fear looking at her; her mouth opened as if to scream, but she made not a sound. I thought her jaw was broken; her mouth was growing bigger and bigger. I couldn't move my arm nor foot to save her, can you imagine it? My own wife!' he said, burying his head in his hands.

'He never married after that,' his sister said, bringing the forlorn tale to an end.

Chapter Eighteen

It costs me nothing to say that I was shaken after the old man's account. No matter if you believe in fairies or not, there was no denying that Jimmy Lenihan was haunted by his loss.

'The woman died of a heart attack,' Ned called to us as we left the cottage. He'd been skulking out by the turf stack, awaiting our departure. 'The rest is in Jimmy's mind.'

I wanted to shout at Ned then. I could remember being told that it was all in my mind and it made me fitfully angry. Harold responded with some platitude and we got back on our bicycles.

'Is everything all right, Anna?' he asked me after a while.

His words startled me, as I was so lost in my own thoughts that I had almost forgotten he was there.

'Of course,' I managed.

'Are you sure this isn't too much for you? Perhaps your leg is paining…' He broke off.

I stopped my bicycle just as we reached the little bridge, and I leaned it against the stone wall. The sun was low in the sky, bringing its warmth onto my face. I took a few breaths, looking down at the swollen river that had long since flooded its banks with brown mountain water.

'It's not my leg that troubles me,' I said. Looking at Harold, I could see that his earnest eyes wanted me to trust him. I had bided my time and watched how he'd interacted with other people in the village. I wanted to be sure that my story would be safe with him. I knew all too well the ridicule of people who were too afraid to believe. Yet Harold treated every tale, every snippet of a half-remembering, with the utmost respect. He never seemed to judge the teller, nor did he hint at his own beliefs. He was a scientist.

'Tell me, Harold, what do you believe?' I asked finally, propping myself up on the stone bridge. The reflection of its arch in the water below made a full, dark circle.

Harold took some tobacco out of his breast pocket and rolled a cigarette, calmly licking it and placing it between his lips before digging out a match that he struck off his shoe. It tickled me when he did such American things.

When he blew out a white-grey breath of smoke, he leaned on the bridge beside me.

'You realise that you are asking me to reveal my conclusions before I have even written my thesis?' he said, with an air of feigned self-importance.

I simply shrugged.

'Well, seeing as you are my assistant, I suppose it won't

hurt,' he said with a smile. 'Although I never had this kind of insubordination with my other assistants.'

Immediately, I felt my heart quicken. I had never even considered the possibility that another girl might have helped Harold with his story collecting.

'So, what were they like then, your other assistants?' I asked, while glancing over my shoulder, as though I were simply making conversation to pass the time.

'Not half as interested as you, I can assure you. Not that I blame them; most of the young men I've met on my travels are more interested in the money than in my studies.'

I exhaled the breath I hadn't realised I was holding.

'So, am I the first girl you've employed then?' I couldn't, or rather I wouldn't, admit to myself why this mattered so much.

'You are the first female assistant, yes. And still the most inquisitive.'

'Well, in that case, please answer the question, Mr Krauss!'

He crossed one foot over the other and searched the skies for a prompt.

'Well, let's see. Having spent so much time with my head stuck in books at Oxford, I now see that it is impossible to learn about the fairy faith in books. The only way to experience it is to spend time in these sacred places and speak to the people who call those places home.'

'Like Thornwood?' I asked.

'Exactly like Thornwood. Every cluster of trees or stack of stones has a meaning and a history known only to that place and its inhabitants. Yet it is a shared history between the Celtic countries, which leads me to deduce that the belief in fairies is almost a doctrine of souls.'

He could see that I wasn't grasping his lofty concepts, but ploughed on in the belief that I would catch up.

'Every place I have visited, all of the Celtic countries, they all share the same beliefs. Yes, there are slight variations particular to each place, but overall, the stories are the same. As I have come to understand it, "Fairyland" is a realm or a place containing the souls of the dead, in company with all other manner of spirit, demon or god. An invisible world.'

'You make it sound so real,' I said.

'But it is real, at least it is to the people who believe they have entered such a world or seen its inhabitants. They often have no training in school or university, but their testimonies are not to be undervalued, for often they are better authorities and more trustworthy than the most ancient manuscript in the British Museum! I suppose my interpretation of their stories gives them some sort of added credibility in your eyes because I am speaking as a scholar.'

'And if you were speaking not as a scholar, but as yourself, what would you say you believe?' I pressed him.

'I believe there is a lot of very exciting research in the area of psychic—'

'Harold!' I said, mildly vexed by his use of flowery language to avoid giving a straight answer.

'Honestly?' he asked, sitting beside me on the bridge. 'I'm not sure what I believe. But it is very difficult to be in a place such as this and not have a sense of the mystic,' he said, looking out beyond the hills that buffer our village. 'But if I was pressed, as I obviously am, I would lean towards the hypothesis that these "beings" are somehow communicating with us. All of this evidence,' he said, tapping the satchel that held his notebook, 'shows that there is a connection between the realm of the spirit and our natural world.'

We shared a contemplative silence then, broken only by the distant screeching of a pheasant.

'Why they choose to reveal themselves to some folk and not to others is still a mystery to me. But your neighbours are right to fear and respect them. They may appear human, but they are not.'

'You say that they are communicating with us, but, what if we wanted to communicate with them?' I was on the verge of telling him about Milly – taking a deep breath and preparing for the shock of diving into the story – when Paddy and a companion I had never seen before appeared on their bicycles.

'How are ye?' Paddy called, but the other one said nothing. 'Are ye on your way home?' he asked me.

I looked to Harold, who concluded that we had done enough for the day.

'I'll see you tomorrow,' he said, giving me that comforting smile I had become so fond of. He waved us off as we cycled down the road towards home.

'This is Danny,' Paddy said, introducing his friend. 'He's a farm labourer.'

'Hello, Danny,' I said. 'Whose farm are you working on?'

They looked at each other and then answered one after

the other that it was in another village and I wouldn't know it. I was far too preoccupied with my own concerns to bother them with questions, but the cat in the barn could tell they were covering something up.

'You might want to decide which farm you're labouring at before we get home to Mother and Father,' I advised them, and cycled on ahead.

In the night, I was woken from my sleep by a battering at the door. I slept in the loft and always felt safely tucked away, high in the rafters, but something about the noise caused my entire body to tense.

'In the name of the King, open this door!' came an angry voice and I pulled the blankets up to my mouth. We have been raided before for making poitín, but never in the middle of the night. Besides, Father doesn't keep the poitín still in the barn any more; he keeps all of the equipment in an old ruin in one of our fields. Just as I thought of this, I heard my father rising to answer the door.

'All right, all right,' he called back, 'give a man time to put on his trousers!'

When he opened the door, about half a dozen men in uniform came into the house and began turning things over.

'What's this about?' my father asked, looking more vexed than I had ever seen him.

'We have reason to believe you are harbouring a young man by the name of Daniel Freeman,' the man in charge said.

I thought of Paddy's new friend, who had sat by our fire and eaten a hearty dinner. But he had left before I came up to bed.

'Who?' my father replied, but I knew that he had already worked it out.

'A member of the Irish Republican Brotherhood, Mister Butler. Do you know anything about that?'

'And what would I know about it? I'm a farmer, not an activist,' he replied, 'and watch the china!' he said, shouting at one of the young soldiers searching the dresser. 'If he was here, he wouldn't be hiding in a teapot, now would he?'

At this stage, my mother and brothers were up and standing in front of the open fire by the settle. The policemen searched the bedrooms and finally had to admit that there was no one hiding with us. There was no apology for disturbing the entire house at such an unsociable hour, but we weren't expecting one.

'What's all this about?' my mother asked.

'There's been a raid on the goods train,' the constable said. 'A well-planned job by all accounts. They made off with two barrels of Guinness, five-thousand cigarettes, two sides of bacon and fifty Christmas cakes. Bloody Fenians,' he said.

We all gasped audibly at the list of goods that had been taken. Satisfying himself that we really didn't know anything about it, he ordered his men to move on to the next house. As soon as they left, my mother shut and bolted the door after them and I climbed hastily down the ladder. Billy instinctively clung to my hip and I held his soft, sleepy head in my arms.

'What have you done?' my father asked Paddy. 'Bringing someone like that into our home!' He gave him a clout around the head, which Paddy had anticipated, and he ducked, missing the brunt of it.

'Leave him, Joe,' my mother said sternly and she went to lift the lid on the seat of the settle. There, to my astonishment, was Danny, looking like a frightened rabbit.

The colourful language that my father used on seeing our secret lodger does not bear repeating. But it was my mother who calmed things down, saying that the soldiers would be back if they heard the ruckus.

'You must go, Danny,' my mother told him, 'you won't be safe in this village now.'

'Someone must have snitched,' Paddy said, feeling sorry for himself. He is fiercely determined to do his bit for the Brotherhood, but as much as my mother supports their cause, she would not have her oldest son join their ranks.

'Paddy, let tonight be a lesson to you. This is not a game and those soldiers aren't playing,' she said to him.

'Listen to your mother, Paddy,' said Danny. 'I'm grateful for your help, but your part in this is over now. Thank you, Mrs Butler,' he said, turning to my mother. 'I'll not forget your kindness,' he added, pulling his cap on his head and stalking cautiously to the back door.

'Hide in the cow shed till you're sure the coast is clear,' my father said with his back to us all. Danny hesitated and gave me the briefest of smiles, then disappeared into the blackness.

That was the last we heard of him, until this morning we found a beautifully iced Christmas cake on the doorstep.

Chapter Nineteen

6th January 2011

'Well, you want to see the tree, don't you?' Marcus said for the second time.

'Sorry, what?' Sarah felt embarrassed, standing barefoot at the door (which she had somehow managed to open properly). She was wearing a short nightdress and not having a bra on rendered her incapable of conversation. 'Just give me ten minutes,' she said, ducking into the bedroom and pulling on whatever clothes she had left crumpled on the bed.

It was very early in the morning, or at least that's what the birds were claiming at the top of their lungs and the lack of sleep was definitely catching up with her. Marcus waited out in the car and she could see his gloved hand tapping the steering wheel as some sort of symphony wafted from his car radio.

'All set?' he asked, as Sarah bundled into the passenger seat. 'It's only about a half hour drive to Fee's.'

'Fee?'

'Oh, Fíona. My better half.'

'I didn't realise you were married,' she said, yanking the seatbelt across her waist.

'I'm not,' Marcus replied, eyes twinkling.

'Oh, sorry, I just assumed,' said Sarah, suddenly feeling very old-fashioned.

'It's not through lack of asking, that's for sure. But Fíona Devine insisted that as long as I'm married to the hotel, she won't wear my ring. So, we've been living in sin for the last thirty years!'

The car took a rather speedy left turn out of the village and out into the wilds of Clare. The countryside was hibernating in its winter cloak of dark-limbed trees and stooping grasses. Sarah tried to imagine how beautiful the place would look in full bloom and wondered if she would ever come back here again. *What if you stay?* a little voice whispered inside her head.

The green Mercedes made its way from the main road onto a glorified path with grass down the middle. Silently praying that they wouldn't meet another car, or, worse, a tractor, Sarah saw an old woman standing by a gateway with a black shawl wrapped tightly around her head. The dark eyes that peered out at her seemed familiar and Sarah shivered under their glare.

'Do you know that woman?' she asked, as the car drove past.

'What woman?'

Sarah checked in her wing mirror and was stunned to find that there was no one there.

'Um, never mind,' she said, trying to block out the suspicion in her gut that those were the eyes that had appeared in her drawing of Thornwood House.

Before long, they pulled into the yard of an old two-storey farmhouse on the right-hand side of the road.

'Is this it?' she asked excitedly, conveniently putting her sighting of the old woman down to shadows from the winter sun and lack of sleep. After all, the last time she thought she'd seen a ghost, it turned out to be a donkey.

'That's the home place,' he confirmed. 'Though I should say it's Devine's Farm – I'm only a blow-in. Herself runs the farm. I'd be neither use nor ornament, or at least that's what she tells me.'

'It's so homely-looking,' she said, gazing at the old sash windows and the giant cartwheel leaning against the gable.

As the car pulled in, a menagerie of animals came to either greet or quarrel with them. A black and white collie barked maniacally and furiously wagged his tail until Sarah got out of the car and patted his head. As if by magic, he fell silent and still, luxuriating in her attention. Then came the geese, which threatened to send Sarah back to wherever she came from with angry hisses and outstretched wings.

'Get out of it now let ye,' came the shrill call of Fíona Devine. 'Welcome, my dear. Sarah, isn't it?'

'Hello, Fíona,' Sarah said, reaching to shake her hand and avoid being bitten by a goose.

'Call me Fee, please.'

Fee had two outstanding features: pure grey hair, styled

in a practical pixie cut that gave her a youthful look, and the palest blue eyes Sarah had ever seen. Her hand felt calloused and well used – the kind of hands Sarah's father would trust. Marcus gave her a quick peck on the cheek and the pair held hands as they walked Sarah to the back of the house.

'We don't use front doors in Ireland – at least not in the country anyway,' Marcus explained. The back porch served as a kind of tack room, filled with every kind of Wellington and coat known to man. This led to the kitchen, an inviting space that blurred the line between well-appointed and cluttered. If there was a rescue centre for abandoned chairs, this was it. The table was surrounded by two carver chairs, a bistro chair, chairs with cushioned seats, various stools and a bedraggled wicker chair painted bright pink. To say nothing of the mismatched Queen Annes that faced each other at the end of the room, providing the perfect spot for reading the books and papers that sat on low tables around them.

'Welcome to our home,' Marcus said, pulling out one of the cushioned refugees for Sarah to sit on. The kitchen table was laid with a plate of scones and there was a fat teapot wearing what looked like a sweater.

'Oh, Fee, you needn't have gone to all this bother,' Sarah said, overwhelmed by the hospitality and silently wishing she'd at least brought some flowers for her host.

'What trouble? Sure it's no trouble opening a pack of scones and a jar of jam. Don't be fooled into thinking I've been slaving over the stove all morning making cakes!' she joked, setting out earthenware mugs and plates.

This no-nonsense attitude made Sarah feel a little more relaxed. Fee explained that she was the first female in the Devine clan to inherit the farm. Neither of her brothers had any interest in farming and they were only too pleased to leave her to it, while they became 'big-shots' up in Dublin.

The pot of tea was emptied and refilled, as they sat and chatted for over an hour. Although Marcus and Fee were the same generation as her parents, they had a completely different attitude to life. The lack of family photos on the walls gave Sarah the impression that they'd never had children and perhaps this was the difference. Child-free couples always seemed a little non-conformist and a lot more relaxed.

'Right, we'll get nothing done today if we sit here stuffing our faces,' Fee announced, pushing back her chair. Marcus instinctively began clearing the table and sticking his hands into a pair of yellow rubber gloves.

'Leave them till later,' Fee said, pointing to the sink.

'When have you ever known me to leave a dirty dish unwashed?' Marcus replied with mock impatience. 'You two go on ahead.'

'I think he has that OCP,' she whispered to Sarah, who couldn't bring herself to correct the woman.

Eventually, they set off by foot to see the hawthorn tree; down an old track that crossed the land of neighbouring farmers. They were watched closely by a herd of black and white cows, chewing the cud in the manner of tough kids in the schoolyard spoiling for a fight. Sarah was glad to see the electric fence stood taut between them. She had been donated a pair of dark green wellies and was chaperoned by the collie who had welcomed her earlier. The day was dull and, according to Fee, smelled like rain, but it was mild and perfect for being outdoors.

'It's just beyond this hillock,' Fee assured her. 'The hawthorn is a sacred tree in Ireland. It looks just like any other tree in the woods, but it has its roots in the otherworld.'

'The otherworld?' Sarah asked.

'Where the fairies are said to reside.' This was said matter-of-factly, as though it was irrelevant whether it was simply superstition or an historical fact.

The roar of cars in the distance told Sarah that the motorway wasn't too far away. It was rough terrain, but as the land began to slope down, Sarah could see the view she had admired in the newspaper back at the airport in Newark. The motorway made a sweeping curve around a small parcel of land, upon which stood the hawthorn tree.

'It looks smaller than the picture,' Sarah said, feeling a bit naive.

'Small and mighty,' said Fee, who could easily have been referring to herself.

As they got closer, Sarah realised that this tree had an inexplicable presence that marked it out immediately. A long tangle of branches wound themselves around in an almost perfect circle and the tree was dressed, appropriately for the season, with dark red berries, which Fee informed her were called haws.

'You can make tea or wine with these,' she explained. 'I'm not much for baking or housework, but I do make good tea!'

Sarah felt a strong urge to touch the tree and cup the little berries in the palm of her hand.

'Careful!' said Fee.

Sarah automatically took a step back, half expecting a fairy to pop up and bite her.

'There are a lot of thorns.'

'Of course, hence the name,' Sarah said, smiling.

A strong wind had begun to pick up. It wasn't exactly how Sarah had imagined it would be and yet there was something captivating about this ancient tree, gnarled and dogged in its determination to stay rooted and strong, despite the changing seasons or the prevailing winds. She admired its tenacity.

'They're at their best in May, when they're in full bloom. Maybe you'll pay us another visit then?'

Sarah nodded, but as she gave Fee a weak smile, she recalled the last time she'd promised to return somewhere. After she'd left the hospital, she and Jack had travelled to Italy, neither of them wanting to be at home. They'd stood with all the other tourists at the Trevi Fountain in Rome, trying to fake a happiness they didn't feel. Following a very unromantic discussion about where all the coins ended up when the city cleaners came by to clear them out at the end of each day, they decided to forgo the tradition of throwing in a coin in order to secure their return to Rome. Sarah felt Jack's reluctance to act like a tourist in his ancestral home very keenly, but maybe she should have thrown that coin into the fountain. Maybe things would have been different. With that, she dug her fingers into her pocket and pulled out a euro coin.

'I should leave something, right?'

'Of course, good on you. We should always leave the fairies a little offering,' Fee replied.

Without any further prompting, Sarah turned and threw the coin over her left shoulder, hoping it would land somewhere in the vicinity of the tree.

'There,' she said, with an emphatic nod.

The pilgrimage at an end, they turned for home and began to pick their way back up the hill. They were welcomed back to the farm by a gaggle of noisy geese and the forlorn calls of sheep in the field beside the house.

'These lot will need feeding now,' Fee said, heading for the old barn at the side of the house.

'Maybe I could give you a hand?' Sarah asked, not wanting to go back to an empty cottage just yet.

There was still no sign of Marcus, so she began helping Fee to pour feed into various buckets.

'Did you find what you were hoping for?' Fee said, handing Sarah some work gloves. 'At the hawthorn tree?'

'I guess I'm not so good at hiding my feelings,' Sarah conceded. 'To be honest, coming to Ireland was more of a last-minute thing. I'm not sure what I was hoping for.'

Fee didn't pry any further. Instead she handed her a bucket of vegetable peelings and gave her the unenviable task of feeding the geese.

'Don't worry, it's the food they're after, not you.'

'Are you sure?' Sarah called back, trying to stand firm against the stampede.

When the bucket was empty, Sarah joined Fee in the adjoining field, where she was pouring feed into long troughs for the sheep. They came at speed from all sides, recognising their mistress immediately.

'You must love living here,' Sarah remarked, looking across the landscape of green fields, stitched together like an old patchwork quilt.

'I wouldn't live anywhere else,' she replied, wiping her brow. 'It can be hard at times, keeping it all going, but I love doing it.'

Sarah couldn't recall ever seeing someone so at one with their environment.

'It's in the blood,' Fee continued. 'My people have been working this land for centuries.'

'I wish I felt that grounded. Sometimes I wonder if I'm connected to anything at all—' Sarah halted self-consciously. What was she doing, talking like this to a complete stranger?

Fee hung the bucket in the crook of her arm and took a step closer to her.

'Just trust this,' she said, tapping her chest, 'and you won't go too far wrong.'

With a sharp inhale, Sarah fought to keep her tears at bay. Some people just knew exactly the right thing to say at exactly the right time. Fee gave her arm a firm pat, just as she had done with the animals to calm them, and Sarah found it strangely reassuring.

'Marcus tells me you've become friends with Oran,' she said, leading them back towards the shed with the empty buckets.

Sarah's face flushed, as though she'd been found out by the school principal.

'It's a small town,' Fee explained with a kind expression. 'Still, I'm glad you two have crossed paths.'

'Why is that?' Sarah asked.

Just then, Marcus made an appearance, jiggling his keys in the air and saying that he was ready to give her a ride back home.

'I'll let you figure that one out yourself,' Fee said with a smile.

On her return to Butler's cottage, Sarah noticed her sketchbook on the table. She opened it to her drawing of Thornwood House, but the eyes she was sure she had seen peering out from the shadows of charcoal were no longer there. Perhaps she'd imagined the entire thing. Turning the page, she smiled when she saw the drawing she'd done of the cottage. She had really captured its essence, the warmth of the hearth, the quaint perspective and the simple furnishings that lent it an uncomplicated air. Oran and his wife must have been so happy in this place, she realised. It was understandable that he didn't want to return here. Too many memories. She and Oran had a lot in common; both grieving, both running away from a past that no longer had a future. But how were you supposed to move on? To mend?

Then a thought struck her – maybe it was Fee's gentle nudge of encouragement, but she decided to act on it before she changed her mind. She tore out the page and, in the absence of a large enough envelope, sandwiched it between two blank sheets of drawing paper and secured it with a piece of string. Writing out the letters of his name suddenly felt weirdly personal but also thrilling. Still, that wasn't the point, she chided herself. She thought about writing a message, or a quote – something clever that would say, 'Hey, I know you've just had the worst experience of your life, but maybe you can learn to love this cottage again?' But that's why she was an artist. She wasn't good with words. She just had to hope her skills were up to the task. Without further ado, she walked to Brian Sweeney's house and left the drawing in the postbox before she could talk herself out of it.

Chapter Twenty

Anna's Diary

13th January 1911

My ankle has healed well enough, though I still have a slight limp. Billy says I'm beginning to waddle like a duck, so I'm doing my best to remedy that. Paddy is keeping a sensible distance from my father, and despite warnings from my mother to keep our family matters private, today I spilled the beans about Danny to Harold before we were even past our gate.

'None of you were hurt?' was his first question.

'Oh no, well, apart from Paddy, that is,' I said, giggling.

'There is indeed a sense that Ireland is on the cusp of something, a rebellion,' he mused. 'And where do you stand on the whole idea of Home Rule?'

I realised then that no one had ever asked my opinion on such a thing and so I thought long and hard about my answer. When I couldn't find the words, I thought of what my grandmother used to say.

'Well, I suppose the English have outstayed their welcome in Ireland,' I paraphrased, 'and there's nothing worse than a visitor who doesn't know when to go home!'

'Very articulately put,' Harold said. 'So, where are you taking me today?'

'The very home of the fairies,' I replied earnestly, 'Cnoc na Sí.'

As we entered the woods, the ground was scarlet with fallen berries from the holly trees, a sign that a harsh winter was yet to arrive. Startled pigeons flew from the branches as we walked by, making slow progress on my newly healed ankle.

'Here, take my arm,' Harold offered, and I hooked my arm in his. 'Any pain?'

'Not much,' I said, trying to disguise my limp.

It was very pleasant, walking along with him like that, arm in arm. Although he has only been in Thornwood for a short time, I have grown accustomed to his presence and have enjoyed our time together. He has made me feel like I am worth listening to.

As we came to the clearing at the top of the hill, Harold stood and admired the view of the village from our raised vantage point.

'God, I love it here,' he said, taking a deep breath. 'I shall miss it when I go back.'

'When must you return to our dear old England?' I said in a very bad English accent.

'Oh, another few weeks, I suppose. Maybe I'll try and stretch it out a bit longer. How would that suit you?' he asked.

I wasn't sure why he was asking me, as if I could influence his plans either way, but I told him that his presence in Thornwood was always welcome.

'Now, Cnoc na Sí,' I said, getting back to the matter at hand.

'Right,' Harold said, taking out his beloved notebook and pencil.

'It's called hill of the fairies because this is said to be where they dwell. People believe that there are excavated passages inside the hill and a palace where the fairies live, in an underground world.' I led him around the hilltop, pointing at hollows and markings in the stones. As children, we believed that every blade of grass was guarded over by a fairy, so it wasn't hard for our overactive minds to imagine forts and dwellings hidden in the smallest of places.

'Some people believe that after consumptives depart this earth, they can be found here, living with the fairies in good health.' I watched his reaction closely. If he truly believed me, I would take it as a sign to tell him all. 'They say that the real body and the soul are carried off together to Fairyland, and those of a changeling substituted in its place. The old body left soon declines and dies. Some say that our loved ones are still alive and well, but we cannot see them,' I said, a lump forming in my throat.

'Hmm, it sounds akin to the hill in Knockma that John O'Conghaile told us about,' Harold said, flicking through his notebook. He stopped then and bent down on one knee, pulling a long blade of grass and rubbing it between his fingers. It was like he was trying to feel the magic of the place or understand the imagination of a people so closely bonded to the earth.

'I envy you, Anna,' he said finally.

'Why do you say that?'

'You see; I merely observe. I study the facts and I write my field notes, trying to make sense of the things I do not fully understand. But you: you are part of this place and its secrets live within you. You walk through this landscape, as I walk through it, but you are as much a part of it as the leaves on the trees. You don't need to try to understand because the knowledge is already in you.'

My heart quickened and my skin grew clammy as my mind settled on my decision. If anyone could help me to find Milly, it was Harold. Without knowing the words, I made to speak, but heard a rustling from behind us and held my tongue.

'Good day!' came a shrill call that broke the peace of the place. My features shifted as I saw it was George Hawley on his horse Seaborne.

'Good day, Master George,' I replied with a smile that hardly fitted the confines of my face.

'Mister Hawley,' Harold said, not in greeting but merely an acknowledgement of his presence.

'You've picked a fine day for a perambulation,' George

said, his shining boots gleaming like the leather of Seaborne's saddle. He always seemed too perfect to be real.

'We're engaged in some important research, so if you don't mind—' I had never seen Harold so reluctant to have a conversation before and even found him rather rude.

'Looking for fairies!' George snorted, which made me feel embarrassed for Harold, when only a moment before….

'Well, I won't keep you then, but my sister and I would like to invite you to a little soirée we're having on the sixteenth.'

I had no idea what a soirée was, but I knew I was invited to it and I wasn't going to miss my chance this time.

'That sounds just wonderful, Master George!' I said.

'Olivia and I are celebrating our twenty-first birthday, so put on your glad rags.'

He gave me a little wink and said he looked forward to seeing us there, but in my heart, I knew his words were for me alone. I felt like my blood was fizzing inside my body as I watched him retreat down the pathway at a trot.

'Isn't it brilliant, Harold? A party at the big house!' I squeaked.

'I'm glad it pleases you, Anna,' he replied, but he didn't look glad. 'I'm not sure if I will attend.'

'Oh, but you must!' I implored. I knew there was no way my mother would let me go to that party without some kind of chaperone, and Harold had almost become one of the family.

'Must I?' he said, looking at me strangely.

'Of course,' I said, searching for a winning argument.

'It's a party!' When that didn't seem to do the trick, I became more creative. 'Miss Olivia will want you there.'

The look he gave me then was one of a tired old man, at his wits' end trying to explain something I would never understand. But he wasn't one to wallow in unhappy moods. The corners of his eyes creased as his smile returned. It was like a warm breeze on a fine day.

'If it will make you happy, then of course we shall go,' he acquiesced.

Needless to say, the excitement of George's invitation put paid to my plan to tell Harold about Milly. It would have to wait for another time, because my mind was suddenly reeling with thoughts of dancing and dresses. I went to the Fox's for my dinner so I could discuss the entire thing at length with Tess.

'You're a right madam!' Tess sulked, when I finally told her all about my meeting with George Hawley and my brief visit to Thornwood House. 'Why didn't you tell me?'

'I wanted to tell you but Mother swore me to secrecy. No one else knows, so you can't go telling Paddy,' I warned her.'

'Why would I tell your brother anything?' she asked, cheeks reddening.

'Now who's calling who a madam? Don't think I haven't seen you giving him those big cow eyes.'

'Anna Butler, take that back!'

We spent a lively evening talking about silly, girlish things with all of the intensity of two women of the world. After we decided that I should ask Paddy about his intentions regarding Tess, conversation returned to the forthcoming magical night at Thornwood House. 'I've nothing to wear, and my mother will hardly let me buy a new dress to go to the Hawleys'. She's forbidden me to go there,' I said, biting my lip.

'So, what makes you think she'll let you go to the party?' she asked, tying up my dark curls in various styles.

'I'm hoping that once I tell her Harold is going, she'll be a bit more favourable to the idea.'

'Oh, Harold now, is it?' Tess teased. 'Harold and George, well, aren't we very grand now altogether!'

I had to laugh along with her. Girls like us didn't meet Harolds or Georges and certainly didn't have the clothes for it, either.

'But can you imagine the finery that will be there on the night? I don't want to make a show of myself, arriving in some dowdy frock.'

'How many days have we got?' she asked.

'Only two days, why?'

'It's going to be tight, but I think we can do it,' she said, having made some invisible calculations.

'Do what? What are you talking about?'

'Well, you're only looking at the two finest lace makers in all of the county! If we can't create a garment fit for a princess, then who can?' She pulled herself up to her full height as she reached to the top of the wardrobe to fetch her sewing box. 'Haven't we spent long enough dressing the gentry? It's about time we had something pretty to wear ourselves.'

'Yes, but I cannot go in a white lace dress. It's not my wedding. All we have is this white thread and it's too late to go ordering it now,' I said, as she handed me her knitting box filled with the wrong colour thread.

'You're right, it's not a wedding. Well, not yet anyway!' We giggled so raucously that her mother scolded us for cackling like hens. 'Leave it to me, we'll sort something out,' she said, and I hugged my friend fiercely before skipping home across the bog with a full bright moon lighting my way.

Chapter Twenty-One

Anna's Diary

14th January 1911

Tess and I began our dressmaking work early this morning. I made sure Mother was out on long errands, and my father and brothers were similarly occupied, so that Tess and I had the house to ourselves before beginning our preparations. I found a plain white cotton dress that my grandparents bought me for a neighbour's wedding a couple of years ago. It is a bit too small for me now, but with a few alterations, I hoped it might do for our purpose.

Tess came with a small sack under her arm and proudly revealed the contents with a triumphant flourish of her hands.

'Onion skins?' I asked, perplexed.

'We're going to dye the thread!' she announced excitedly, fetching a pot and filling it with water from the barrel.

'Do you know how? Have you done it before?' I asked, helping her.

'Well, not exactly. But I heard Nelly O'Halloran at the post office telling Eileen Gallagher that her mother-in-law used to do it all the time with the wool before spinning it,' she said confidently.

'It'll be fine.'

I didn't share her optimism, but for lack of any better ideas, I took on the role of her assistant, while the head dressmaker gave the orders. We boiled the yellow onion skins and let them simmer in the pot for half an hour. Then we soaked the thread and the cotton dress in hot water before placing them in the dye, being careful to remove the skins first. We reheated the water and, using an old wooden spoon, stirred the pot to ensure the colour spread evenly. When we took it out to rinse it under cold water, no one was more astonished than I to see we had created a bright gold dress and matching thread.

'Tess, it's magical!' I cried with sheer wonder.

'Told you it would work,' she said, although she did seem surprised with the results herself. 'Now, we must hang them out to dry, maybe in the shed where no one can see? she suggested.

'Well, that's the first part done,' I said. 'Now all we have to do is turn this plain cotton dress into a ball gown.'

'You are not going to that house!' my mother announced, as she poured a pool of buttermilk into the mound of flour on the table. She never uses a bowl when making bread, instead she builds a wall of flour and pours the liquid into a central moat. Gradually, she coaxed the mixture together with circular movements of her right hand, held in the shape of a claw. She always throws in an extra handful of raisins too, in case anyone might think she is ungenerous. 'Did you throw them in from the door?' she says to me, if I ever make the bread without enough fruit.

'But I'll be with Harold,' I whined for the umpteenth time. 'He'll be my chaperone.'

'I don't care if the Pope himself is with you, you're not going to that house, Anna Butler, and that is final. Now bring in some more turf for the fire and get those notions out of your head.'

I went outside and took the thread and my old cotton dress down from the rafters in the shed. They had dried beautifully and were just waiting to be spun into a fairy-tale gown. I held them in my hands and felt like the sorriest girl in the world.

'Well, there's no use in sulking,' I said to myself. So I packed them in a bag and called to my mother that I was going over to Fox's. She made some protest about my gallivanting, but I shouted back that going to Tess's house hardly qualified.

'She's forbidden you then?' Tess said, seeing the gloomy look on my face. I just nodded and threw myself on her bed. 'She didn't find the dress, did she?'

'No, but sure it's all a waste now.' Muffled by her pillow, my voice came out small and childlike.

She dawdled for a moment and when I looked up I noticed a bashful look on her face.

'What is it?' I asked.

'Well, I was wondering, did you talk to Paddy?'

'I didn't get a chance yet. He's been avoiding the place since the whole Danny incident. But I promise, I'll get him on his own tonight.'

Tess took the golden threads and the dress out of the bag, marvelling at how well they looked.

'Jeez, we didn't do a half-bad job, did we?'

'It was you really, Tess.'

Her countenance changed utterly when she received a compliment. Her features looked almost angelic, as if butter wouldn't melt in her mouth. Most of the time, she seems on the verge of having an argument. Maybe it comes from growing up in such a large family, but she is always on the defensive. Her jealousy gets the better of her, despite the fact that she has more than most. But when you're too busy coveting your neighbour's goods, you cannot see your own blessings. At least that's what Father Peter taught us in catechism.

'Let's make the dress anyway, Anna. Sure, what have we got to lose?' she said, nudging me with her elbow.

'It's a lot of work for nothing.'

'Don't be such a poor mouth; sure, there'll always be some dance or other coming up. Besides, my mother always says you never know what will happen from one day to the next and wouldn't you be raging if you suddenly got to go to the party and you didn't have a dress?' she said, holding out the thread.

'You're a good friend, Tess Fox.'

'Yes, I am,' she replied matter-of-factly. 'And it just so happens that I've already sketched out a pattern, so get your crochet needle out and start working!'

We worked for hours, until my fingers were creased with indentations from my needle. Tess let out the dress at the seams and started sewing the delicate lace around the edge of the neck and the sleeves, creating a beautiful overlay of crochet flowers and teardrops. I couldn't quite believe the progress we had made, but when I looked at the clock, I screeched to see how late it was. I rushed off home across the dew-soaked fields, sure that my mother would be waiting up to give me an earful. But it was Paddy who was sitting by the fire when I got home, staring blindly at the embers.

'Is everyone asleep?' I whispered, looking about me like a thief.

'Don't worry; Mother said she'll have a few choice words for you in the morning,' he said.

We both threw our eyes up to heaven in sibling unity. I took off my coat and my boots and pulled on a pair of my woolly socks that were warming by the fire.

'How do you fancy a hot cup of cocoa before bed?' I asked, putting a pan on to boil.

'I wouldn't say no. So, what have you done to get Mother riled up?'

'Well, I haven't been harbouring a wanted man, if that's what you mean,' I answered, slyly. As the milk began to bubble, I took it off the heat and added the cocoa powder.

'No, you're just swanning around the countryside, chasing leprechauns.' He took the steaming cup from my hands and blew lightly on the surface.

'Don't make fun of me, Paddy, you know I don't like it.' He had believed me about Milly once, but the years had robbed him of his sensitivity to such childish things.

'I'm not making fun of you; I'm just trying to make you understand. There are more important things going on in the world, Anna – you can't have your head stuck in the clouds all of your life.'

What's wrong with having your head in the clouds? I wanted to say. It certainly isn't doing Harold any harm. But he is a man – a man with means, not a farmer's daughter. He can do as he likes. So, I kept quiet because I knew what Paddy was doing. He was trying to toughen me up for the big bad world, in that annoying way that older brothers do. Thinking they know best. As if I am not already keenly aware of how unfair life can be. I decided to change the subject.

'Are you courting anyone, Paddy?' I asked, blowing on the hot drink.

'Like I'd tell you!' he said, almost choking on his cocoa.

'Well, I know someone who fancies you.' I was acting all smug in my knowledge, but it was pointless if he wasn't going to play along. After enough time had passed, I pressed on. 'Do you want to know who it is?' He was a great card player and you could never tell if he was bluffing. 'It's Tess,' I said finally, unable to hold my tongue. He just stared into the fire, giving nothing away. 'Well? Do you like her?' I asked.

'As if I'd tell you,' he said again, this time with a smirk, and got up to go to bed.

Chapter Twenty-Two

8th January 2011

'Jack.' Sarah said his name and it felt like saying a secret out loud after years of keeping it in. Her entire body froze when she saw his number on the screen.

'Hey, I just wanted to call and see if you're okay. Meghan told me you were in Ireland…' He left the sentence hanging, waiting for his wife to offer an explanation.

'Yes' was all she could manage. There was no easy way to say why she had ended up on the other side of the Atlantic, and besides, why should she explain herself to him? Sarah had grown weary of trying to make things palatable for everyone around her.

She decided to say as little as possible. "I'm … yes. I'm pretty good, actually.'

'Oh.'

'You sound disappointed!' Sarah was suddenly spoiling for a fight, but she wasn't sure why.

'Jesus, Sarah, I just … I was worried, that's all. I still care about you. That's okay, isn't it?'

Sarah hung her head and tried to wipe the anguish she felt from her face. Jack's concern had become a stick she used to beat herself with. *Look how kind and thoughtful he's being – shouldn't that be enough?* she would think to herself. Yet with time and distance, she was starting to realise that his 'caring' was just suffocating and disabling. She didn't want him belittling her trip to Ireland and she could already hear that patronising tone in his voice, as if she couldn't cope without him.

'I don't know.'

'Right, well…'

He was winded, she could tell. Normally, his Mr Nice Guy routine could charm her out of any argument. She let herself be cajoled and accepted her role as the one in the wrong. The one who had to change or do better or say sorry. Perhaps she had been too afraid of losing him. But she had lost something far more valuable and his approval didn't seem to matter so much anymore.

'It's too late to ask me if I'm okay, Jack. I haven't been okay for a long time. But you didn't want to hear that, did you? Did you think that by avoiding me, you could avoid what happened?'

'Sarah, honey, I never meant…' He trailed off and sighed heavily. 'Look, blame me if it makes you feel better, but you shut me out, too.'

'I shut *you* out? Don't you remember what you said to me after the hospital? You said you weren't able to deal with my pain as well as your own! Who says that, Jack?

Who says that to their own wife? I've spent the past two years trying to hide my grief from you, in case you got upset. We should have been grieving together but you completely abandoned me and I'll never forgive you for that.'

Sarah hadn't realised that she was shouting. She was shaking, but it felt so liberating to finally tell him the truth. Notwithstanding the thousands of miles that stretched between them. Perhaps he had already hung up. Then his voice came down the line, almost unrecognisable.

'You're not the only one who lost someone!' With that, the phone went dead.

Sarah was still shaking by the time she made it to the store. They didn't sell hard liquor, so she bought two bottles of white wine and a packet of cigarettes.

'I'll take that box of chocolates, too,' she said to the girl behind the counter, who put the makings of a pity party into a plastic bag.

'No resolutions, then?'

'What?'

'You know, for the New Year. Most people give this stuff up,' she said, handing Sarah her change.

'Well, I'm not most people,' Sarah said. She shuddered at how this young girl must see her: a grumpy middle-aged woman with a chip on her shoulder the size of Texas. *Screw it*, she thought to herself, *why should I go out of my way to make these people like me? They couldn't possibly know what I'm going through and frankly, it's none of their business anyway.*

The eternal dusk that seemed to be January in Ireland closed in upon her as she walked back to the cottage. The low-lying clouds made it feel as though the sky started about five feet above her head. There were no cars on the road, so she opened one of the bottles and took long, satisfying gulps. She pulled the cellophane off the cigarette pack and coaxed one out with her lips, like a horse searching for sugar lumps. She hadn't smoked since college, but her body was suddenly craving nicotine. The first inhalation almost choked her, as it caught the back of her throat by surprise. How had she enjoyed these things? A quick slug of wine helped to put the fire out and, determined to kick-start the habit, she took another drag, albeit shorter this time. What was the point in making her body a temple, anyway, she wondered defiantly? Being good never seemed to do her any good. So, she might as well be bad.

'You'll be the Yank, I suppose,' came a voice out of nowhere.

Sarah spun around to find the old woman in the dark shawl standing behind her.

'Where… How did you…?'

'You're fond of the old drop, I see?' said the woman, looking pointedly at the open bottle in Sarah's hand. ''Tis bad luck not to offer a drink to your neighbour.'

Sarah was dumbstruck. She couldn't say why, but the woman frightened her. Her wiry frame was crooked with age and her face, although mostly covered, was deeply lined and sprouting grey hairs on her cheeks and chin.

'I've seen you before,' she finally managed to say, but the woman was only interested in the bottle.

'I'll tell you your fortune for a drink.'

Sarah would have given her the bottle anyway, just to be rid of her. The woman held it to her lips and swallowed almost half of its contents before letting out a loud belch.

'I thank ye,' she said, offering the bottle back to Sarah.

'It's okay. You keep it.' Sarah winced at the thought of putting her lips where that horrible woman's had been. 'Wait, how did you know I was American?'

The old woman ignored her, as her eyes glazed over and she appeared to go into some kind of trance.

'You have the stench of death on you,' she said. 'I see blood. No heartbeat.'

Sarah stepped back from her.

'How could you say such a thing?'

The woman's eyes turned on her and she seemed lucid once more.

'I have the sight, I don't choose what I see.'

'Just stay the hell away from me,' Sarah said, breaking into a half run. It was only when she was almost at the cottage that she permitted herself to look back. The road was empty. Her fingers felt numb and twice their size as she fumbled with them at the front door. Tears were already blurring her vision. Once inside, she locked the door behind her and planned on never opening it again.

∾

It was dark outside when she heard the knocking at the front door. Curled up on the couch, she hadn't even managed to light the fire and now she was shivering with the cold. The second bottle of wine she'd bought had barely touched the sides. The knocking came again, a little louder this time. That old woman had really shaken her up. What if it was her again? She got up and stood beside the door, listening for anything that might betray the identity of the person. When the knocking came again she almost jumped.

'What do you want?' she shouted angrily.

'Uh, don't want to bother you. It's me, Oran. I just…'

'Oh, shit,' Sarah said, trying to open the door. For once, it came easily.

'Hi,' he said, a lopsided smile on his face. He was holding a piece of paper. Her drawing, she realised. On reading her expression, his features changed. 'Sorry, I shouldn't have dropped in like this, it's clearly not a good time.'

Sarah could well imagine how she looked. Eyes red from crying, a blanket wrapped around her shoulders, hair in need of a wash.

'No, it's fine, it's just…' What could she say? That she'd had a fight with her ex, been scared half to death by some crazy old woman and spent the last two hours drinking in the dark?

'I just wanted to say thanks. For the drawing, I mean,' he said, looking slightly sheepish.

'Oh, yes, of course, I…'

'It was really thoughtful. Anyway, I'll leave you to it,' he said, already halfway down the path.

'But—' she began, then realised she was now sounding desperate on top of looking hysterical.

He raised a hand that may have meant, 'I totally get it' or 'I've had a lucky escape', Sarah couldn't decide which. She closed the door and slumped down against it. That was probably the first time he'd wanted to come inside the cottage since his wife died and she'd spoiled it. She let her head knock back against the door in frustration. Seeing him standing there, holding her drawing in one hand, the other hand in his pocket, all she wanted to do was reach out to him. *Even a broken heart still feels.* She'd read that somewhere. And in her own mixed-up way, she thought that by fixing someone else's, she might heal her own.

'Idiot,' she said, smacking her forehead with her palm.

Chapter Twenty-Three

Anna's Diary

18th January 1911

I have so much to write down about the events of the
Hawleys' party and what happened in the days afterwards.
I can still scarcely believe it all…

I woke early on the day of the party to a cold gale
blowing in from the north, for the wind had shifted during
the night. I couldn't sleep for thinking about Master George
and the party at Thornwood House, and my dress. I lit the
candle by my bed so I could do some drawings. Tess had
suggested a fishnet lace to cover the arms, and she had
borrowed a beautiful satin ribbon in ivory that would finish
the waist perfectly. I thought about what a coincidence it
was to meet George up at Cnoc na Sí again. Was it foolish to
believe that he had gone there with the hope of seeing me? I

didn't think it was possible for a man like George to be enamoured of someone like me? He could have his pick of girls, but he had asked me to come to the party, so surely that had to mean something.

When my morning's work was finished, I found Harold waiting for me at our gate. He was clapping his hands against his body to keep himself warm, despite the fact that he wore a large woollen overcoat, gloves and scarf. The sight of him made me smile. Yanks are accustomed to a bit more comfort, I imagine. Yet he loves our land, even if it doesn't always love him back.

'Good morning, Anna!' he called, as I walked up the lane, scattering the hens that scratched the ground for food.

'Have you been waiting long? You should have come in to sit by the fire.'

His dark hair was greased back and his spectacles glinted in the morning light. I suddenly felt shy in his presence and my breath caught in my throat. I never imagined myself being acquainted with a scholar. Wasn't it the strangest thing that two people as different as ourselves, from the opposite sides of the world, had crossed paths?

'Then I would have missed the enlightening conversation I had with Nora Dooley,' he said, adjusting his scarf.

I would have thought missing a meeting with Nora Dooley was a blessing, but perhaps she had a story for him.

'Are you familiar with the woman they call the seeress – a Maggie Walsh?'

The hairs on the back of my neck tingled. So, there was no avoiding her, then.

'Yes, I know of her.'

I said nothing further and Harold looked at me the way our dog Jet looks when straining to hear a far-off sound.

'She lives beyond Cnoc na Sí,' I told him, after a time.

'Well, we'd best make a start then,' he said, turning the wheel of his bike towards the road.

We cycled along in silence for a while, something that never seemed to bother Harold, one way or the other. Still, he must have known by then that I can't stay quiet for long, so it was just a waiting game.

'She's not very, how did you put it once … reliable.'

There. I had said my piece. Let him make his own mind up after that.

'Why do you say that?'

God, but he was forever asking questions, I thought to myself. Then quickly remembered that he was paying me for this very reason and flushed with embarrassment.

'Didn't Nora Dooley tell you?' I asked. If I had spoken to my mother this way, she would have accused me of 'being smart'. I didn't mean to be, not with Harold of all people, but it was the thought of visiting Maggie Walsh that made me uneasy.

'Not exactly,' he said, putting on his brakes. I stopped too, in the middle of the road. 'She told me that this … seeress helped her to see her husband. Her dearly departed husband. Apparently, she required only offerings of food and—'

'And did she tell you that she was brought before the magistrate for it? Having everyone believe that she could bring back their loved ones from the Fairy World, just by fattening them up?' I suddenly realised how high-pitched my voice had become. They were not my words, but my mother's. She had warned me against Maggie Walsh on more than one occasion. 'That woman preys on people's sorrow,' she had said.

'Yes, she did mention some trouble with the law. But she insisted that she had seen her husband, walking the fields at dusk. She said it was a small price to pay, giving Maggie the food to bring him back.'

'That was no more John Dooley than the cat! She stole their clothes, the deceased's clothes,' I said, blessing myself. 'That's how she did it. She dressed up some young one, so it looked from a distance like the person who had passed. It was just trickery. She cheated Nora Dooley and more besides.'

I had said more than I wanted to. We walked along the road a bit and leaned our bikes against an old tree trunk at the bottom of Cnoc na Sí.

'We'll have to walk the rest of the way,' I said in almost a whisper. I didn't know if I was betraying myself, Harold or Milly by my outburst. It is true that Maggie Walsh has been accused of swindling decent folk, but I wasn't sure if I truly thought her a cheat or a liar, and for some reason, I didn't want Harold to think that either. Or rather, I didn't know what I wanted.

'You know, we don't have to take sides, Anna. My job is to document these stories and present the facts. All you're doing is helping me to shine a light on this place; it's not up to us where the shadows will fall.'

The smile returned to my face. I felt just like I did after

confession, absolved of all my sins and free of blame. It wasn't until that moment that I realised the weight I had been carrying, ever since I agreed to help Harold collect his stories. I worried that Harold's view of this place rested entirely on how I presented it. Yet, as much as he relied on me to understand Thornwood and its inhabitants, I wasn't sure I could rely on myself. Still, I had to put my misgivings away as we set off up the winding path, over the hill and beyond the trees.

Our faces were ruddy and our eyes gleaming from the wind when we descended the far side of the hill. The sky was a dark bruise overhead and I prayed the rain would hold off. If you don't know where to look, you can easily walk right past Maggie Walsh's abode without knowing it. She lives in an old *bothán*, a one-roomed cottage, whose walls are disguised with green moss and lichen. The roof, what there is of it, badly needs thatching and the one narrow window at the front hardly lets in enough light for her to see her own hand in front of her face.

A croaking jackdaw skulked high in the branches of a beech tree, keeping a close eye on us. I looked doubtfully at Harold, but he seemed more curious than daunted. He stepped towards a dark depression in the wall that he assumed must house a door. It opened just as he went to knock upon it. Maggie Walsh was a terrible sight. I couldn't put an age on her, or tell whether it was the elements that had lined her face or simply time. She was a rake of a woman, and the skin hung in folds around her eyes and her mouth. Her hair was like twine made of silver and charcoal strands, tied in a long plait down her back.

Even her clothes were like rags, I noticed, bleached of their original colour long ago and the rips left unrepaired. I lost all my manners and just stood there, mouth hanging open.

'You've brought the American, I see?' she said in Irish.

I looked at Harold and hunched my shoulders.

'Indeed, I've heard all about your story collecting,' she said, still in Irish, motioning for us to come inside. Harold ducked under the lintel and I followed in his wake. The stench of the place almost forced me back out; a damp, earthy smell tinged with burning hair and something putrid that choked the air. She took an ember from the fire with the tongs and lit the tobacco in her pipe.

'So, you know why we have come to visit you?' Harold asked.

'This is a land of whispering grasses, Mr Krauss. There's not much happens in Thornwood that I don't hear about.'

I translated her answer for him. My eyes were still adjusting to the dark when I spotted two green eyes staring at me from a height. I jumped instinctively, making Maggie laugh.

''Tis only the cat, girl. Sit yourselves down,' she insisted, but when I looked for somewhere to perch, all I could see in the darkness were some upturned crates with old pieces of cloth on them. Whatever her schemes in the past, they hadn't made her rich.

'I would like to talk to you about the fairy faith here in Thornwood,' Harold began, taking his notebook out of his satchel. I doubted whether he would be able to see the page in this dim light. 'You've probably heard, I've been travelling all along the west coast, meeting the locals and exploring this magnificent landscape.'

I translated the entire thing for her, but she didn't seem to be listening to me. Maggie tapped the pipe against her lips, twisting into a wry grin. She was intuiting more than his words.

'Aye, I can see it working on you, lad,' she said, eyeing him closely. She had switched to English with a thick accent that sounded like Cork or Kerry to me. 'Don't stay in Ireland for too long, story collector, it'll catch you.' Her hands grabbed the air and she cackled wildly to herself. Even in the dark I could see the black of her fingernails. I hoped Harold would be quick about his business; I did not want to tarry a moment longer in that place.

'I have met with some of the older generation on my travels; there are those who believe fairies are the spirits of our dead friends,' he continued, ignoring her remark and pulling at his shirt collar.

Maggie took a long draw from her pipe and puffed out clouds of smoke, like a chimney in slack winds.

''Tis true, they say that if you have many friends deceased, you have many friendly fairies,' she agreed, nodding her head. 'Then it's equally true that if you have many enemies deceased, you have many fairies looking to do you harm.'

'Do you have any contact with The Good People yourself?' he asked.

'Contact? Ho-ho, do you hear that, girleen, contact!' She hugged herself with the laughter.

'Nora Dooley told me that you could bring the departed back from the dead. From the otherworld. Is that true?'

She took a moment to answer, the laughter gone out of her now.

'They came here looking for comfort and I gave it to them. 'Tis true, I have the gift to see what is unseen on this earth and I did my best to restore those that had passed over. It doesn't always work. They decide, not I.'

The familiar sound of Harold scratching the words into his book seemed to hypnotise the woman.

'I have another *scéal* for you, story collector.'

We both looked up, like dogs waiting for more crumbs.

'But it's not for the girl's ears, or anyone else from this village. I swore I would never tell a soul in this land and I have kept my word.'

'I will treat your testimony with the utmost confidentiality,' Harold said, straightening his spectacles.

'You'll be keeping my name out of it?' she asked in plainer language.

'You have my word. It is the story I'm after, nothing more.'

They both looked at me and it was clear my presence was no longer required. I'd be lying if I said I wasn't relieved to be leaving that hovel. I stood to go, resisting the urge to brush the dust from my clothes.

'I'll be waiting at the top of the hill,' I said, 'where the rocks are,' but already I was thinking of the whin bush at the rear of the *bothán*, perfect for hiding.

I made myself as comfortable as I was going to get, huddled behind the thorny bushes, which, thankfully, blocked the wind. I had tramped off in the opposite direction for what I thought was long enough to fool them, then cut back along the ash trees that backed onto the *bothán*. It was difficult to hear what they were saying within, but as luck would have it, the thatch was balding at the corner of the low roof, showing bare rafters. If I strained towards it and the wind eased off a bit, I could hear well enough.

'I warned them, you know, about cutting that tree,' she said. 'For all the good it did.'

'What tree?' I heard Harold ask.

'The hawthorn, up at Thornwood House.'

My ears pricked up like a horse. Did she have a story about the Hawleys?

'But sure, no one wanted to listen to Maggie Walsh then. It was a few years after that, late one night, when I had an unexpected visitor. The rain was pelting down on the thatch and the thunder booming. You wouldn't have put your dog out in it. There was a hard rap on the door and when I opened it, there she stood, all her finery drownded, like a rat. Desperate, she was. That's how they all come in the end, to see the cailleach. The hag. The witch. When no one else will help them.'

'Lady Hawley? She came to you for help?'

At that very moment, the bothersome jackdaw cawed at some unseen threat in the distance. I tried shushing him, waving at him and finally sticking my tongue out, which seemed to do the trick. He spread his wings and flew south to the river. I settled my breath and cocked my ears again, until the murmuring of their voices became clear again.

'"They're not natural," she kept telling me. Those twins had her driven half mad. Her eyes were red raw with crying, her whole body shaking. She knew they weren't right.'

'How do you mean?' asked Harold.

'She told me straight: "Those two imps are not the babies I birthed. They squeal and suck my milk like two piglets, wailing day and night as if the devil himself possesses them." She no longer recognised them and claimed they were not of her blood.'

My pulse quickened and I scrambled closer to the hole in the roof, getting scratches on my hands and face from the brambles for my trouble.

'I see. And why come to you, why not attend a physician?'

'Oh, you can be sure that I was the very last person she came to. The doctor told her to rest, that 'twas all in her mind. But her maid was canny and brought her here. I had seen it before, young mothers who hadn't protected their child with the iron, so I knew what had to be done.'

'I'm sorry,' said Harold, 'what had to be done?'

'Well, story collector, when a mother no longer knows her own child, there can only be one explanation. A changeling.'

The words were carried to me on the wind and crawled inside my ear; I shook my head to empty them out again, but it was no good.

'You know what a changeling is, story collector? The Good People steal a healthy human child and they replace them with one of their own. Sickly things they are, always hungry, always bawling, never thriving. Local women know to put irons above the crib for protection, but Lady Hawley didn't have the knowledge.'

I gulped down my shock and hoped they hadn't heard me.

'She said she would do anything to have her own children returned to her. So, I set about banishing those creatures back to where they came from.'

'And, um, you succeeded in your endeavours?'

'Musha, I tried. The only way to get rid of a changeling is to put it in harm's way. The fairies won't see their own suffer. They'll come to claim their changeling and return the human baby. There are ways,' Maggie said, her voice lowering again to a murmur, leaving gaps in her story.

'—and the foxglove. I've witnessed them putting the fairies out of the child with fire, or drowning, but Lady Hawley wouldn't agree to that. So, I told them to bring the twins to the top of Cnoc na Sí on the next full moon. I had one of the travelling men make me a small box, big enough for the two of them, and we dug out a hollow for them in the ground.'

'Wait a moment, I'm not sure I'm following you here,' I heard Harold say. 'Are you suggesting that … forgive me, are you saying that you harmed the children in some way?'

'Of course not! I placed them in the little box and fastened the lid. That way, no wild animals could get at them. Then we waited for *na daoine maithe* to come and claim them.'

'You … buried them? Alive?'

I could hear the alarm in Harold's voice and clasped my hand firmly over my mouth in case a scream would escape.

'Ara, they weren't buried, couldn't I still hear them howling as we walked away and hid further off in the bushes, waiting for Them. But it was all for nothing. The maid took a fit of panic and ran back to the house, telling his lordship what we'd done. He rushed up there with a crowbar and took those changelings back, before the fairies had time to return the real Hawley babies. He beat his wife that night and threatened to send us all to the gallows.

'But his pride saved us. He couldn't have everyone knowing what his wife had done. So, the maid was paid for her silence, I swore blind that I would not tell a soul to save my own neck and sure, poor Lady Hawley was dragged back home. The very next day they found her, her skull cracked on the ground. Believe me when I tell you, story collector, there will never be any luck in that house. It's cursed and the family with it.'

I fell back onto the grass, feeling dizzy and a bit sick. It couldn't be real, I told myself. Everyone knew Maggie Walsh was soft in the head and spiteful to boot. She must have been making it up, for Harold's benefit. For all I knew, she was probably asking him for food or money in return for this little performance. And it wasn't as if Lady Hawley was alive to put things right.

Yet I wondered what Harold thought. Did he believe her? Harold, whom I could now hear saying his farewells, brought me back to my senses. I made a dash for the hill and felt the muscles in my legs burning as I climbed upwards, away from Maggie and her scary stories.

Harold spoke not one word about his meeting with Maggie Walsh, while I chattered the whole way back through the woods, pretending not to have heard a thing. The thought of those two babies – half buried; half alive; half fairy – and their mother half mad, throwing herself to her death. It was too awful to be true. If it was true, the Hawley twins were lucky to still be alive and anyone could see that they were very much human. Poor Lady Hawley must have been in an awful way to go along with such a desperate plan. How distressing, to imagine one's children stolen and replaced by changelings. Perhaps Mother had been right all along and it was best to give Maggie Walsh a wide berth.

The walk home brought us back to more familiar surroundings and with every step we put a welcome distance between ourselves and the awful tales of the seeress. We came across my father digging and preparing the soil for spring sowing in one of the fields. He had our old horse Aengus with him, so named after the Scottish man that sold him to us at the fair. As the afternoon sun set low in the sky, the image of man and beast and nature working in unison was a striking sight. We waved over at him and he took the opportunity to break from his work.

'*Bail ó Dhia ar an obair*!' I called out the traditional blessing – God bless the work.

'Afternoon, Mister Butler,' Harold said, his American accent softening slightly.

'How are the workers?' my father asked, wiping his brow with a handkerchief.

'I couldn't, in all good conscience, call what we do work when I see you and Aengus here in the field,' Harold said.

'Well, you're welcome to have a go, if you'd like.'

I looked at Harold's pristine shoes and trousers and thought my father had taken leave of his senses.

'Can I?' Harold said, with all the enthusiasm of a young boy. I could well understand that he too wanted to forget about Maggie Walsh and her ramblings.

Before my father even answered, Harold had hopped over the wall and began tucking his trousers into his socks. I leaned against the wall, giving myself a good vantage point. Aengus turned his large head around and looked at Harold, already doubting his fitness for the task. Taking hold of the reins, Harold gave a very American 'Yeehaw!' Unfortunately, Aengus didn't understand American and just stood there, motionless. I laughed openly, causing Harold to redouble his efforts. He shook the reins and gave a resounding 'Giddyup!' Aengus must have taken pity on him, and moved forward at such a pace that he caught Harold by surprise, pulling him hard and tipping him over onto the earth with a thud. I had to clasp my hand over my mouth to stop my laughter ringing out across the field. My father had no such manners and let a roar out of him, as he reached out an arm to help Harold up. The poor man was covered in muck, but true to his character, he still had a good-natured smile on his face.

'She's got some horse-power, hasn't she?' he said, patting himself down.

'Eh, don't let Aengus hear you say that, he's a boy!' I said, trying not to laugh.

He climbed back over the wall, trying his best to hide any humiliation.

'Well, that was fun!' he said at last, laughing heartily himself.

'Oh, Harold, you'll have to use a lot of cologne when you go to Thornwood House tonight,' I said. I froze when I realised what I had just said and I could tell by Harold's expression that he was now thinking the same thing. My words were like a fisherman's net, dragging up the memory of Maggie Walsh's story.

'So, you'll be off rubbing shoulders with the landed gentry this evening?' my father joked. 'From paupers to kings.'

'Oh, I'm not so sure about that, but yes, George Hawley has invited us to dinner, to celebrate the twins' birthday,' Harold explained.

'Us?'

'Anna and I,' Harold said, looking at me.

'Anna? My Anna, up at the big house?' my father asked, hardly believing his ears.

'Mother said I can't go,' I told them both, my shoulders hunching.

'And why ever not?' my father asked.

I could have told him the truth then, but a devious part of me that I was hitherto unaware of decided to hold my tongue.

'You'll be accompanying her, won't you, Harold?' my

father asked. 'That's settled then. Don't you worry, Anna, I'll talk to your mother,' he said kindly.

My heart was near bursting. Tess had been right; I was so glad that we had continued to work on the dress. But if we were to have it ready for the evening, we would have to work hard and fast. I told my father that I would be over with Tess getting ready, so he could have time to talk with my mother alone. There would be a fierce battle of wills between them, so I had to be sure to make myself scarce.

'I was going to borrow the priest's gig this evening, so I can come and pick you up,' Harold offered.

'I can't wait,' I said, pedalling away as though my bicycle had wings.

Chapter Twenty-Four

'It's like a fairy tale,' Tess said, as we put the finishing touches to the dress. The bodice had a high-necked collar, trimmed in bands of lace with crochet flowers. The satin ribbon which trimmed the waist had long streamers that trailed down the length of the skirt, and we had altered the back of the dress with hook and eye closures. The skirt was also trimmed with little teardrops that fluttered with movement. Tess pinned my hair into a beautiful bun that swirled, with strands of hair overlapping and curling underneath. Finally, it was time to try on the dress. I put it on over my slip and she hooked the clasps at the back. When I turned around, I thought she would burst with excitement.

'How does it look?' I asked, although she had clearly made her feelings known.

'It looks like the fairies themselves spun gold into a dress!' she laughed. She walked around me, appraising our work and her own design, turning me this way and that and snipping any loose threads.

There was a small looking-glass on the wall that Tess held up for me so I could see my very first ball gown from every angle. I felt every inch the princess, and my eyes began to blur with tears of sheer delight. 'I'll never be able to thank you enough for this, Tess,' I said. 'Oh, but I tried to talk to Paddy on your behalf. He wouldn't give anything away,' I said regretfully.

'I didn't get a chance to tell you, he was here this morning,' she said, her lips curling into a mischievous smile. 'He asked me if I'd like to go to the dance with him in Ennis next week!'

'Oh, I'm so pleased!' I squeaked.

We spent so much time admiring ourselves and the dress that I was very late arriving home. Although I had a beautiful dress, I still had to wear my old winter coat over it, but that couldn't be helped. At least I could take it off when we got to the party.

I saw the gig in the driveway and knew that Harold had made it before me. I realised then that being late was a blessing in disguise. Whatever debate was taking place between my parents would have to be glossed over in Harold's presence and that would certainly work in my favour. I entered the house and at once saw my mother's face. Hidden beneath her neutral features, I recognised a look of pure infuriation. I feared I might pay for my duplicity later on, but for tonight, I had my permission.

'You look stunning,' Harold said, getting up from his seat. He was immaculately turned out himself in white tie and tails, holding his top hat between his fingers. He held me in his gaze, just as he had done the first day we met. My feelings were getting a little mixed up. Did I simply see him as the scholar or something more? But I couldn't think about it just then, with everyone looking at me.

'Oh, this is just my old coat,' I said, undoing the clasps to reveal the beautiful dress underneath. My mother gasped audibly and I wasn't sure, but I thought my father's eyes were watering.

'Where did you get that?' my mother said, the anger in her voice giving way to appreciation.

'Tess and I made it,' I said, doing a little twirl.

'Magnificent,' Harold said.

'Well, I'm sure there won't be one other woman at this shindig who's made her own dress,' my father said, adding, 'Don't we have a talented daughter, Kitty?'

'Oh yes, very talented,' my mother agreed with a slight edge to her voice, but she had to concede that we had done a good job. As she disappeared into her bedroom, I thought perhaps she was even angrier with me than I'd realised. However, she reappeared with a little box and, without a word, handed it to me.

'What's this?' I asked.

'My pearls,' she said simply. 'Be careful with them now.'

I opened the plain black box and saw the beautiful pearl earrings with the matching necklace. They were an ivory colour that matched the sash at my waist. They were Granny's pearls, and Father had given them to her when they got engaged.

'I can't wear these!' I protested, feeling slightly overwhelmed.

'Well, you might not deserve them after the stunt you pulled,' my mother mumbled as she fastened the clasp at the nape of my neck, 'but let no one say my daughter wasn't turned out properly,' she said, standing back and admiring the necklace.

As we shuffled out the front door, I could hear my mother whispering a warning to Harold. 'Look after her now, won't you?'

Parents will always be worrying, but I didn't think I needed protecting. Not that evening. Waving us off from the doorway with the light from inside surrounding them, my parents suddenly seemed very small and vulnerable. I had a strange feeling that I was leaving home forever and would never view the old place in the same way again. Harold helped me into the gig and, thankfully, seemed a little more skilled with the horse and trap than he was with Aengus and the plough. The stars hung from the navy blue sky like glittering eyes, a heavenly audience to this magical night. It was cold and frosty and when we spoke, our words evaporated in clouds of white smoke before our faces. I fidgeted with my hands, as though their very existence was a recent discovery, requiring all of my attention.

'Is this your first party?' Harold asked.

'It's my first … everything!' I replied, glad for the distraction. 'Do you think they'll all be wondering what a farm girl is doing at Thornwood House?' I asked.

'I don't think anyone would mistake you for a farm girl this evening, Anna,' he replied softly. 'But you shouldn't let these people intimidate you. You come from a fine family, with a good reputation and honest values. You should be proud of your home,' he said, completely missing my point. 'In fact Anna, I'd like to—'

'I am proud of my home,' I interrupted, 'but I want George, I mean Master Hawley, to see me as a lady,' I said, sounding foolish even to my own ears.

'I see.' He returned his focus to the road ahead.

'And I know Miss Olivia will be eager to see you, too,' I went on, cheering his mood. In fact, that was how the rest of the journey continued; Harold quietly nodding while I chatted nervously.

As we passed through the gates to Thornwood, I could see the drive ahead lit with flickering torches. It was so magical and as we drew closer to the house, I could hear music playing that would have rivalled the fairies' for its sweetness.

Harold pulled the reins and our carriage came to a halt at the foot of the steps of the grand house. He quickly hopped down and before I had a chance to navigate my way out of the seat without straining the seams on my new dress, he was there, offering his hand. I stepped down onto the gravel drive, feeling for all the world like a real princess.

'My lady,' he said, bowing formally and then giving me his arm.

When we entered the house, the sound of glasses clinking and guests laughing filled my ears. I rushed to give my old coat to the servant and Harold placed it with his own overcoat. He did look dashing in his finery, his dark hair combed back and his piercing eyes taking in the scene.

He'd removed his spectacles and he looked younger somehow, less serious. I can say without vanity that our arrival caused a ripple of curiosity among the revellers. We were obviously newcomers to this annual gathering and being young and gay was certainly in our favour. Concerned that I must look like a frightened rabbit, I plastered a frozen smile across my face as we passed through the crowd and nodded our way to the centre of the house.

'Good evening, Mister Krauss,' said the schoolmaster, Mr Finnegan, with his lady wife smiling at Harold but looking askance at me. I lifted my nose in the air and acted like visiting Thornwood House was a regular occurrence for me.

We stood in the little alcove by the side of the staircase, where I was finally able to breathe.

'Well, Miss Butler, how do you find it?'

'It's wonderful, isn't it, Harold? Everyone looks so magnificent and cheerful.'

A young girl with a frilly cap and apron offered us a drink from a tray full of pretty glasses. Harold took the red drink and so I followed suit. I watched the other ladies in the room and pursed my lips to take a sip, but the taste did not deliver what the colour had promised. Instead of a sweet, fruity drink, it was a dry, heady concoction that burned my throat. I left my glass on a little shelf and turned to find another server offering us tiny parcels of food. I picked up one that I recognised as smoked salmon with some sort of cream and devoured it.

'Mmm, that's delicious!' I said to the server, who seemed

unaccustomed to being spoken to. I took two more and he gave me a serviette to place them in, winking at me as he did so. I smiled back and encouraged Harold to try the salmon.

'No, thank you, I'm not very hungry,' he said, sipping his drink.

'How can you drink that?' I asked, licking my fingers.

'You don't have a taste for wine then?'

'That's wine? Ugh, it's disgusting,' I said, finishing off my little salmon picnic.

We surveyed the party from our little hideaway and I felt like a watchful fox hiding in the long grass, safe from scrutiny.

'Well, we can't hide behind the stairs all evening.'

'Really?' I said. My breathing had only just returned to its normal rhythm and I liked watching everyone from the safety of the shadows. There was Doctor Lynch and his wife, who wore her hair piled on top of her head and sparkling jewels at her neck. Miss Olivia flitted amongst the crowd, tilting her head at everyone and laughing raucously at what must have been a very funny joke. She didn't have to pretend to be a lady, so she could behave how she liked. Her dress was a flattering silk gown in primrose yellow with soft blue flowers embroidered on the bodice. It complemented her dark hair and I had to force myself to stop staring at her. There was still no sign of George, so I agreed with Harold and ventured back out into the throng.

We walked across the hall and followed the sound of the music to the ballroom. The grandeur of the room surpassed anything I had seen in the rest of the house. Three large chandeliers hung over the crowd of dancers, with strings of cut glass sparkling and shimmering in the candlelight. The great windows were dressed in opulent, blue-velvet curtains trimmed in gold and the ceiling was painted with scenes of tiny cherubs looking down at the proceedings. I never knew that people could live in such splendour and finery.

'Would you care to dance, Miss Butler?' Harold asked. He really did look very handsome. I was eager to dance, but I wasn't sure of the steps. 'I'll show you.'

When he took me in his arms, something shifted between us.

As he led me around the floor, I began to realise that perhaps he wasn't the meek and mild man I had once thought. Ever since his arrival in Thornwood, I had always felt like the one in charge, showing the bewildered American around the village. But this was his domain now. He expertly twisted and turned me in his arms, smiling all the while and looking like the proudest man in the room. Perhaps he had let me think I was leading him, when all along he was leading from two steps behind.

'I am the luckiest man here,' he said, making me blush.

I was lost in my thoughts, the music, the dance, when I saw a large hand tapping Harold on the shoulder.

'Mind if I cut in, Krauss?' came the voice of George Hawley, who looked equally pristine in his tails.

Harold hesitated, reluctant to let go of my hand. But George just stood there, staring him down with a toothy grin. Harold finally moved away and George suggested to him that he might ask his sister to dance. I looked across the room and saw a rather stony-faced Olivia staring at us. But Harold was nothing if not mannerly and so he crossed the room and asked her to dance.

George took me in his arms with a proprietorial grasp that, following Harold's gentle touch, rather shocked me. I had dreamt of this moment for so long, yet now that it had arrived, I could hardly believe it was real. My body refused to move to the music and I hung in his arms like a lifeless doll. His face was almost blinding in its beauty, and in a room filled with the prettiest girls in the west of Ireland, I felt unworthy of his attention.

'You look good enough to eat,' he said rather daringly and he spun me with a carelessness that required all of my balance to counter. No one had ever spoken to me like that before and if it hadn't been the Master himself speaking, I would have considered it impertinent.

'Thank you for inviting me,' I said shakily. I couldn't let my family down by forgetting my manners. 'And my ankle has healed perfectly, thanks to you,' I continued, although he didn't seem to be listening.

'Good, good,' he agreed, then pulled me closer to him. 'I've been thinking about you ever since that day, Anna, and no matter what I do, I cannot seem to banish you from my thoughts.'

My head felt dizzy with his words. George Hawley was thinking of me? It was simply too good to be true.

'Have you thought of me?' he asked, whispering the words in my ear and sending shivers down my neck.

'Yes, Master … I mean, George. Yes,' I said, biting my lip.

He spun me around again and the room became a blur. We both laughed and he danced with me faster and faster until we were at the other side of the ballroom, where the glass doors opened out onto the garden.

'Let us take a walk in the moonlight,' he said, grabbing a bottle and two glasses from a table in the corner.

I wasn't sure that we should leave the party and I turned around to see if Harold was in sight. I craned my neck and stood on tiptoes, but I couldn't catch a glimpse of my chaperone.

'It's a bit cold out tonight,' I said. It was a feeble protest, for I already knew I was going to go with him. I was under George Hawley's spell and I wasn't fooling either of us.

'Here, take my jacket,' he said, placing his black dinner jacket over my shoulders.

We walked across the gravel to a little stone building with columns and a domed roof, facing the fast flowing river. The swollen waters looked black as ink, reflecting shimmering droplets of moonshine. He led me into the little edifice, where there was a stone bench.

'Mademoiselle,' he said, taking out a handkerchief and placing it on the bench for me. 'Would you care to take a seat?'

'Thank you,' I said, pulling his jacket tighter around me. The house looked beautiful from here, all aglow with twinkling candlelight.

He lit a cigarette and poured what he called champagne into the glasses. I hoped it wouldn't taste as bad as the wine and sipped only a thimbleful just to be sure. But it was light and sparkly and put bubbles in my nose.

'Do you like champagne, Anna?' he asked, already pouring himself another glass.

I nodded my head and he smiled knowingly.

'Well then, like me, you have very sophisticated taste,' he said.

When some time passed and he had finished smoking his cigarette, he turned to me and asked if I was always so quiet.

'No, in fact, normally I can't stop talking!' I assured him. 'I think perhaps I'm a little nervous,' I said, to which he replied that I should take another sip of champagne.

'I think it was more than serendipity that caused our paths to cross up on the hill the other day,' he said, moving closer. 'I'd been hoping to see you again.'

'I had to stay at home until my ankle healed,' I explained, but he had already moved on.

'You have beautiful hair, Anna, do you know? Dark like a raven's,' he said, touching my curls and wrapping them between his fingers. His body was leaning against mine now and instead of feeling any chill, I suddenly felt my body flush with heat. Before I knew what was happening, he ducked his head and pressed his lips against my neck. It tickled something terrible and it was all I could do not to laugh out loud. I squirmed out of his reach and while it wasn't an altogether unpleasant experience, I didn't want him to think I was one of *those* girls.

'Don't you like kissing?'

'I don't know, I've never…' I stumbled over the words.

'Never been kissed?'

I couldn't answer and just shook my head.

'Just one kiss then, on the cheek. You owe me that at least.'

It struck me as a strange thing to say, that I should owe him anything. But he was already nuzzling my cheek with his nose, like a horse might. I thought I would faint from the rush of blood that seemed to fill my body only to instantly leave it. His lips searched my face and slowly found my lips and softly, he kissed me over and over. My mind was reeling! Everything I had ever dreamed about was actually happening. 'Wait till I tell Tess!' I thought to myself. 'I wonder if I'm doing this right?' was the next thought. Then, quite unexpectedly, he pushed his tongue into my mouth. I was shocked and tried to pull free, but his large hands had a grip of my shoulders.

'Um, wait,' I gasped.

He began pouring out more champagne and thrust the glass into my hand. I put it to my lips in order to delay any more of his advances and drank deeply without thinking.

'Maybe we should go back inside?' I suggested, my words flowing a little more freely. I was slightly out of breath and feeling a little uneasy about what he might be expecting from me. I wanted him to like me, but I wasn't sure how far I was prepared to go.

'Sure it's a beautiful night, Anna, come here and let us keep each other warm,' he said, wrapping his arms around my waist. It felt nice, but it also felt reckless. I had heard enough sermons from Father Peter to know right from wrong.

'I'm sorry, but it's not proper,' I said finally. 'Of course I like you very much, but—'

The kissing began again, but this time he wasn't slow or gentle.

He seemed to be in a terrible rush and I squealed when he bit my lip. 'Master George, please. I don't want to do this any more.' He raised his head and it took me a moment to recognise him. His eyes had become large and almost black-looking and his beautiful mouth had changed utterly. His lips were curled back, which gave the impression that his teeth had grown an inch in length. He looked frightening.

'Playing hard to get, are we? Yes, I like that, Anna,' he said, his features changing from a smile to a grimace. 'You know how to get a fellow going, don't you?'

He grabbed me again, harder this time.

'George, please, I cannot,' I said, trying to compose myself. Things seemed to be moving very fast and I wasn't sure how to get back to where we were. Yes, I had loved him from afar for years, but now, here, something didn't seem right. The gentleman who had carried me on his horse when I wounded my ankle had all but disappeared. Or changed. Maggie Walsh's shocking words returned to me: 'a changeling'. Was this George's true nature, something I was too blind and stupid to see? I had to get away and so I made to leave the seat.

The hunger in his eyes turned to a ravenous rage, and in an instant, his hands were all over my body, touching wherever they pleased. As I pushed them away, they only found another part of my body to invade. I fought and kicked, realising now that I was in trouble, but his fierce bulk overpowered me. He tore at my pretty dress, ripping all of the delicate stitches Tess and I had sewn.

'Stop it, stop it!' I shouted, my voice strangled and unrecognisable to myself, like a trapped animal. I had never felt so helpless. I had trusted him. Like a fool I'd trusted him because of his name, because of who he was. Who would believe he was capable of such violence? Who would believe me?

These dreadful thoughts forked my mind like lightning as I struggled against him. I couldn't catch my breath, and when I tried to scream again, my voice kept catching in my throat. It was like a very bad dream, where you try to move to help yourself, but you cannot. As he fumbled with his own clothes, I took the chance to try and push him off me, but he slammed me down on the stone seat and smacked my head against it. Things grew darker then, but I could still feel his hands, everywhere.

Then, something very strange happened. He moved back from me and took his hands away. I looked up bleary-eyed and saw that he was swatting something away from around his face. Within seconds, his arms were flailing about and he was cursing whatever it was that was attacking him.

'Anna! Anna, help me!' he shouted.

I attempted to lift myself up from the bench, but the inside of my head felt like it was swimming. I tried to steady my gaze and suddenly became aware of a buzzing sound. George was being stung over and over again, by bees. I thought how strange it was to see a swarm of bees in the middle of winter; I couldn't make sense of what was going on. He stumbled to his feet and I could see that the swarm was growing bigger and bigger. No matter how hard he tried to bat them away, it made no difference, and he pulled his jacket off me to cover his head.

'Leave me alone, you vile creatures! Please, someone help me!'

I felt sure that someone from the house would hear him, but no one came. When I looked back at George, I couldn't make out his features any more for he was covered in a black fury of bees. The buzzing filled my ears with a roaring hum. I was slumped on the seat, unable to do anything but look on. George's body was entirely covered and just as his screams became intolerable, I saw him tumble backwards into the black river. The flow was fast and ferocious and within seconds he was gone.

Chapter Twenty-Five

9th January 2011

S arah looked up from Anna's diary and stared at her own reflection in the dressing-table mirror. She could hardly believe what she'd just read. 'Poor Anna,' she whispered, touching the surface of the last page she'd read. Her fingertips traced the handwriting, as though she could reach out through time to comfort the girl.

She had brought her morning cup of tea to bed to soothe her hangover and, judging by the light, it was now almost noon. Her entire world had reduced down to the diary, Anna and the extraordinary events that had taken place at Thornwood House. The whole event was described in such heart-wrenching detail that Sarah felt, not for the first time, like an intruder reading the pages.

Lurking in the background of Anna's story was the mention of the seeress. She sounded uncannily like the old woman Sarah had met on the road the day before. But it wasn't possible, was it? Maggie Walsh would be long dead. A shiver ran through her at the mere thought of that woman. And what of George Hawley? Clearly this was a man who used his position to act above the law. He should have been tried and sentenced for his crimes. Yet, as strange as it seemed, was it possible that there was another law of the land or nature, keeping score of his wrongdoings? Sarah couldn't make sense of it. Where had the army of bees come from? Her mind was reeling with these questions when a hard knock at the front door almost made her jump.

'Hello,' came a far-off voice. Sarah was still in her pyjamas and felt sure her three-day-old hair looked a fright. She didn't want to see anyone today. Her head was throbbing and her mouth tasted like something had died in there. She would just sit tight and wait for them to go away.

'Hello! Anybody home?' came a familiar-sounding voice..

'I'm coming!' she called out reluctantly, pulling on a cardigan and scraping her hair up into a bun.

She saw Hazel through the window, wandering down the garden path and practising a few Irish dancing steps while she waited. She looked graceful and agile, her long legs decked in multi-coloured leggings.

'Well, hello there,' Sarah said, leaning against the half door. Her voice sounded an octave lower than usual. 'Do you want to come in?'

'Eh, well, I thought we could go to see Ned Delaney. He's giving a talk at the library in Ennis.'

Sarah instinctively touched her hair and her unmade

face, as if this would obviously excuse her from any last-minute excursions.

'Well, I hadn't really planned… Ned who?'

'You know, the fella who got the motorway moved and saved the hawthorn tree? The Fairy Whisperer?'

It still fascinated Sarah that you could go around calling yourself a fairy whisperer in this country, as if it was the most natural thing in the world.

'Oh, right. Of course.'

'You said that's why you came here,' Hazel said in that direct way that only young people can. From anyone else's mouth, it might have sounded like an accusation.

'Absolutely. That's absolutely what I said.' It seemed there was no getting out of it. 'Does your father know you're here?'

'Of course. But it starts at three, so—'

'Give me ten minutes. Make that twenty. Actually, you better come in!'

Ennis was a quaint little town, despite the misty rain that gave a muffled quality to the place. Every street was like a picture postcard, with its brightly coloured shops, all squished up together as if posing for a photo. They caught the bus from outside the church at Thornwood and Hazel spent the journey pointing out various spots of interest, like her school and the local GAA pitch.

'So, it's like American football?'

'No, that's more like rugby,' Hazel said patiently.

'But you can pick the ball up with your hands?'

'Yes, but you have to keep bouncing it.'

'Then, it's like basketball? But there's no hoop.'

'Sort of. There's a goal, but you can score points over the bar.'

'Um…'

And so the journey went, until twenty minutes later when they found themselves in the thriving town of Ennis. Sarah was glad of the distraction and the painkillers she had swallowed before leaving the cottage. It was bad enough arguing with Jack and getting stupidly drunk, but recalling the awkwardness between her and Oran made her cringe. Not to mention Anna's story, which had affected her more than she realised.

'Have you ever heard of a woman by the name of Maggie Walsh?'

'The old seeress,' Hazel replied, without missing a beat.

'So she's well known, then?'

'You could say that. It's said that she haunts the village, but I've never seen her myself,' she said in a tone that implied disappointment. 'Why? Have you seen her?'

Sarah shook her head in a way that said, *of course not, don't be silly*. Perhaps Hazel was comfortable with the idea of ghosts popping up in broad daylight, but Sarah certainly was not.

Hazel led the way to the library, which was nestled behind a pretty little church in the centre of town. She could see lots of parents and children filing in and realised that this might be a bigger event than she had first thought. At least she was spending the day with real live people. When they got through the doors, chatter filled the air like a thick fog. There was a sense of anticipation and Sarah was quietly surprised that all of these kids had abandoned their screens for the afternoon to hear a man talk about fairies.

Chairs were set in a semi-circle around a plinth, and scatter cushions covered the floor in front. A woman appeared from nowhere, stepped onto the plinth and asked everyone to take their seats, as the *seanachaí*, Mr Delaney, was due imminently.

'What's a *seanachaí*?' Sarah asked.

'It's like a storyteller.'

As the chatter dissipated and everyone took their seats, Sarah felt like she was at the theatre. The show began when the Fairy Whisperer made his way from the back of the room, his walking stick solemnly echoing his slow march towards the stage. Sarah could not hide her fascination at the enigma that appeared before them. If the audience hadn't remained so quiet and attentive, she would have burst out laughing. On the stage was Ireland's answer to Gandalf, only significantly shorter. The man, who could have ranged anywhere in age from forty to a hundred, was hardly visible behind his impressive beard, which parted from his mouth like walrus tusks. He appeared to be balding, yet a shock of static-filled hair surrounded the back and sides of his head like a halo of silvering briars. Even his eyes were obscured by a pair of old-fashioned spectacles, holding lenses so thick that it was difficult to tell if he had eyes at all.

A couple of giggles erupted here and there, more from excitement than anything else. He held what looked like a gnarled wooden staff in his hands and, thumping it on floor, he began.

'An old man told me once – and he was a reliable old man,' he said, pointing a finger at the audience, in case we suspected otherwise. 'He said to me, "Ned, the fairies are just like us; the person sitting next to you could be one of them and you wouldn't know it." Isn't that a frightening thought? That they can take any shape they like.'

He let that unnerving thought settle about their ears for a while, as Hazel and Sarah looked nervously at each other and at their neighbours. Far from the Disney-inspired fairies that Sarah had assumed this talk would be about, it seemed to be more of a cautionary tale. She noticed a young boy sitting beside her, who began to curl himself into his father's arms. The father smiled nervously, possibly reconsidering his choice of outing.

'Now one early morning, a man was on his way to the fair to sell his horse, when he passed by the gates to a grand house. A little man appeared from inside the gates and asked how much the man was selling the horse for. He said he hoped to get eight pounds and the little man laughed and said he knew someone who would pay forty pounds for the horse. Sure, the man thought he was half cracked, because that was two years' wages at the time. But it didn't take much persuasion anyhow and he followed the little man up the drive. Instead of a great house, though, the man brought him to a tunnel and down they went, deeper and deeper into the earth. The man became afraid at this point, but he couldn't turn back, for with all the twists and turns he was sorely lost. So, he had no choice but to keep going.'

Ned was an amazingly articulate and animated storyteller. Every line was accompanied by actions and facial expressions that drew the adults in, as well as the children. Sarah had never witnessed anything like him. She looked about the room and saw the crowd were enraptured by his tale.

'Finally, they came to a stable and the little man told him to leave the horse there and to come to the great hall to get his money. There he found a party of hundreds of gaily dressed people, all feasting and making merry. A man who was sitting at the top of the hall handed him a bag of gold for the horse and invited him to stay for his dinner. Well, the smell of the food was making his mouth water and so he agreed to stay and sat down at the end of a long table. A young woman came around to serve him his food, but she gave him a warning. She said, "If you eat even a morsel of this food, you will never be able to leave this place." With that, she was gone. The man thought this was very strange, but as his wife had often told him, it was better to be safe than sorry, so he didn't touch the food. The man who had paid him the gold roared down to the back of the room, "Why do you not eat?" And the man answered that he couldn't – his wife would have his dinner ready when he got home. "It's rude not to share in our feast," the man tried again. But still, the man refused. On his third refusal, everything in the hall changed. The beautiful people transformed into ugly, terrifying creatures and the man ran out of there as fast as he could.'

At this point, Ned Delaney leaped into the air and began

running on the spot, the terror in his eyes as evident as if he was being chased himself.

'Next thing he knew, it was morning and he had fallen asleep outside of his own front door. His wife came out and asked him where he had been all night. He thought to himself that he must have had too much to drink in the pub, but when he felt the weight of gold in his pockets, he knew that he had been with the fairies.'

A pregnant silence remained in the room for several moments after the story ended. Sarah could not have been more convinced that this event had actually happened if she had been there herself, such was Ned Delaney's conviction. She wondered if everyone else had fallen under his spell. With a sudden clap of his hands, he brought the room back to themselves and finished his story with the statement: 'And that's as sure as I'm standin' here!' for good measure.

The room broke into a rapturous applause then and Ned took several short bows. He told story after story in the same engaging style, about haunted places, fairy paths and holy wells, his bushy eyebrows working overtime. When he finished, a queue began to form rapidly, as children and adults alike lined up to have him sign their books and have selfies taken. Hazel had a copy of his most recent book, *The Good People*, and they both joined the line snaking around the bookshelves.

He seemed like a man from another era and Sarah wasn't sure how to address him when it came to their turn.

'Hello, Mister Delaney,' she settled on in the end.

'Is that an American accent I hear?' he asked.

'Yes, I'm from Boston. Via New York.'

'Well, you're very welcome to County Clare,' he said, 'and it's Hazel, isn't it?'

'Yeah, how did you remember my name?'

'Well, with a very special name like that, I wasn't likely to forget! And sure yourself and your father were a great support at the protest.'

Sarah could see Hazel glowing in the light of his recognition. He was obviously a highly respected man around here, even if people wouldn't openly admit to believing his stories about The Good People.

As he wrote a message on the inside page of Hazel's book, she told him that Sarah was very interested in the hawthorn tree that had changed the route of the motorway.

'That's why she came here,' she told him.

'Oh well,' Sarah said hesitantly, 'I wouldn't go that far!' She laughed nervously at the two women queuing behind her.

'We've had visitors from all over the globe, haven't we, Hazel?'

'Well, I don't want to take up too much of your time,' Sarah said, 'but actually, you wouldn't happen to know anything about, um, bees?' Sarah lowered her voice, as if talking about bees would make her look odd in a roomful of people listening to fairy tales.

'I could tell you a lot about bees,' he said, giving a sly wink. 'What is it you'd like to know?'

'Well, you know, just general bee stuff. Or like, folklore?'

Unperturbed by the impatient families behind them, Ned Delaney settled into his explanation as though they had all the time in the world.

'There is a lot of folklore surrounding bees and there was a tradition here in Ireland and across Europe known as "telling the bees". Now, telling the bees was a custom in which the bees would be told of important events in their keeper's lives, such as births, marriages, or departures from the household. If the custom was omitted or forgotten and the bees were not "put into mourning", then it was believed a penalty would be paid.'

'What kind of penalty?' Hazel asked.

'Oh, such as the bees might leave their hive, stop producing honey, or even die in some cases. In ancient times, the bee was believed to be the sacred insect that bridged the natural world to the otherworld. There are stories that the fairies would have commanded the bees to do their bidding.'

'You mean, the fairies could control the bees; use them to … attack someone?'

'Indeed yes, if that is what they wished. If you don't mind me saying, these are very particular questions, Mrs—?'

'Harper, Miss Harper. Sarah.'

'And she found a diary, in a tree,' Hazel added, singing like a veritable canary.

'Gosh, look at the time! We really ought to be getting back,' Sarah said, shooing Hazel towards the exit. 'Thank you so much, Mr Delaney, lovely to meet you,' she called as she made her way outside.

Chapter Twenty-Six

Anna's Diary

18th January 1911

Seconds after the bee attack on George, I opened my eyes, but all around me was quiet. I started to wonder if it had all been a very bad dream, but then I saw her standing in front of me, just like that day she came to my sick bed.

'Milly!' I cried, and the tears began to flow. I sobbed great heaving gulps of tears and shivered with the shock of it all.

'He's gone now,' she said, coming close to me but not touching. 'I cannot stay, Anna, but you're safe now,' she explained, looking behind her as though there was someone there.

She was still in her yellow summer dress, but as my eyes focused, I could see that she was not the same Milly at all.

There was something unnatural about her skin; it shimmered pale green, then yellow, then white, like the bark of a silver birch. And although she sat perfectly still, she was moving. No, it was not she who moved, but tiny, winged creatures, fluttering about her. Like white butterflies, they encircled her head and nested in her tangled hair, which was crowned with twigs and leaves. All along her arms, their wings opened and closed and yet she seemed undisturbed by their presence. I had the sense that my Milly had returned to the earth, returned to nature. She belonged to the otherworld now and she would never be my Milly again. She was forever altered, unreachable.

'You saved me from him,' I said, with a tremble in my voice.

We both looked back towards the river, but there was nothing to see any more.

'I— I shouldn't have come here at all,' I said, finally understanding the chain of events. 'Mother said not to come and if I hadn't, he— George…' I broke off, unable to say the words.

'Hush now, sister. George Hawley's destiny was written long before he met you,' she replied, sounding wise beyond her years. 'You are not to blame.'

I thought I could hear the sound of someone coming and the look on Milly's face confirmed it.

'Milly, please wait! I'm so sorry … so sorry for never having the courage to say goodbye,' I whispered frantically.

'You have nothing to be sorry for, Anna. I have to go now and you must stop looking for me,' she said, placing her hands over my eyes.

'But Milly, I miss you with all my heart!'

I felt my body shuddering as she closed my eyes and whispered, 'Remember what I always told you.' When her hands disappeared, I found myself quite alone. Next thing I knew, Harold was beside me, asking me if I was all right.

'What's happened, Anna? You're shaking,' he said, taking off his own jacket and wrapping it tightly around me. 'Your dress… Where is George?' he asked, looking out into the darkness.

The mere mention of his name sent me into hysterics. It wasn't long before Olivia came in search of Harold and as she sauntered across the lawn, she called out something about a foxtrot. I bent my head and tried to pull the remains of my dress around me. I could not look her in the eye after what had just happened.

'Oh!' She stopped short of the stone building, a look of surprise on her face. 'I see you have found your little farm girl,' she said haughtily.

'She's in shock, I need to get her inside,' Harold said.

'Has my brother given you the push?' she said, mercilessly. 'Oh, you didn't really think he was interested in someone like you, did you? How quaint!' She threw her head back and let out a wicked laugh, as Harold lifted me up and bundled me past her.

'Please, don't take me into that house,' I said, my teeth chattering.

'But I have to get you into the warmth, Anna,' he said softly.

I looked up into his eyes and begged him wordlessly to heed my wishes.

'Right, let's hurry to the stables and I'll get the carriage.'

I didn't know I was in shock then. Harold explained it to me later, how the mind cannot make sense of things straight away. I thought perhaps I had dreamt it all. Everything that had happened from the moment I stepped out onto the lawn that night seemed unreal. I climbed into the carriage and didn't speak a word, while Harold attached the harness to the horse. He covered me in both of our overcoats, but I trembled ceaselessly. I suddenly thought of the maid from Cork. She had been right all along. I had seen with my own eyes how the charming Master George could turn into a monster and I felt ashamed for not believing her. Had she been pregnant with George's baby? I swayed with sickness at the thought of how we had all gossiped about her, assuming that she was telling lies and never believing the man capable of such deeds.

The journey passed in a blur, but as we neared our cottage, my eyes began to fill with tears. It seemed like only moments ago I had left this place, young and innocent and full of dreams. Now I felt as though nothing good could come of the world again. I felt naïve and stupid, wearing a handmade dress and Mother's pearls. As I thought of them, my hand reached to my neck. The pearls were gone.

'Mother's pearls!' I screeched, giving Harold a terrible fright. 'I've lost them; I'll have to go back.'

'Shh,' Harold soothed, 'don't worry about that now. I will go back first thing in the morning and look for them,' he said, stroking my hair gently.

I knew he was trying to comfort me, but I had to move away from him. I didn't want to be touched.

'I should probably wake your mother – she'll want to look after you,' he said, tactfully.

'Jesus, no! Don't do that, Harold, please,' I begged. 'I can't tell my mother. She never wanted me to go to that house, and she was right,' I said, the tears falling anew.

'Well, I have to do something, Anna. I can't just leave you on your own,' he said. 'And you need to tell someone.'

The only place I could think to go where I would feel safe was with Betsy in the barn. I told Harold to leave the carriage on the road, so as not to wake anyone. We walked quietly to the rear of the cottage and found Betsy tucked up on a bed of straw, her warm, earthy smell filling my nostrils with familiarity and calm. I lit the storm lamp and found my little milking stool and an old wooden crate for us to sit on. There was a threadbare blanket left hanging on a hook that Harold took down and placed across our laps.

'Are you sure you're warm enough?' he asked.

'Just about,' I said, smiling sorrowfully at him. 'This is the best place for me to be now.'

Harold looked around at the tiny barn with its whitewashed walls, wooden beams and stone floor covered in straw.

'I like it,' he said, in good humour. 'One could grow accustomed to the smell of manure, I'm sure. So, do you want to tell me what happened between you and George?'

I took a deep breath.

'Can I tell you about Milly first?' I asked. 'You see, I've been wanting to tell you about my sister since you first came here, but I wasn't sure if I could trust you. Now I know that I can, and you need to know about Milly before I can tell you … the rest of it.'

'Your sister? I didn't know you had a sister,' Harold said, looking surprised. 'Does she live in Thornwood?'

'She lives in Cnoc na Sí,' I replied, 'with The Good People.'

I remained silent for a time, letting my words take shape in Harold's mind. The only sound was that of Betsy breathing and chewing the cud. Her nose glistened in the lamplight and she didn't seem perturbed by our presence at such an hour.

'You'd better tell me the story from the beginning,' Harold said, as he searched fruitlessly for his pencil and notebook, forgetting that he was in his top hat and tails and not in his usual uniform. He smiled at me and I took a very deep breath, as though preparing to dive into the depths.

'Emily – Milly – was the eldest in our family, a year older than Paddy. In fact, she was more like a second mother to all of us and she looked after me like her own little baby doll. I idolised her, became her little shadow and pestered her and copied everything she did,' I said, taking big gulps of air to prevent any more tears. 'She taught me how to climb the big oak tree at the edge of our land. As I got more courageous, she would let me go ahead and anytime I got scared or felt unsure of my footing, she would say, "Sure I'm only a step behind you." That was our secret message then. Anytime I had to do something that frightened me, she would whisper it to me and I knew I'd be all right.

'When she was eleven years old, she became ill with consumption. She had to stay in Mother and Father's room – isolation, the doctor called it. Oh, we all hated that, because we couldn't go in to play or cuddle with her or anything. She took her meals alone in there and only my mother was allowed to go in, for the consumption is fierce contagious,' I explained.

I have always found it hard to talk about Milly, but it gave me comfort then, especially after what had happened at Thornwood House. Seeing her again, so suddenly, made it as though our years apart had never happened. I hardly mentioned her name at home, for I never knew if the memories would make my parents sad or, worse still, angry.

'To my fledgling mind, I never thought it possible that someone so young could die. I'm not sure I ever really understood that she was gone, forever.'

'I'm so sorry, Anna,' Harold said, trying to take my hand, but I still couldn't let him touch me. 'Grief is a dark labyrinth to navigate, even when you are an adult, but to lose someone so close as a child … it's understandable that you struggled to comprehend it.'

'My mother says it's because I didn't go to her funeral,' I said, staring into the gloom, as if I could see the past replaying itself in the shadows. 'I ran away that morning and climbed the big oak tree on the boundary of our farm. I went there every day for a month after she died, because I kept thinking she would be there, hiding from all of us, and then we'd skip back home, laughing and forgetting everything.'

Harold instinctively reached his arm around me again, but pulled away with an apology. I knew he was trying to comfort me and I desperately wanted to let him, so I gave him my fingertips to hold.

'Anyway, I got sick myself after that. My poor parents were so worried that I would go the same way as Milly, but, by the grace of God, I recovered. Something happened during that time, though;, something that no one wishes to talk about now. I was very ill with a fever and could hardly recognise the faces that were more familiar to me than my own. I remember one day, in the height of summer, when the rays were shining brightly through the window, I heard Milly calling my name. I was so happy to hear her voice and so delirious from the fever, that I didn't question it. She was bright and happy and her voice sounded like silver bells ringing. I couldn't speak, but somehow it didn't matter. She told me that she was with The Good People now and that she was quite content. That was when she told me about the magical palace hidden under the earth of Cnoc na Sí,' I said, and Harold nodded his recollection of our conversation.

'I so longed to speak with her, to ask her forgiveness. All these years I've been so ashamed of myself. Before the wake, we were all supposed to go in and say our last goodbyes, but I just couldn't do it. I couldn't bear to see her … changed. I was terrified of how she would look and couldn't bear having that image of her in my mind forever. I think I convinced myself that she wasn't dead, that this wasn't final. My mother tried to persuade me. She kept telling me it was for my own good to see her laid out, but I refused. I could not go into that room and my guilt kept me from the funeral. I just wanted to tell her I was sorry. But the next thing I knew, she was gone as suddenly as she had appeared and I was once again alone in my bed. When I told everything to my mother, she just patted my head and told me that the fever was breaking. No one believed me and it was after that I stopped talking for a time. Although Father says I've been making up for it ever since!' I said, managing a smile.

'You poor girl. Well, I can assure you that I do believe you, every word. I'm glad you trusted me enough to tell me,' Harold said, squeezing my fingers. 'I'm sorry you never got to speak with her again.'

'Oh, but you see I did, tonight!'

'You saw your sister, at Thornwood House?'

The sight of Milly, or the girl who used to be Milly, with the dark-winged creatures fluttering around her head, flashed before my eyes.

'I-I saw her, I think.' I hesitated. 'She stopped George. The bees.' I realised that I wasn't making much sense. 'I know it was her, Harold,' I said, with renewed belief, 'because she told me our secret message. She said, "Sure I'm only a step behind you."'

I wanted to end it there, but I knew that if I didn't tell Harold everything there and then, I never would have the courage to do it again. So, I told him what passed between George Hawley and me; how he had tried to force himself upon me, even though I kept begging him to stop. I told him of how I'd watched helplessly as George was attacked by a ferocious swarm of bees, his screams quietened finally by the river.

'Do you think what the seeress said was true? About the Hawley children being changelings?' I asked, wiping my swollen eyes.

'Maggie Walsh? How did you...?' Harold shook his head, with the makings of a smile on his face. 'Were you eavesdropping? I should have figured that out when you didn't ask me any questions afterwards. Normally you're like a dog with a bone!'

I smiled meekly at him, pleased to be reminded of the girl I was before the party.

'Changeling or not, anyone who could do that to another human being is not a man, in my book,' he said.

I grew weary with the weight of it all. My throat was sore from shouting and crying and I eventually let my head rest against Harold's shoulder.

In the early hours of the next morning it was still dark, but Betsy's internal clock knew that it was almost time for milking. She made a big show of raising herself up on her feet and then let out a long, low bugle call. I must have drifted off, for the noise made me start and I came to realise that Harold was holding me, tightly wrapped in the coats and the blankets. I felt self-conscious and embarrassed now by our conversation, but he must have spent those hours thinking things through, and, thankfully, he had a plan.

'Don't concern yourself, Anna. I will look after everything. Just go into the house quietly and change into your working clothes without waking anyone. When you come out, milk Betsy as usual and in the meantime I will go back to Thornwood House and search for the pearls.' He held my shoulders as he spoke to me, intent on my understanding every word. 'I will go back to my lodgings to change and meet you back here in a few hours, all right?'

'Indeed, I'll go about my chores as usual and I won't say a word to anyone,' I agreed. I was trying to be strong like him, although I dreaded my mother's questions. 'But what about George, do you think he's…?'

'Don't worry about that now,' he said in a practical voice and began the entirely pointless task of folding the old blanket, which was covered in straw and God knows what else. I could see that he was troubled but doing his best to conceal it from me.

He set off only when I had promised him that I was up to the task. I did everything exactly as he had told me. I crept into the house and quickly deposited my coat and dress under my bedclothes. Seeing my beautiful dress torn and dirty almost set me off again, but I couldn't allow the tears to fall. I pulled on an old jumper and skirt, which took so much longer than usual with my shaking hands. My hair was still caught up in the pins Tess had so carefully placed there. I pulled at the curls, but a sharp pain reminded me of the gash at the back of my head. I dipped a flannel into the basin of water on the washstand and dabbed the blood, which had dried into my hair. I couldn't see what I was doing and finally decided to tie a scarf over my head. When

I came downstairs, I put some turf on the fire and set a pot of water on to boil, just before my mother entered the room.

'Well, did you enjoy your party?' she said in a tone that made it clear she still disapproved of the whole thing.

If only I had listened to her. I felt a knot in my gut when I told her that I had spent a lovely evening at Thornwood House, and apologised if I was late coming home.

'And was Master George there?' she asked, setting the table for breakfast.

'Of course he was there,' I said sharply. 'Sure, isn't it his house?'

A quick glance from my mother was enough to bring me back to my senses.

'I'm sorry, I'm just tired,' I said, making for the back door before she could ask me anything else.

'Did Harold see you home?' my father called to me, as he rose from the bedroom, pulling his braces over his shoulder.

'Yes, yes,' I said, rushing out the door and back to the safety of the barn.

I took my time milking Betsy, for every time my thoughts returned to George's hands ripping at my dress, the tears threatened. I had to press my fists into my eyes to stop them. The poor animal was bewildered by my fitful actions, and gave me a wide-eyed look. My hands refused to work properly and in the end, little Billy was sent out to search for me.

'Mammy wants to know if she should drink her tea black this morning,' he said, kicking an old horseshoe across the yard.

'Tell her that I'm going as fast as I can,' I said irritably, wiping my eyes with the end of my skirt.

Billy spent some time watching me, then came over and crouched beside me.

'I know where there are some kittens,' he said, out of the blue.

'Do you now?' I said, my heart softening. His beautiful brown eyes were so full of innocence, I wanted him to stay that way for ever.

'Mmm-hmm. I can show ya if ya like,' he offered. 'They're black and white, but one is all white with a black ear and another one is all black with four white socks!' He looked to me for a reaction; as if this was the most unexpected thing in the world.

'Well, isn't that something?' I said, swallowing the lump in my throat. 'Four white socks! What are the other ones like?' I continued, realising that his simple conversation was keeping my hands steady and the bucket full. He chatted happily by my side and we arranged to go and see the kittens after breakfast.

It was a well-timed plan, because all through breakfast, the questions about Thornwood House and its inhabitants multiplied. Paddy was the least interested, but Mother, Father and Tommy were fascinated with the idea of their little Anna attending a party at the big house.

'Well, for a girl that was dying to go to a party, you're certainly very quiet about it,' my father remarked.

I just smiled meekly and poured more tea. I couldn't blame them; had things turned out differently, I would have been only too pleased to relay every minute detail of the evening. As it was, I could hardly eke out more than one-word answers to their questions. The thought of waiting around the house for Harold to return was excruciating. The kittens were up at Gallagher's farm – the cottage bordering the Thornwood estate – so I knew I would be able to see him passing on the road from there.

I set off with Billy on the crossbar, his head turning constantly, as his young mind found novelty in every mundane occurrence. The sight of a hare racing across the field, or a robin following our journey along the hedgerows, or a cloud that took the shape of a fox.

'You're my little darlin',' I said to the crown of his head and he just nodded, like I was pointing out a truth as obvious as both of us having brown eyes.

When we reached Gallagher's, Billy slipped down from the bike and took off at speed for the barn. I knocked gently on the back door and was greeted by Rosie Gallagher, who said we were more than welcome to take a kitten if Billy wanted one.

'The mother is great for catching mice,' she assured me, so I said I would run it past Mother before getting Billy too excited.

After spending half an hour in the barn playing with the kittens, we came into the house for some tea and brown bread. The clock on the mantelpiece showed that it was almost noon and there was still no sign of Harold. I asked Rosie if Billy could stay with her a little longer, while I picked up some bits and bobs in the village.

I set off on my bike, hoping at every turn that I would see Harold coming towards me. The day was bright and cold and my fingers were red with frostbite as I gripped the handlebars tightly. My chest was tight and my breathing quickened as I came ever closer to the gates of Thornwood House. Flashes of George's face, contorted and frightening, came to my mind. I could still feel his weight upon me, trapped like a helpless animal beneath him. I had to put on the brakes and stand on the road for a moment while I tried to suck air into my lungs.

Pushing the images out of my head, I thought of Harold and how kind he had been. I remembered dancing with him in the ballroom before George had cut in. The very thought of him calmed me and my breathing returned to normal. I smiled to myself and realised that I was longing to see him. I got back on my bike and pedalled quickly up the road and passed the imposing gates of Thornwood House. But I braked hard again upon hearing the commotion from the big house. I looked up the long avenue and saw the police wagon coming down the drive. A tight fist gripped my heart. I realised that they must have discovered George was missing and had begun the search. I dropped my bicycle in the ditch and concealed myself behind the concrete pillar of the gate to watch the police wagon go by. To my utter dismay, I saw Harold in the back, his face white as a sheet. He was flanked by two officers, so he couldn't see me when I jumped from my hiding place and tried to wave at him. I turned to look back up at the house and saw Miss Olivia in the distance, her arms folded and a look of pure loathing on her face.

I cycled in a blind panic to the priest's house beside the

church. I burst through the back door without knocking and caught the poor man at his lunch.

'I'm sorry, Father, but you have to help me,' I pleaded breathlessly.

'What in the name of God has you in this state, Anna Butler?' Father Peter asked, putting down his knife and fork.

'It's Harold, Father, they've arrested him!'

'Arrested Mr Krauss? For what, girl? You're not making any sense.'

'George is missing and I think it's all my fault,' I replied. 'I don't know exactly what happened, but I saw Harold being taken away from Thornwood House in a police wagon.'

Father Peter rubbed his chin in contemplation, then touched the wooden cross that hung on the wall beside the door.

'Well, that can't be right. There must be some sort of a mistake,' he decided finally. 'I was up at Thornwood House myself this morning. Terrible business. Young Master George was found dead in the early hours,' he said, blessing himself.

I swayed and leaned against the wall. I knew it, deep down I knew it. But to hear the words said aloud made the awfulness of the situation more real. George Hawley was really dead.

'God knows they weren't Catholics, but they deserve our prayers at a time like this. Poor man drowned in the river, probably after one too many bottles of champagne if you ask me,' he said, gossiping like a fishwife.

This is all my fault, I whispered to myself. 'Can you take me to see him, Father? I must speak with him.'

'To the gaol?'

'Yes, the gaol. If I could cycle that far I would,' I said. He agreed, reluctantly, and prepared for the road in his slow, deliberate way. I couldn't stand still. I walked in and out of the doorway ten times, but my agitation did nothing to hurry the man, who was accustomed to going at God's eternal pace. When we eventually set out on the road, it was late afternoon and the clouds had begun to roll in.

Chapter Twenty-Seven

10th January 2011

'He said to call over anytime,' Sarah said silently to her reflection, which didn't seem convinced. 'I'm just being neighbourly,' she said, aloud this time, determined to make up for the last time they met. Sarah turned and finished brushing her hair while looking out of the window. The weather had already changed three times that morning, from sunny to cloudy and then hailstones. How did the Irish dress for this weather? At home, if it was sunny, you could pretty much bank on it staying that way for at least the rest of the day. She pulled on her coat over a bright red knitted dress and slipped the loop of an umbrella over her arm before heading off down the road.

She'd had one of her 'night terrors' last night, as Jack used to call them. It made her sound as though she were a child going through a tedious phase. He had never shown much compassion for her anxiety. Or maybe he just didn't have it in him to console her as well as himself. Either way, it left her feeling as though she had to hide her panic attacks from him. That was probably half the reason she began leaving the apartment at night and jogging the streets. And drinking. But here, she was learning to sit with them – or sit through them at least. It somehow felt like progress, the fact that she wasn't running away from them anymore, but she couldn't be sure of that. There had been so many false starts, when she thought that maybe she was turning a corner or moving on to the next stage of grief. People liked to have road maps, even when it came to the human condition. She used to joke with her sister that she was leaving 'Denial Boulevard' and heading for 'Anger Junction'. But in reality, she didn't know where she was. Everything she did seemed to be wrong. But coming here … something felt strangely right about it. All of the coincidences, uncovering Anna's story, meeting Oran and his daughter, Marcus and Fee, and the most enigmatic of characters, Ned Delaney. She wasn't sure what it all meant, but it felt something like living again.

'Ah great, you've saved me a journey,' Oran said as he opened the front door, but his tone belied his words.

'Howdy, neighbour, I just thought you might be free for a coffee or…'

Sarah could see Hazel halfway up the staircase shaking her head vigorously and mouthing the words 'I'm sorry'.

'Is there something wrong?' Sarah was confused by the fact that she wasn't being invited inside. Was he angry with her?

'Yes, Sarah, actually,' he said, nervously running his hands through his hair and finally stuffing them in his pockets. 'I just can't believe you brought Hazel to see that man yesterday.'

'I brought *her*!' came a shout from the stairs.

'I thought I told you to stay in your room,' he shouted back. Sarah expected him to finish the sentence with 'young lady', which made her smile, as that was something her parents always said when she was in trouble. Looking back at Oran, she swiftly rearranged her facial expression into that of a responsible adult.

'I'm sorry but Hazel told me she had cleared it with you first.'

'She's a kid, of course she's going to say that.'

'I'm not a kid, I'm a teenager!' came the argument from upstairs.

'Right, well, maybe I should just go, then,' said Sarah.

A moment passed where neither of them said anything. Sarah silently wished that she had kept right out of their business and just barricaded herself in the cottage until it was time to go back to the States. Which was when, exactly? Was she just hiding herself away in the middle of nowhere, losing herself in other people's problems? She hardly knew these people and yet here she was, trampling all over their carefully guarded lives, like the stereotypical loud-mouth American.

'Look, I'm sorry. I shouldn't be blaming you,' he said, scratching the back of his head and talking to the floor.

All of his bluster was gone now and replaced by a weariness Sarah could almost taste.

'It's okay, you've got a point. After everything you told me, about Hazel and the fairy stuff, I should have thought. I'm sorry, Oran. I guess I was just glad of the company and she's such a passionate young girl.'

'Manipulative, you mean.'

'I'm sure you don't mean that. She's just strong-minded and that's a good thing.'

'Not when you're her father, it's not.'

Hazel's bedroom door slammed shut and Sarah looked up the stairs to where the girl had made her retreat.

'I better leave you to it,' she said.

'Maybe we could still have that coffee? Unless I've frightened you off with all our family drama,' he said, standing back to let her in.

She stepped over the threshold, promising herself she wouldn't stay long. Max the dog made a great fuss of the visitor while Oran filled the kettle.

'How did you find out anyway?' Sarah asked as she took off her coat. Was it her imagination or did he give her dress a second look before clearing his throat?

'One of the neighbours saw you both and of course they couldn't wait to quiz me about Hazel's new friend,' he replied, the last part in air quotes.

So this was life in a small town, she thought to herself. From her vantage point at the head of the kitchen table, she couldn't help but look at the large framed photograph of Oran, a younger version of Hazel and, of course, Cathy. She was determined not to bring up another touchy subject, but she couldn't shift her gaze from the beautiful woman with a contented smile on her face and dark, playful curls tumbling behind her.

'I thought it was a mistake. Can you believe that?' he said, nodding towards the photo.

'Sorry?'

Oran brought over two giant mugs of tea and a packet of shortcake biscuits under his arm.

'Cathy,' he said, looking at the photograph. 'I actually thought my father was going senile, talking about Cathy's death. At the time, I think it was the only way my mind could make sense of the words. "She's gone," he kept saying. "How could she be gone?" That's all I could say.'

Sarah was surprised by his candour. She wasn't sure how to react and so she decided to just hang back and let him speak. It seemed as though he needed to get this out and that he hadn't been able to do it up till now.

'A heart attack. I remember telling them in the hospital that she was too young, only thirty-five. I could hear my voice saying the same thing over and over. They must hear that sort of thing all the time. Relatives not understanding … unable to process the fact that it was already too late for arguments or reasons. She died in the ambulance.'

'My God, Oran, I am so sorry.'

'It was Hazel who rang for an ambulance. She was only seven years old. I can't imagine how that must have been for her. They'd been walking on Cnoc na Sí, you see. They both loved it there.'

The only sound in the kitchen was the ticking clock. Briefly, Sarah wondered if Hazel was still in her room, or listening on the stairs, as she had so often done herself as a young girl. Grown-ups always just assumed that you weren't listening.

'If I'm honest, I thought it would kill me. The grief. But you know what's worse? It doesn't kill you. You go on, living … surviving, whether you want to or not. And Hazel —' His voice caught in his throat.

'She's an amazing girl,' Sarah said, tentatively wrapping her hands around his.

'But can you see now why I don't want her getting involved in all this fairy nonsense? In the beginning, I thought it was a distraction, but when she started having those visions…' He trailed off, still reluctant to talk about it.

'Visions?'

'It's only happened a handful of times,' he said, trying to mitigate the situation. 'She says she can see Cathy, talk to her.' He buried his face in his hands.

'Look,' said Sarah cautiously, 'I know it's not my place and please don't see this as interfering; I'm just playing Devil's advocate. But maybe she's trying to find a way of dealing with her grief?'

'What? By pretending she can see her? Talk to her? It's crazy, Sarah, and you shouldn't be encouraging her.'

'I'm not, Oran, I'm just trying to listen to her.' She knew how it sounded as soon as she said it and braced herself for the response.

'Meaning I'm not?'

Sarah took a deep breath. Anyone who had an ounce of sense would keep their mouth shut, but she figured she'd already crossed the line; no point back-pedalling now.

'It's natural; the urge to protect your child. But I don't

think you can protect her from this, Oran,' she said eventually. 'I think that Hazel is trying to deal with this in her own way and that's different to yours. Maybe there's a way you can both try to help each other?'

Sarah could see that Oran was fighting the urge to argue with her, to defend himself. Who would tolerate a stranger walking into their house and telling them how to parent their child? A long time passed before he spoke again.

'I just didn't want her to have to grow up so quickly. I wanted to shield her from it, but now that I'm hearing myself say it out loud, it sounds ridiculous. How can you stop a child from missing their mother?'

You couldn't, Sarah wanted to say. Just like you couldn't stop a mother from missing her child.

'Did your father tell you about the diary I found? It belonged to a girl who lived in the cottage.'

'Wow, that was really seamless. I hardly noticed you changing the subject at all,' Oran said, a wry smile on his face.

'Sorry, I'm just trying not to intrude on your private life any more than I have.'

'No, I'm … I'm glad you did.' Oran nodded his head and sucked in his bottom lip as he looked to the floor for inspiration. 'I shouldn't be dumping all of this on you anyway. I suppose if I had any sense of decency, I'd be embarrassed.'

'Don't say that. I've wasted too much time being polite with people. Better to be open about things.' She said this more to herself than anything.

'Okay, well, next time, we're delving into your closet for skeletons.'

Sarah's heart jumped a little. Hearing him say 'next time' felt so good; it was the skeleton part that sent a chill through her.

'Let's stick to neutral ground, for now. I was wondering if maybe you knew anything about the Butler family?'

'Not really, to be honest. The sale of the cottage was through an agent and it had been empty for a long time before we bought it. I could ask my father though, or my grandfather. He's in a nursing home now. His body is weak but his memory is sharp as ever.'

'I'd appreciate that.' She put down her cup of coffee and got up to leave. 'But now I really must get back, I have some calls to make,' she lied.

On the way out, she spotted her drawing of Butler's cottage standing proudly on a shelf above the stove.

'I'd forgotten the beauty of the place,' he said, catching her glance. 'Thanks for reminding me.'

After Sarah had left, Oran climbed softly up the carpeted stairs and knocked on Hazel's door, ignoring the large 'Do Not Disturb' sign she had made herself, featuring a skull and crossbones. Max, despite countless warnings not to go upstairs, trotted up behind him.

'Go away!' came Hazel's firm response.

'Um, I would, it's just that Max wants a quick word.' Right on cue, Max began scratching at the door, another indictable offence that Oran was willing to overlook. Just this once.

The key turned in the lock and two large eyes peeped out through a crack. Max, determined to gain access, nudged the door persistently with his nose until Hazel gave in.

'Not on the bed!' they cried in unison, but Max, helplessly drawn to the soft folds of the duvet, ignored their pleas.

'I think maybe we need to talk,' began Oran and they both sat on the bed, careful not to squash Max.

'It wasn't Sarah's fault.'

'It's no one's fault. That's the point. None of it is your fault, or mine. Or your mother's.'

The words Oran had always wanted to say, and Hazel needed to hear, quietly worked their magic.

'All this time, I thought I was protecting you. These visions of your mother, I thought they were … unhealthy. But maybe I was wrong.'

She looked up at him with a mixture of relief and hope.

'I know it sounds weird, Dad, but it was kind of comforting, like she was keeping watch over me.'

'Was?' Oran picked up on her use of the past tense.

'I had a dream last night. She told me that I wouldn't be able to see her anymore, but that she would always be here, just a step behind me. Then I woke up and, I dunno, I just felt different.'

Oran pulled her into his arms, her tears falling softly on the wool of his sweater.

'Are you okay?' he said, after some time had passed

'I guess. I just miss her.'

'Me, too, sweetheart. Me, too.'

They spent the afternoon lying on her bed with Max, talking about silly things they remembered. Like the time they found a mouse in the attic of the cottage and Oran set a trap with cheese. Yet every day he checked the trap, the cheese was gone but there was no sign of the mouse. It turned out that Hazel and her mother were stealing the cheese to save the poor mouse's neck.

'I couldn't figure out how the mouse was doing it!' he said, laughing at the memory. 'Cathy literally wouldn't hurt a fly.'

'Sarah's nice, isn't she?' Hazel asked out of the blue.

'M-hmm.'

'She seems a bit sad, though.'

'What makes you say that?'

'I dunno, I just feel like sometimes she's hiding something. Maybe she's homesick.'

Oran wondered if Hazel was already possessed of women's intuition, or if he was just hopelessly oblivious to other people's problems.

'You know, I gave her *The Fairy Compendium*,' Hazel said suddenly.

'Oh, really? But that's your favourite book.'

'I know, but guess what? It turns out the guy who wrote it came here to Thornwood and he met the girl who wrote the diary Sarah found,' she explained. 'She lived in Butler's cottage, just like me.'

'That's interesting. So, does Sarah believe in fairies, too?'

Oran asked, hardly believing he was saying this with a straight face.

'Those who don't believe in magic will never find it.'

'Wow, that's pretty profound, Hazel. When did you get so clever?'

'It's Roald Dahl, Dad! Honestly, you really should try reading a book every now and again!'

Chapter Twenty-Eight

L ater that evening, Sarah was pacing the length of the cottage, which, considering its size, wasn't very far. There was a missed call from Jack on her phone, which blinked incessantly, demanding some sort of response. She wanted a drink badly, but she knew it was just making things worse. She couldn't put it off any longer; it was time to face up to the truth and stop hiding. But she didn't want to go it alone. Picking up her phone, she googled the number of a local cab firm. She waited by the front door, the top half open. Looking out, she spotted two beams of light illuminating the road like searchlights, and when the cab's engine came within earshot, she already felt reassured.

'Well, this is a lovely surprise!' said Fee. She stood back from the door and motioned Sarah to enter. In contrast to the dark night outside, the farmhouse glowed warmly in soft lamplight.

'I'm sorry for just landing in on top of you like this, Fee. I should have called first.'

Fee batted away the social niceties, which immediately put Sarah at ease. She automatically flicked on the kettle and spooned some loose tea into a pot that waited patiently on the worktop, ever ready for an impromptu cup of tea.

'No Marcus this evening?'

'He's with his mistress,' she said, the soft skin around her eyes creasing. 'Works all hours at that hotel.'

'But you don't mind?'

'Why would I? It's what he loves and it keeps him happy.'

Fee and Marcus made everything look so simple. It seemed as though nothing could unglue them.

'My husband called.'

'Ah.' Fee poured the tea into earthenware cups and opened a biscuit tin boasting a variety of treats.

'This tea is delicious!' Sarah gulped down the soothing warm liquid and they both sat in silence for a while.

'I'm starting to wonder if maybe I got things wrong. It was something he said…' Sarah's voice caught in her throat. 'We never really spoke about it, you see. I mean, we did, but it was always with a forced kind of politeness. It's like we were two strangers, trying not to offend each other.'

'I understand; you end up saying what you think they want to hear. There's a fear in all of us, that we'll lose the relationship. But I suppose we end up losing ourselves instead.'

Sarah couldn't figure out what it was about this woman, or this place, that made such profound conversations seem commonplace. In all of the time she had been seeing a therapist, she had never felt comfortable enough to open up about things. Some people were just better listeners than others.

'Fee? Can I tell you my story? Because if I don't I think I'll go mad!'

Fee simply squeezed Sarah's hand. 'You're safe here.'

The house was warm, with a scent of dried flowers and fruit. Sarah put her elbows on the armrests of the wooden carver chair and joined her hands on her stomach, with her fingers interlaced. 'We thought that once we got past the first trimester everything would be okay,' she began. 'Jack went crazy buying things – a Moses basket, a crib, a car seat. The house was full of baby things and I added to it with enough outfits for triplets! We were completely prepared to bring life into the world, but not for … well, not for what happened.' Sarah's hand instinctively covered her mouth, a last attempt to physically stop the words. Her fingertips traced her dry lips, over and over, while Fee sat quietly across from her. Once her mind had settled on the decision, she continued.

'I'll never forget the look on the ultrasound technician's face. The panic. Someone else came into the room and I heard the words "placental abruption". I wasn't sure what that meant, but I knew it wasn't good. Then she spoke about a stillbirth and … well, there was no mistaking that. It felt like taking a deep breath in and never being able to breathe out again. They induced me the next day. I hadn't expected it to be so silent in the delivery room. I ached to hear my baby cry, but there was nothing. Emptiness. They said we could have as much time as we wanted. They told us to take photos and Jack kept her handprints and footprints. I felt like I was being crushed; I had no baby and yet my body was flooding with hormones and milk.'

Sarah sucked in great big gulps of air; her ribcage shuddered with the effort. A wooden fruit bowl at the centre of the table held her gaze. She could tell it was handmade, like her father used to make on his lathe. She needed something to focus on and so she stared at the grain in the wood, anchoring herself.

'The nurses kept repeating their mantra, "You can try again, honey." Like I was trying to win a stuffed toy at a fairground. No,' she shook her head, 'when I lost Emma, I lost all of the possibilities her little life had promised us. Feeling the warmth of my daughter's body against my skin; inhaling her own unique scent; hearing that little guttural noise babies make when they sleep; hearing her laugh…'

She pressed the palms of her hands harder together and shook her head free of something that had been holding her captive. There were no tears now; she had done her crying. Now she just needed to be heard.

'My daughter,' she said, her voice finally giving way. 'My daughter,' she repeated, louder now. 'I feel like I can't even say I had a daughter! It's like everyone wants me to forget about it, just move on like she never existed. But she did; I carried her for seven months,' she said, finally freeing her hands to beat them against her belly. 'I felt her moving inside of me; I planned our future. But now I have to pretend like it never happened. Try again. And we did try again, Jack and I, but I couldn't get pregnant. Unsurprisingly, they said it was the stress. My fault again!'

Fee moved her chair closer and put her hand on Sarah's shoulder.

'It's nobody's fault, love.'

'Then we stopped trying altogether. We were just two people with a dead daughter in common, a daughter we couldn't talk about. In the end, we were living around the edges of each other. I know he wants to move on, start a family. Maybe now he will. I guess that's why I was going home, to grieve properly. But in the end, I knew it would be the same thing – my parents tiptoeing around my feelings and me not wanting to hurt them any more with my pain.' Sarah suddenly thought of her conversation with Oran; maybe they were all just trying to protect her. So why did it feel like she was being silenced?

Finally, it was all out. She went to take a sip of tea, but it had gone cold. Fee emptied her cup and poured her a fresh one, piling a large spoon of sugar into it.

'You poor woman,' she said at last. 'But you're on the right path now.'

'What makes you so sure?' Sarah couldn't help but think of the panic attacks and the alcohol she'd used to drown them. 'I'm not sure I'm even on a path.'

'Well, it sounds to me like you're finally allowing yourself to grieve for your loss. Grief is like a hard lump inside of you,' she said, tapping her gut. 'It will stay there, hard like a rock, unless you begin working to soften it.'

Fee got up from her seat then and began searching in the bottom cupboard of a dresser. She pulled out jars with handwritten labels and brought them to the table.

'It will never go away completely, but instead of a

hardness, it can become a tenderness. Your heart will make room for your memories and you won't be afraid of them any more.'

'How did you get to know so much?' Sarah said, with a little laugh. She felt raw and open, which, to her surprise, felt lighter than her previous state.

'Ha! It's life, my dear. We all get schooled in the end. Now let me show you something.'

Fee opened the jars of what looked like potpourri, filling the room with a generous scent of the outdoors preserved.

'Remember I told you that the berries from the hawthorn are a tonic for the heart? It helps lower cholesterol, manage blood pressure, that kind of thing. Well, this preparation is also beneficial on an emotional level, like a DIY heart-repair kit! A more resilient heart helps us to spring back from heartbreak and venture forward on a new path, without so much fear and heartsickness.'

She explained all of this while spooning some of the dried herbs into a small brown paper bag.

'So, you're telling me that this is a magic potion to heal a broken heart?' Sarah asked, failing to keep the doubt out of her voice.

'You're wise to be sceptical, but sure, it's worth a go, isn't it?' Fee replied, smiling wisely.

'Are they rose petals?' Sarah asked.

'Indeed, the rose has always been associated with matters of the heart and the white rose signifies the end of a life.'

Sarah took a deep breath.

'Rose petals help with insomnia, too. They calm the

nerves. Roses can open the heart and prepare it for a new beginning,' Fee continued encouragingly.

'Will this really work?'

'It's already working,' Fee replied, glancing at the empty teapot.

Sarah's mouth opened and widened into a smile. Could it be true? The berries from the very hawthorn tree that had been the catalyst for her impromptu escape to Ireland were now in her cup, warming her body and healing her heart.

Chapter Twenty-Nine

Anna's Diary

18th January 1911

By the time we arrived at the gaol, the heavens had opened and lashed down such a torrent of rain that I was soaked through to the skin. The tall stone building was the colour of slate, with two pompous pillars guarding the entrance. An unwelcoming edifice, to be sure, but I imagined that was the point. Scurrying through the front door, I must have looked like a river rat with my hair stuck onto my face. I was immediately caught by one of the Royal Irish Constabulary, a moustachioed man wearing a uniform with impossibly shiny buttons.

'Slow down there, Miss,' he said, trying to herd me towards a desk.

'I have to see Mr Krauss,' I said, my wet hair dripping

onto the paperwork in front of him. He looked up at me with an expression of mild disgust and probably would have thrown me out if it weren't for Father Peter arriving in my wake.

'One of my parishioners is being held here and he has requested an audience with his priest,' Father Peter said in his tenor voice that always commanded respect.

'An audience?' the constable repeated. 'Who do you think you are, the Pope?' he jeered and one of the other officers joined him in a good long laugh at Father Peter's expense.

After a short contest of wills, the constable relented and allowed Father Peter through. I followed quietly, but a long arm blocked my way.

'Not you, young one, unless you're going to tell me that you're a nun!' said the constable, laughing without managing to smile.

'Please Sir, you don't understand, I must speak with him!' I said, becoming delirious with impatience and worry. My eyes were red and sore from crying, but the thought of Harold alone in a cell brought the tears forth anew.

'Don't worry, my girl,' said Father Peter. 'He can speak to me in confidence and if there is anything he should want you to know, I will pass it on to you.' He looked on me kindly, then, his watery blue eyes assuring me that everything would come out right in the end. I sat down on a hard wooden bench by the door and waited. I was shivering, sitting there in my wet clothes and one of the other officers kindly brought me a hot cup of tea. My hands were shaking so badly that I could hardly bring the cup to my lips. My mind reeled, trying to piece together the events of last night and this morning.

The waiting was interminable, leaving me alone with my guilty thoughts. I jumped when the door finally swung open and Father Peter came out. I could tell by his ashen face that the news wasn't good, but he refused to discuss the matter until we were back outside.

'I must contact Mr Krauss's superiors in Oxford,' he said, as he climbed into the carriage and flicked the reins. The rain had eased up to a light mist, not that either of us took much notice.

'What's happened, Father? Why have they arrested him?'

'He asked me not to burden you with the details, Anna, but he wanted me to assure you that all will be well. So you're not to worry,' he said, with a quick smile that belied his own anxieties.

'Father, I know you are a priest and that confessions are confidential, but you have to understand; I'm the reason that Harold went to Thornwood House this morning,' I explained hurriedly. 'You see, I lost my mother's pearls there and he offered to go back and retrieve them for me. He shouldn't have been there at all!'

Father Peter pulled hard on the reins and brought the carriage to a halt.

'I know how you lost your pearls, Anna.'

I fell silent, wondering how much Harold had told him about George's actions. I could never have told anyone about that night, not least because he was Lord Hawley's son. Who would believe me? And even if they did, they would not look favourably on me for it. If it hadn't been for Harold coming to me as soon as it happened, I would have taken the secret to my grave.

'But why did they arrest Harold? He did nothing wrong,' I said.

'I'm sorry, Anna, but I promised the man I would contact his professors at Oxford first. He needs all of the help he can get now—' He looked as though he instantly regretted what he had said. 'We will pray for his release,' he added, secure in the belief that prayers would serve as a calming balm to our worries.

He commanded the horse to walk on and the carriage lurched forward. I squeezed my eyes tightly shut and made a fervent prayer to Our Lady, but my thoughts refused to keep quiet.

'What do you mean, he needs all our help? Do they think he had something to do with Master Hawley's death?' I persisted. 'I have to know, Father.'

Father Peter pulled on the reins again, earning him a loud and impatient whinny from the horse.

'*In ainm Dé*!' he blustered, calling on the Lord for patience. 'Miss Olivia witnessed you leaving the party with her brother last night and gave her testimony to the police this morning. When they found the pearls scattered on the bank, they thought they had their culprit.'

'Me?' I asked, my eyes widening in disbelief.

'Yet when Harold arrived at the scene and became aware of their investigations, he confessed to having had a scuffle with Master George himself and that he accidentally fell into the river.'

A wave of nausea swept through my body and I had to throw my head to the side of the carriage quickly before a watery bile spewed from my mouth. I could hear the priest admonishing himself for having told me.

'I didn't do it, Father. It was an accident, he fell,' I explained, stammering.

'I know, I know; Harold explained as best he could,' he said. 'Listen to me, Anna. You cannot speak of this to anyone. I know you're troubled, but it won't help his cause if people start gossiping. Do you understand me, girl?'

'Yes, Father,' I said, trying to compose myself. 'I'm all right now, 'twas just the shock,' I said.

'I want to get back to the village and send a telegram immediately. Can you make your way home from there?' he asked.

'Of course, Father, don't worry about me.'

I spent the entire journey planning what I would do next. Harold was in gaol because of me and so it was my responsibility to clear his name. The only problem was that I couldn't tell the truth. Who would believe that an army of fairies set upon Master Hawley and drove him into the silent river? I couldn't even tell my family, for the mere mention of Milly would cause them all to fear for my sanity. Not to mention the unspeakable shame I would bring on my parents if people knew what had transpired between Master Hawley and me. It did not matter that he had attacked me; I would be seen as disgraced in the eyes of anyone with an ounce of moral standing. One only had to look at how people had reacted to that poor maid from Cork. Harold knew this, and sacrificed himself to save my reputation. He also knew that Father Peter was bound by the confessional to keep our secret and I wouldn't make his incarceration in gaol a futile exercise by betraying him.

There was only one person who could help me, yet as I walked up the avenue, I knew she would be the last person to do my bidding. As I walked up those cold, wet steps, I had to bury my hands in my pockets to keep them from shaking. Thornwood House was a very different place now. While it was never exactly welcoming, its allure and sparkle had worn off, like a broken spell in a fairy tale.

'Miss Olivia is not available at the moment,' the butler said with his snooty accent.

'I just want to … offer my sympathies,' I said, the words sticking in my throat.

'I'll pass on your message,' he replied, standing like a sentinel at the door.

I wasn't going to give up that easily and told him straight that I planned to station myself on the front steps until she saw me. As he was about to close the door on me, I heard her shrill voice coming from the bowels of the house.

'Tell Miss Butler I'll see her in the library,' came the orders, leaving the butler red-faced.

It was disconcerting, walking back into the house where, only the night before, I had entered with all the excitement of a debutante. I kept my head turned and didn't look at the doors leading to the ballroom. I had to keep my nerve. After all, I was here to represent Harold.

Olivia was the picture of a graceful mourner, dressed in a black gown, which only accentuated her pale, papery skin.

She was slim as a whippet and moved about the room with effortless grace. She was drinking whisky from a crystal tumbler and had her back turned to me as I entered the room.

'I'm sorry for your trouble, Miss Olivia,' I said, hesitantly.

She responded with a hollow laugh and turned to me with a wild look in her eyes.

'You're sorry, are you? Well, that makes everything better then, doesn't it?'

I wasn't sure what to say to that. I began to wonder if coming here was a mistake.

'Miss Olivia, I am sorry, and I've come to ask you if you would please tell the police they've made a mistake in arresting Harold. He didn't harm your brother; you know him, he couldn't hurt a fly. It was an accident, you see, Master George had too much to drink and—'

'Shut up, you stupid girl!' she shouted at me with the vehemence of a wild animal. 'I know perfectly well who is responsible for my brother's death and she's standing right in front of me. Brazen as you like.'

I opened my mouth to respond, but the words wouldn't come. All of a sudden, I became that little girl hiding in the tree, unable to speak.

'You had to have them both, didn't you?'

I shook my head in bewilderment.

'Oh yes, poor Anna, the innocent farm girl. Well, I'm not fooled by your guile,' she seethed. 'It wasn't enough that you seduced my brother, but you had to lead Harold along, too.'

'W-what are you saying? Th-that's not right, I thought George … I thought he liked me but h-he tried to…'

'Hah! Don't come the innocent with me, Anna.' She laughed scornfully. 'We both know that's what you wanted.'

My body was shaking with rage, yet the words still wouldn't come.

'But you weren't satisfied with just one man. Oh no, you had to play them both against each other.'

'That's ridiculous, I wouldn't do that!' I shouted, finally. 'Harold was only trying to protect me, don't you see?'

'There's the temper that murdered my brother. Now we see your true colours,' she said maliciously. 'It's too late for poor little Harold though, isn't it? Well, he was a fool to fall for you and now you've destroyed his life and taken my brother's,' she said bitterly.

'Think what you like about me, Olivia, but you know Harold is innocent.' She had turned her back to me again, but I carried on. 'Please don't punish him for not returning your feelings.'

'How dare you! Who do you think you are, coming to my house when my brother's body is barely cold?' she said, her breathing laboured. 'You should be rotting in prison for what you did, but if Harold wishes to take your place, then that is his choice. It's nothing to do with me. Now get out of my house before I have you arrested for trespassing!' On hearing our raised voices, the butler hurried in and wasted no time in grabbing my arm and yanking me towards the hall.

'It was an accident, I swear to you! Harold didn't kill

him and neither did I,' I shouted. 'You'll be letting an innocent man hang.'

That was when I saw Lord Hugh Hawley standing at the top of the stairs, leaning on the banister and looking like a broken man.

'Get that peasant girl out of my house,' he bellowed, like a thundercloud. 'She's not fit to speak my son's name.'

'Lord Hawley,' I called out, as the butler wrestled me to the door. 'Please, Sir, I beg you to listen!' He wouldn't even deign to look at me and with a final shove I was out on the front step with the large wooden door slammed in my face.

Chapter Thirty

I recovered my bicycle from where I had left it and stopped at Gallagher's to collect Billy. Rosie brought me inside and showed me my little brother, fast asleep in front of the fire with the little kitten in his arms. He was the picture of sweet innocence and I didn't like to disturb him.

'Why not stop for your supper?' Rosie asked kindly. 'You can dry your clothes by the fire,' she added, feeling my damp coat and hair.

I was so tired that I let her take care of me like a little child. She had a baby of her own, Ruán, who was sleeping soundly in his cot. Her mother-in-law, Eileen, was knitting away quietly in her rocking chair, making the domestic scene a calm and peaceful place to be.

'Where's Gerard?' I asked her, as she gave me some of her old clothes to wear while we set mine to dry.

'Oh, he's gone to the market in Limerick with a few cattle,' she said. 'I used to miss him when he'd go away for the night, but ever since I had Ruán, I just enjoy the peace now!'

I smiled at her honesty, and pulled a lovely warm jumper over my head. We ate a hearty dinner of stew and boiled potatoes. The food and the warmth made me drowsy and I couldn't rouse myself to make the journey home with Billy.

'If you don't mind my saying, Anna, you look terrible,' Rosie said. 'I'm not sure if you should go out into the cold again.'

'I'll be fine now in a minute,' I assured her, trying to raise my eyelids as my head drooped lower and lower towards the table.

'I'll tell you what, why don't you stretch out on the settle for a while, let the food go down and then I'll walk you home myself,' she suggested.

Billy would be happy to stay as long as the kitten kept him company, playing with Eileen's wool on the floor.

'Maybe just for a minute then,' I agreed.

As I lay my head down, the tightness in my muscles finally gave way and I was lost to sleep.

My dreams were disturbing and frighteningly real. George Hawley's face loomed at me from above, with terrible teeth like a wolf snapping at me. I dreamed that I was drowning with him in the dark waters and I gasped for breath. I felt like I was being carried by hundreds of arms and hands, taking me who knew where. I woke up with a start, covered in sweat. It was already light outside and when I looked around the room, I couldn't figure out where I was.

'Mother!' I called out, and Rosie came rushing to my side.

'You're all right now, hush,' she said, calmly.

'Rosie, I'm so sorry, I must have slept the whole night through,' I said, trying to lift my head. 'Where's Billy?'

'Easy now, cratúr, it's been two days that you've had this fever,' she said softly. 'I sent Billy home with Paddy that first night.'

'What? Two days, that's not possible,' I replied, frustrated with my inability to get up. My limbs felt like heavy sacks of potatoes.

'The doctor said you were to stay put until the fever had passed, we couldn't risk taking you home and catching another chill,' she said, tucking the blankets around me and handing me a cup of warm water and honey.

'The doctor?' I screeched.

'Yes, he came with Father Peter,' she said, drawing back the curtains.

'Did he have any news? How is Harold?' I asked eagerly.

'Calm yourself, Anna, you mustn't get excited now.'

'Listen to me, Rosie, you are so good to look after me. You've even given me your room,' I said, looking around me.

'Gerard's still grumbling about having to sleep on the settle!'

'Thank you for your kindness, but I have to go and help Harold,' I explained. 'You've heard that he was arrested?'

Her face changed then to an inscrutable mask.

'What is it? Has something happened?' I asked,

throwing back the covers.

'He's gone, Anna, they've taken him to Dublin,' she said in an apologetic tone. 'He'll be tried there in the morning.'

My head felt as though it would burst open with the pressure.

'You mean, Harold's been alone in that gaol all this time, and I've just been lying here?'

'But sure, the doctor thought you had pneumonia,' Rosie explained, trying to make me see reason. 'Besides, no one other than the priest was allowed to see him.'

'You don't understand, Rosie! Harold took the blame for me; they thought I killed George,' I said, searching around for my clothes.

'You?' she shrieked incredulously. 'Sure, why would anyone think that?'

I gave her a grave look and she finally gave up the battle to keep me in bed.

'I didn't do it Rosie, it was, it was an accident. But please, don't repeat this to anyone. I must go!'

I stumbled about the room getting dressed and tried to ignore the uneasiness that had come between us. She sat on the edge of the bed, eyes trained on the floor.

'Tell me, did he try to, you know, force himself on you?' she asked softly.

I couldn't answer, but my silence was enough confirmation for her. She didn't seem surprised or shocked, merely nodded her head resignedly.

'You, too?' I asked.

She quickly wiped a tear from her cheek and fussed with my coat.

'I'll ask Nana to mind Ruán and I'll cycle back to the house with you,' she said, pulling on her own coat.

We spoke no more about it, but shared the wretched silence of two women with a common injury.

When I got home, it felt as though there was a death in the house. I felt sorely out of touch, having missed two days of goings on. My mother and father were sitting at the table – something they rarely did outside of mealtimes.

'Is there any news?' I asked desperately, almost out of breath after such a light exertion.

'What are you doing out of bed?' my mother scolded and sat me down immediately beside the fire. 'You'll catch your death,' she said, rather hysterically.

'Please, Mother, don't fuss and just tell me about Harold.'

My father gave me a strange look and then looked away out the window.

'You can't believe that he did it!' I said accusingly. 'Father, you know him, he—'

'I know, I know,' he said, hushing me. 'I knew the moment I heard it that there must have been some mistake.'

I was so heartened that they had not lost their trust in Harold. In that moment, I felt such a rush of love for my parents. They had always valued Harold's good character above all else and from this belief they could not be shaken.

'What *did* happen that night, Anna?' my mother asked. 'Did you see Master George?'

'Yes, I did see him and I'm the sorrier for it. But I promise you, Mother, neither Harold nor I had a hand, act or part in his death.'

'I don't need telling what I already know,' she said, smiling at me.

'So what are we going to do about it? Rosie said that his trial is tomorrow and he is already on his way to Dublin.'

My parents looked away again, their faces inscrutable.

'What is it? Have his professors come from England to help him?' I asked.

No one seemed in any hurry to answer me.

'I'd best be heading home,' Rosie said, sensing that this was now a private matter.

My mother got up and walked her to the door, whispering that the less she knew about it, the better it would be for her and her family.

'You're really worrying me now,' I said to my father, sitting beside him at the table.

'Paddy went to see you in Rosie's last night,' he began solemnly. 'You were very sick with fever and, well, you were babbling a bit.'

'Oh.' I wondered nervously what I had said and how much of it Paddy would have told Father. 'Where is Paddy now?'

'Do you remember the young fella that came here, Danny was his name?' my mother asked.

'Of course, from the Brotherhood.'

'Well, when he left here, he told Paddy he was in his debt, and if he ever needed anything…'

'I told him not to go getting mixed up with that lot,' my father said, his anger rising.

'What are they doing?' I asked, my eyes darting from one to the other.

'Harold will be taken to Brooklodge station to catch the steam train to Dublin,' my mother explained.

'Surely they can't be planning on stopping the train,' I said, incredulous.

'Oh, Anna, I'm not sure what they're planning, but my heart's been in my mouth all morning,' she said, wringing her handkerchief in her hands.

I put my head in my hands. I was too weary to cry any more and besides, what good would tears do? My dearest brother, who had never gone against the law in his life, was now planning on helping a prisoner escape trial. I cursed my stupid pride, believing that George Hawley could ever love anyone but himself. Believing that he was a gentleman. I was risking the lives of the people who truly cared for me, and all because of my foolishness.

'When will we know?'

'The train leaves at noon,' my mother said.

My father scraped back his chair and put on his cap before heading out the door with Jet at his heels.

'He's best keeping busy,' she said, 'and we should do the same.'

All I wanted to do was run as fast as I could to the train station, but it was pointless. I'd never make it and even if I did, what could I do? I had to trust that Paddy and Danny would rescue him and not end up arrested themselves. I remembered something the seeress said, about having a friend amongst The Good People if you had a friend departed. I silently offered up a desperate plea to Milly.

'Save him, Milly. Please save him.'

Chapter Thirty-One

11th January 2011

S arah spent the afternoon walking Cnoc na Sí. She was on tenterhooks reading about Harold and Anna, but as there were only a few pages left, she was trying to make them last. She didn't want the story to end just yet. Possibly she was avoiding the truth – that perhaps this story wouldn't have the outcome she hoped for. But that seemed to be the nature of things. You made your plans, but life had other ideas and somehow you had to make peace with that. Find the meaning in it and let it change you. Fighting to stay the same was the problem. It felt like everybody wanted the old Sarah back, including herself. But a part of her died that day with Emma and she would never be the same woman again. And maybe that was okay.

Following her conversation with Fee the night before, she felt more at peace with herself than she had done in a long time. The day was bright and crisp and there was still some ground frost in the shadows on the forest floor. She was smiling to herself, thinking how coming to Ireland had been the right thing after all, when her phone buzzed in her pocket.

'Meghan, I've been meaning to call,' she said, wincing at the lie.

'Have you been meaning to call our parents, too? Because they won't stop pestering me. "When's Sarah coming home, Meg?" "What's she doing in Ireland, Meg?"'

'I'll call them, I promise. I've just been … working through some stuff,' she said, sitting down on an old log covered in moss.

'Well, when *are* you coming home?'

'Um … I'm not sure. Soon. Maybe.' She could almost hear her sister's eyes rolling, judging her for her seeming lack of direction. Yet she *was* finding her way, just on her own terms.

'Don't get me wrong, I'd love to visit the Emerald Isle, but in the depths of January? I can think of warmer escapes, like Barbados.'

Sarah smiled. Her sister had a point. Turquoise waters and warm sandy beaches sounded like bliss, but she wouldn't trade.

'Oh, I don't know, this place has its charms.'

Meghan took a beat before reading between the lines.

'There's a guy, isn't there?'

'What? No!' she said, laughing. Then reconsidered. 'I mean, there is someone but—'

'I knew it!' Meghan replied gleefully, always happy to be

proved right. 'I want to hear everything about him from the beginning and don't leave anything out.'

It was so good to hear her sister getting excited for her. They hadn't had much to laugh about lately.

'Meghan, you won't believe this, but I've just spotted him.' Oran was wearing his conservation officer uniform and Max was weaving between the tree trunks behind him.

'What? Where? What does he look like?'

'On the trail, he's coming right towards me.' Sarah said the words like a ventriloquist in case Oran could read her lips.

'I need photos, Sarah? Are you listening, don't hang—' Meghan's voice cut off as Sarah hit the red button and put the phone back in her pocket.

'Hi.'

'Hello, again,' she replied, standing to greet him, slightly embarrassed that she had been caught talking about him.

'How are things?'

'Good, good. And you?'

'Good,' he said, a broad smile on his face.

'That's good.'

He nodded and then they both began to laugh at themselves.

'Oh my God, what's wrong with us?' she joked, burying her face in her gloved hands. It really was like being a teenager again. The chemistry between them was so strong, there was no point in denying it, but it was also incredibly awkward because neither of them had made a move to act on it, or even acknowledge its existence. If her eighteen-year-old self could see how immaturely she was acting right now, she would have been embarrassed for her.

'Are you working?' she said, nodding towards the device in his hand that looked like something between a GPS and a camera.

'Just collecting some data for a biodiversity project we're hoping to get off the ground soon.' Max reached up his paws, waiting for Oran to throw a stick, which he duly did.

'It's good to see you,' he said, making direct eye contact, which almost took her breath away.

'It's good to see you, too,' she said, smiling like a loon. The tension was unbearably delicious.

'Which way are you headed?'

'The same direction as you,' she said, her cheeks burning. *Who needs Barbados?*

Quite unexpectedly, Oran had reached out his hand to her and without hesitating, she clasped it and fell into step beside him as they began walking up the hill. They didn't speak for a while; it was enough to just walk together, hand in hand. It felt natural and Sarah didn't want the trail to end. Max ran off searching for who knew what in the undergrowth and when they came to a wooden gate that provided a view all the way down to Thornwood village, they both stopped to take it all in.

'I love this place,' she said simply.

'It's not bad, is it?' he replied, interlacing his fingers between hers.

The warmth of his touch felt so good, she wanted to melt into him. But it wasn't only that; he held a warmth inside, a kind of genuineness that made her feel like she could be herself around him. She didn't have to try to be somebody else in order to impress him, something she could now see had been a major problem with Jack. She had never felt like enough for him and when they lost Emma, she had taken that as confirmation.

Oran turned to look at her and slowly raised his other hand to her cheek, tracing a line down along her jaw.

'I never thought I'd want to do this again, till I met you,' he said.

Only now could she fully admit to herself how many spare moments she had spent wondering what his lips would feel like; his hands pulling her closer, his fingers tangling in her hair. Should she hold back? Would this spoil things? How long had they been locked in this awkward silence?

The warmth of his mouth on hers came as a sweet surprise. He must have been thinking about it too, all this time. Everything felt new, the way he held her, the taste of him, the softness of his lips and the texture of his stubble against her skin. Yet, within minutes, it felt like all she'd ever known. Oran.

When they finally stopped kissing, they looked at each other and smiled. *Could this really be happening?*

'Oran, there's something I need to tell you. *Want* to tell you.'

'I'm listening,' he said, stroking her hair and not pulling away.

'I know I told everyone I came to Thornwood to see the hawthorn tree, but that wasn't true. I came here to grieve. I lost my daughter, Emma. She died in my womb.'

It was the first time she had spoken about it using those words. It felt like she was finally owning her experience. No more hiding. No more pretending.

'Sarah, my God, I'm so sorry,' he said, hugging her tightly. He didn't ask any questions. He didn't need to.

'Maybe there is some unseen magic in this place,' she said, finding an old tissue in her pocket and wiping her nose. 'Finding Anna's diary … I didn't realise it at the time, but the guilt she was carrying around over her sister, Milly, I've been feeling that too. I blamed myself for what happened. As Emma's mother, I should've protected her from harm. But Anna has helped me to see that guilt is just a way of not allowing yourself to grieve. Because once you start to grieve, you really have to accept that they're gone.'

Oran sighed deeply and nodded.

'Grief is a dark labyrinth.'

'What did you say? Is that a quote from somewhere?'

'I don't know,' he said, looking puzzled.

'It doesn't matter,' she said, smiling to herself and stepping back into his warm embrace. Unseen magic indeed.

Chapter Thirty-Two

Anna's Diary

18th January 1911

Waiting for news is a kind of penance in itself. The seconds ticked away on the clock, but somehow it felt as though time wasn't moving at all. I didn't feel as though I could perform any task around the house, but my mother, God bless her, kept us busy for hours on end, washing clothes, peeling vegetables, making bread and scrubbing the floor. It was time to start lighting the lamps when Paddy finally burst through the door. He looked exhausted but happy and although I wasn't certain, he smelled of alcohol.

'Where the hell have you been!' my mother shouted at him. 'Your father's been worried sick.'

'I met him in the top field just now, told him everything,' he said, slumping down on the settle to catch his breath.

'Well, tell us, will you!' I said, rushing to his side. 'What did you do?'

Tommy and Billy sat on the floor in front of him with crossed legs, as though it were story-time at Butler's.

'Danny brought three other lads with him – when I told them that an innocent man was being framed for the murder of an Anglo-Irish lord, they were only too happy to help,' he said, chuckling to himself.

My mother thumped him then, furious that he failed to see the seriousness of the situation.

'You big eejit, you could have ended up in jail yourself,' she said.

'I didn't do anything, Mother, Danny was the man of action. All I did was stand watch, not that I could see very much.'

Every time he stopped for breath I wanted to throttle the story out of him. Billy's kitten came to investigate this new arrival.

'Who's this?' Paddy asked, and as Billy began to explain where Suzy the cat came from, we both thumped him.

'Did you free him?' I asked.

'We were waiting at the station for them. The paddy wagon arrived with two officers in the front and one in the back with Harold. We weren't sure how we would take him, but two of Danny's fellas had shotguns and—'

'Shotguns!' my mother screeched, with her hand to her mouth. 'Sure, ye could have been killed,' she said, blessing herself and whispering a few supplications to Our Lady.

'Mother, wait till you hear. We didn't need the guns at all in the end. We had hid ourselves up on the bank on the opposite side of the platform, so we had a good view of Harold as they led him out of the back of the wagon. Danny told me to keep a lookout for any other armed officers who might be lurking unseen and they slid down the grassy bank, making their way behind the storerooms. But as soon as they did, there was a terrible ruckus outside when Higgins – you know, the pig farmer?' he asked, looking at my mother.

'Yes, yes I know him.' She nodded, still clutching her rosary beads.

'Well, he was trying to get his animals onto the siding with the loading bank and sure they got loose on him. There were pigs and piglets running about and squealing their heads off, all over the platform. Of course that started the women screaming and running and I could see the boys peeping out from behind the storeroom, looking for their chance to pounce.'

'My God, ye're so brave,' I said, shaking my head as Mother passed him a plate of food.

'The officers were already distracted,' he continued, tearing mouthfuls of bread and slurping milk from a cup. 'But to add to our luck, didn't the train let out an almighty cloud of steam – filling the platform with a thick white smoke. I could see nothing after that, until I felt a clod of turf hit me on the head. And wasn't it the boys leading Harold in his handcuffs away across the fields. I ran then like the clappers.'

My mother and I stayed silent for a moment, letting his story sink in. She got up first and gave her eldest son a tight hug, almost depriving him of air. Then she kissed the top of his head and gave him a good hard smack across the face.

'What was that for?' he said, slightly dazed.

'That's for the shotguns,' she said. Reaching up to the top of the dresser, she took down the old bottle of poitín and poured him a glass. 'That's for helping your friend.'

They smiled at each other then and all was right with the world, in their eyes at least.

'So, he's safe?' I asked, not satisfied with the story ending where it had.

'He's on his way to Cork. He'll get the ferry back to America from Cobh in the morning,' he said, throwing back the drink.

'America? He's not going back to London?'

'It's too dangerous. He decided he's better off going home. Don't worry, Anna, he'll be safe now.'

'Yes. Safe,' I repeated. I would never see Harold again. The thought took my breath away. I would never get to say goodbye. I couldn't bear it.

'But I didn't even get to thank him,' I said in a voice that was almost a whisper.

'You haven't thanked your brother yet, either,' my mother pointed out. 'I'll go out to call your father in for his tea,' she said, happy to return to normality.

'Of course. I'm sorry, Paddy,' I said, getting up and wrapping my arms around him. 'How can I ever thank you enough for what you did? And Danny – it was such a risk.'

'Ah sure, I had to do something, I couldn't let an innocent man go to gaol,' he said. 'Not after what you told me.'

'I don't remember anything,' I said. 'What did I tell you, Paddy?'

'Only what you should've told me as soon as it happened,' he replied, gruffly. 'I would have drowned that bastard myself if I knew he laid a finger on you.'

I turned away from him then, ashamed of the whole sorry affair.

'People like him always get their comeuppance,' he assured me, 'and that sister of his won't come to a good end either. She would have happily put Harold's neck in the noose, if it suited her.'

'I wish I'd never met them, Paddy, either of them. I've been such a fool,' I said, burying my head in my hands again.

'Don't be blaming yourself, Anna, he was a brute of a man,' Paddy said, stroking my back.

'I didn't realise, until it was too late.'

'I know, it's not your fault.'

'You misunderstand me, I'm not talking about George,' I said, sniffling. 'It's Harold. I didn't realise— I mean, I didn't know how much I…'

Paddy patted down his trouser pockets and after a long search, found what he was looking for.

'Here,' he said, handing me a piece of paper. 'He wrote this for you.'

I took the crumpled paper from his hand and saw my name written in a neat script on the front. I looked up at my brother, who smiled at me, then I ran up to my bed to read it in private.

Dearest Anna,

I pray you are well. Paddy told me of your illness and I have to say I feel some responsibility, letting you stay out in that cold shed all night. Alas, things did not go as I had planned. I'm afraid I was too late to retrieve your pearls from the grounds of Thornwood House; the authorities had already confiscated them and were taking them as evidence of your struggle with Master Hawley. Well, the rest is a matter of record now I'm sure, but please offer my apologies to your mother in regard to the pearls.

It was very good of you to come with Father Peter; he told me of your fervent appeal to the officers to see me and I have to say it gladdened my heart to hear of it. I deeply regret what happened that night at Thornwood House and if there was any way I could change the past and protect you, I would. I should have protected you, Anna, but my jealousy blinded me. You see, I believed that you could read my intentions the way you read the weather in the clouds, but I have had much time to ponder it and now realise that you could not have known. I have loved you, Anna, from the first moment we met at your front door. I have loved you and enjoyed every moment we have spent together in the places you call home. And God forgive me, but I thought my heart would break in its love for you that night you fell asleep in my arms.

You will think me cowardly now, professing love in a letter when I am about to leave the country. But I want you to know that as soon as I reach my home in the States, I will write to you and if you are willing, arrange for your passage to join me here. I must away now, your brother and his 'colleagues' have been so charitable to me and we don't have much time.

Love always, Harold Griffin-Krauss

Chapter Thirty-Three

12th January 2011

That was the last entry in the diary, the remaining pages were blank. Harold's letter, worn from repeated reading, was folded and kept in the back cover. Sarah's eyes were blurry with unshed tears. Surely that couldn't be the end of the story? But no matter how many times she turned the diary over, or searched the box in which she found it, there was no more. Only an unused ticket for a passenger ship to America. Was it possible that he had returned to Ireland? Sarah wasn't ready to accept that these two people, who were so obviously in love, would never see each other again. Sadly, *The Fairy Compendium* made no mention of his personal circumstances, only that it was published in 1912.

There was a soft knocking at the front door. It was late in the evening and she hadn't been expecting anyone. She opened the top half of the door and saw Oran standing there in the rain, soaked to the skin.

'What are you doing here?' she asked.

'Drowning, if you don't let me in!'

'Oh, right, sorry!' she said, fiddling with the latch on the door.

Once inside, he kissed her all too briefly on the cheek before shaking himself out of his wet coat. She hung it on a hook on the back of the door, where it slowly dripped a pool of water on the welcome mat.

'It's bucketing down,' he said, warming his hands by the fire and shaking the rain from his hair. He looked so handsome, it was difficult to focus or behave like a normal person when she was around him.

'Can I get you a cup of coffee or anything?'

'Do you have anything stronger?' he asked with a sly grin.

'Eh, no, actually, but I do have a magic potion if you're interested?'

'Why not,' he said, sitting on a stool by the hearth. He looked completely at home and yet, somehow, unsettled.

'Are you sure you want to be here? I mean—'

'I know what you mean,' he said a little brusquely. 'It's time.'

Sarah filled a pot with Fee's hawthorn and rose-petal concoction and carried it over on a tray.

'I was thinking a lot about what you said, up at Cnoc na Sí. Leaving this cottage,' he said, looking around at the cosy interiors, 'moving back in with my father... I suppose I've been punishing myself in a way. Since Cathy died.

Sometimes I feel like I'm not entitled to a happy life anymore, if she's been denied hers.'

Sarah ached to hold him, but she sensed that this was something he needed to say out loud and she didn't want to interrupt.

'I've never allowed us to move on. Hazel and me. I've kept us frozen in time, frozen in our grief. It's like you said, I've just been avoiding it.'

She couldn't help herself. She held out her hand and he took it gently, bringing to his lips.

'It took you coming here to see it.'

'Well, misery loves company,' she said, lightening the mood with a bit of sarcasm.

'Anyway, enough of that,' he said. 'Let's try some of this magic potion.'

Sarah let go of his hand and set out some cups.

'How's the diary going?' he asked, watching her pour the strangely pink tea.

'As a matter of fact, I just finished it,' she said, with a tinge of disappointment. 'There are no more entries after Krauss goes back to the States. Unless there were other diaries and I just haven't found them.' She decided not to mention the various searches she'd carried out, peeking in the attic, inspecting loose floorboards and even checking other trees for clues.

'I spoke to my grandfather. His mother was the postmistress in Thornwood, so they knew all of the goings on in the village.' He took a mouthful of tea and clicked his tongue against the roof of his mouth, trying to discern the flavour.

'So, are you going to tell me the end of the story?' Sarah asked.

'You've grown quite attached to Anna and Harold, haven't you?'

'They're like the Romeo and Juliet of Thornwood,' she said, lamely.

'Oof, look how they ended up!'

Sarah responded with a frown.

He threw another log on the fire, sending sparks up the chimney.

'Are you sure you want to hear this?' Oran asked, doubtfully.

'Why, is it not a happy ending?' She was suddenly very aware of how invested she had become in their story. But it wasn't just a story; it was real life, which always had a way of not sticking to the plot.

'Well, it might not be the one you're hoping for.'

Sarah took a deep breath and a large gulp of her drink. She thought about her own life and how, if someone read about it one hundred years from now, it might sound desperately sad. But reality wasn't so clear-cut. Life was like a great painting; if you only focused on one part, you would miss the full picture.

'I suppose no one's life turns out the way they think it will,' she said, and they held each other's gaze for a moment longer than necessary.

'My grandfather was only a boy at the time, but he knew all about the American and his fairy book,' he began. 'He was a bit of a celebrity in the village and after the whole debacle with George Hawley, his name became infamous.'

'Yes, I read that it was Anna's brother and some men from the Irish Republican Brotherhood who freed him before the trial.'

'Well, not long after he left, Anna's mother died very suddenly.'

Sarah's hand went to her chest with shock.

'But she was so young, wasn't she? How did it happen?'

'He didn't say. Seeing as Anna was the only woman in the house then, she stayed and looked after her father and her brothers. The two eldest, Paddy and Tommy, fought in the First World War. There was a belief at the time that fighting in the war would help to achieve Home Rule, but of course it didn't and those who fought with the British were labelled traitors when they returned.'

'Gosh, maybe I don't want to hear this,' she admitted, but nodded at him to proceed. 'No point in coming this far and leaving the story unfinished.'

'As for Thornwood House, Lord Hawley died during the war and the estate was inherited by a distant cousin in England who never even bothered to come and inspect it. Olivia Hawley lived there at their discretion, but having no income or stipend herself, she had to let the staff go. The estate had accumulated vast debts; many of the tenants left after George's unsolved murder. There were rumours, superstition that the land was cursed. Olivia lived like a hermit, completely alone, and most people thought her mad. Her body was eventually discovered when an agent for the family came to put the property up for sale in the 1940s. No one knew how long she had lain dead on the stairs, with only the rats for company.'

'Oh, my God, that's horrendous!' Sarah said. 'I can't say that I was her biggest fan after reading the diary, but no one deserves a death like that.'

'Understandably, the house has been left derelict since. It was handed over to the Office of Public Works in the sixties, but as you saw for yourself, the restoration plans aren't exactly "afoot". My grandfather insists the place is haunted. Who knows, maybe he's right.'

'So, Anna didn't go to America? Did she ever see Harold again?' Sarah asked, crestfallen.

'Well, according to my grandfather, boat tickets arrived from America every year until the war, but Anna never collected them.'

'That is so sad,' Sarah said, not bothering to conceal her feelings for a couple she had never known. 'She put her family before herself.'

'Like I said, it's not the ending you were hoping for,' he agreed. 'And of course, Harold could never return here, what with the warrant out for his arrest. But Anna did marry, after the war. He was a Dublin lad – fought in the war with Paddy Butler. Grandfather couldn't remember his last name, but said everyone called him Danny.'

Sarah shook her head in disbelief. Danny, the rebel who had helped Harold to escape. Anna had chosen to marry the very man who had risked his life to save her one true love.

'Our wills and fate do so contrary run,' she said.

'Beautifully put.'

'It's Shakespeare,' she said, smiling.

'Well, I doubt he sounded as good as you.' He looked away for a moment, suddenly self-conscious. 'Anyway, that's how these things tend to go; just when you think you know where life is taking you –' he paused for a moment '– it throws you a curveball.'

'Aha, you've been brushing up on your American.' She nodded approvingly.

Oran gulped down the rest of the tea and a pensive silence descended on them both, as they watched the flames of the fire sway and spark.

'So, that's all I can tell you. Anna moved to Dublin after that,' he said, putting his cup down.

'Poor Harold, it must've broken his heart to leave. And to think they never saw each other again ... I wonder if they corresponded at all? I just can't believe that's where the story ended.'

'Hmm. I guess people didn't really do long-distance relationships back then. It's different nowadays.'

She hoped he meant that.

'I feel like he rescued her, in a way. All that time she'd been waiting for someone to help her resolve her trauma after her sister died.'

'Sounds like they rescued each other. She showed him how to see the beauty in the ordinary.' As he said this, he looked around at the cottage, as though seeing it for the first time.

Sarah suddenly felt a little exposed, as if Oran were seeing right through her.

'What about Billy?' she asked, clearing her throat.

'Billy took over the farm when Anna married. He never married and he sold the cottage when he moved into a nursing home.'

Sarah looked a bit deflated to Oran, as though she were still waiting for something more. Then he thought about what his daughter had said. He stood up and walked over to the space on the seat next to hers, in what he hoped was a nonchalant move.

'And what about Sarah?' he asked. 'How does her story end?'

'You mean do I go back to Boston? Or New York?'

'Or stay in Ireland a while longer…' he suggested, with an irresistible smile.

'I honestly don't know what I want to do, Oran. This trip wasn't exactly planned.'

'Well, a bit of spontaneity never hurt anyone.'

'You sound like Fee!' She laughed. 'It must be this tea, gives you all the answers.' Sarah wanted to speak from the heart, even if it meant risking everything. 'I can't promise you anything,' she said. 'I need to stand on my own two feet for a while, rediscover what it is that used to make me … well, me.'

He gave her an encouraging nod. Maybe it was okay to open up.

'I can't ask you to wait for me, Oran—'

'Whether you ask it or not… I will,' he said, before tenderly kissing her lips.

All of a sudden, everything felt easy. The struggles of the past were over. She could finally let go and let herself be loved.

The tea had worked its magic yet again.

Chapter Thirty-Four

20th June 2011

The evening sun angled through the high, cathedral-like windows of the gallery, filling the space with a golden light. This was the time Sarah relished most, just before the guests arrived to view the work. She walked slowly from one end of the room to the other, straightening the frames by a fraction here and there, the only sound her own footsteps on the bare concrete floor. When Jack arrived, carrying a tray of glasses, she knew she'd made the right decision.

So much had changed since she left New York and blew into Shannon airport. She smiled at the recollection. Those days had been all about running away. Whether she had left to escape Jack or to find herself, it didn't really matter in the end. She had found something else in Thornwood, something she hadn't realised she was looking for. Purpose. In the weeks following that unexpected night with Oran,

Sarah spent a lot of time walking in the woods and fields around the cottage. Perhaps it was just as the seeress had said: if you stayed in Ireland long enough, it would catch you.

The idea had been right under her nose all along, if only she had known where to look. Sarah was convinced that the true inspiration behind Harold's pilgrimage to Ireland was an attempt to recapture his mother's spirit. Losing her at such a young age had unquestionably shaped his life and led him to this most unusual of paths. She found it strange to think that they were all being guided by invisible hands to find meaning in loss.

Harold was of the belief that The Good People were the departed souls of our dearly beloved, their voices reduced to a flutter on the breeze or the musical babbling of a brook. He wasn't just collecting fairy stories – he was keeping the memory of his ancestors alive. Perhaps that was why some people were so willing to believe in fairies. Maybe they were trying to hang on to something, or make believe that there was more to this life, beyond death. Sarah understood that, all too well.

Instinctively, she set about continuing his work the only way she knew how. She sharpened her pencils, opened a blank page and let the descriptions she had read in Harold's book translate into living, breathing characters of all shapes and sizes. She revisited the library in Ennis and found out about the National Folklore Commission, which was set up by the Irish Government in the 1930s to study and collect oral traditions of folklore from around the country. Were they inspired by

Harold's work? Quite possibly. All that was missing was a visual representation of these beliefs. The idea fell into place so easily, she was amazed she hadn't thought of it before.

The feel of the rough paper under her fingertips and the motion of drawing with a pencil gently brought her body and her mind back to a place of calm focus. For the first time in a long time, she had the satisfying feeling of being exactly where she was supposed to be. Were The Good People helping her or was she helping them? It didn't do to over-analyse such things. The physical and the spiritual worlds were so tightly bound together in Thornwood, it was impossible not to be affected by it.

She took several deep breaths and brought her mind back to the present.

'Happy?' Jack asked, handing her a glass of something fizzy, which she declined.

'I will be, when everybody gets here.' She checked her watch again, then reached for a bottle of water.

'I'm glad you came back. I thought I'd lost you to the wilds of Ireland for good,' he said, clinking his glass against her plastic bottle.

'Don't get too carried away, I'm only here for the free gallery space!' They both laughed. It was a relief to be back on good terms.

'What time are your parents getting in?'

'They're on their way – Meghan's driving them. Dad has a thing about flying, you remember.'

Another awkward moment, jostling their relationship from past to present.

'Your work has really progressed,' he said, keeping the conversation on neutral ground.

Sarah was tempted to say, 'I've progressed', but decided it might sound petulant.

'I found something I'm passionate about,' she settled on, looking around the room at the lively drawings of The Good People.

'They're not your typical fairy creature, are they?' Jack said, stepping closer to inspect a drawing of a water nymph. 'Some of them are a bit gruesome!'

Sarah smiled triumphantly. She was keenly aware of her country's reputation for turning Irish folklore into something to be ridiculed. Visions of *Darby O'Gill* and *Finian's Rainbow* came to mind. No. Sarah was adamant that her drawings would render The Good People in their true light. Not pretty little Tinkerbells, but wizened old faces with sharp teeth and twigs for hair. Capricious creatures whose inclination towards good or evil turned on a sixpence.

'They are the manifestations of all that is unseen in this world, Jack, they're not meant to be supermodels!'

'My mistake,' he replied, holding his hands up as if under siege.

'Seriously though, thanks for curating the exhibition. I was worried it might be a bit, well, weird.'

'Honestly? It is a bit weird, but I'd rather that than nothing at all.'

She took his hand briefly, hoping to convey in one simple gesture how much he had once meant to her. They had visited Emma's grave together on her return to New

York. They looked through her memory box, treasuring the photos and the tiny footprints that would never know the feel of the ground beneath them. Things would never be as they once were between them, but acknowledging the truth was preferable to the lie they had been living.

The bell rang at reception and she jerked with apprehension.

'I'll get it. Can you check if this one is straight? I can't trust my eyes any more!' she said, making her way out to the front of the gallery.

She hurried down the stairs, hoping that her family would arrive before everyone else. Sarah couldn't wait to share her work with them, particularly her father. She hadn't seen them in such a long time and the last few weeks in New York had made her even more eager to reunite with them.

And there he was. Oran Sweeney in midtown Manhattan. He stood on the other side of the glass, a smile on his face, shrugging slightly. It took Sarah a moment to unlock the door, a quirk that had become something of an affliction.

'You came,' she said simply, holding the door ajar.

'Well, you sent the ticket,' he replied.

She shook her head. 'I … I can't believe you're here!'

She stepped out onto the street and into his arms, into their life together. Yes, she'd made the right decision. It felt like coming home. They embraced for quite a long time, Sarah smiling inwardly, for she hadn't sent any ticket at all.

Acknowledgments

I wrote this book as a love letter to old Ireland, our ancient beliefs, traditions and folklore. Heartfelt thanks go to my family and to my ancestors whose stories I have drawn upon to create the magic of Thornwood. I was greatly inspired by the real Harold, Walter Evans-Wentz, who came to this country in search of the mystic and captured all of Ireland's beauty and mystery. To *na Daoine Maithe*, who transformed a wish left at the roots of an old hawthorn tree into reality, thank you! Finally, to the entire team at One More Chapter, thank you for your incredible support and for putting storytelling at the heart of everything you do.

Read on for an extract from *The Lost Bookshop*

On a quiet street in Dublin, a lost bookshop is waiting to be found…

For too long, Opaline, Martha and Henry have been the side characters in their own lives.

But when a vanishing bookshop casts its spell, these three unsuspecting strangers will discover that their own stories are every bit as extraordinary as the ones found in the pages of their beloved books. And by unlocking the secrets of the shelves, they find themselves transported to a world of wonder… where nothing is as it seems.

The Lost Bookshop: Extract

Prologue

The rainy streets of Dublin on a cold winter's day were no place for a young boy to dawdle, unless that very same boy had his nose pressed up against the window of the most fascinating bookshop. Lights twinkled inside and the colourful covers called to him, promising stories of adventure and escape. The window was packed with novelties and trinkets; miniature hot-air balloons almost reached the ceiling, while music boxes with mechanical birds and carousels twirled and chimed within. The lady inside spotted him and waved him in. He shook his head and blushed slightly.

'I'll be late for school,' he mouthed through the glass.

She nodded and smiled. She seemed friendly enough.

'Just for a minute,' he said, having fought the urge to go inside for all of three seconds.

'A minute it is.' She was behind the counter, taking more

books out of a big cardboard box. She glanced over at his untucked shirt, his mop of hair that had managed to evade a comb for quite some time and mismatched socks. She smiled to herself. Opaline's Bookshop was a magnet for little boys and girls. 'What class are you in?'

'Third class in St Ignatius,' he replied, craning his neck to look up at the wooden airplanes suspended mid-flight from the vaulted ceiling.

'And do you like it?'

He scoffed at the thought.

She left him leafing through an old book of magic tricks, but it wasn't long until he approached her desk and began looking at the stationery.

'You can help if you like. I'm sending out invitations to a book launch.'

He shrugged and began mimicking the way she folded the letters and stuffed them into the envelopes with a little too much enthusiasm. He wrinkled his nose with the effort, changing the constellation of freckles that spread out to his cheeks.

'What does Opaline mean?' he asked, pronouncing it with far too many syllables.

'Opaline is a name.'

'Is it your name?'

'No, I'm Martha.'

She could tell that he wasn't satisfied with that as an explanation.

'I can tell you a story about her, if you like? She didn't like school very much either. Or rules.'

'Or doing what she's told?' he suggested.

'Oh, she especially didn't like that.' Martha smiled conspiratorially. 'Here, you finish jamming those letters into envelopes and I'll make us some tea. A good story always begins with tea.'

Chapter 1

London, 1921

I let my fingers run along the spine of the book, letting the indentations of the embossed cover guide my skin to something tangible; something that I believed in more than the fiction that was playing out before me. Twenty-one years of age and my mother had decided that the time had come for me to marry. My brother, Lyndon, had rather unhelpfully found some dim-witted creature who had just inherited the family business; something to do with importing something or other from some far-flung place. I was barely listening.

'There are only two options open to a woman your age,' Mother pronounced, putting down her cup and saucer on the table beside her armchair. 'One is to marry, and the other to find a post in keeping with her gentility.'

'Gentility?' I echoed, with some incredulity. Looking around the drawing room with its chipped paint and faded curtains, I had to admire her vanity. She had married beneath her station and had always been at pains to remind my father, lest he forgot.

'Must you do that now?' my brother Lyndon asked, as

Mrs Barrett, our housemaid, cleared out the ashes from the grate.

'Madam requested a fire,' she said in a tone that showed no inflexion of respect. She had been with us for as long as I could remember and only took orders from my mother. The rest of us she treated like cheap imposters.

'The fact of the matter is that you must marry,' Lyndon parroted as he limped across the room, leaning heavily on his walking stick. Twenty years my elder, the entire right side of his body had been warped by shrapnel during the war in Flanders and the brother I once knew stayed buried somewhere in that very field. The horrors he held in his eyes frightened me, and even though I didn't like to admit it, I had grown fearful of him. 'This is a good match. Father's pension is barely enough for Mother to run the house. It's time you took your head out of your books and faced reality.'

I clung tighter to my book. A rare first American edition of *Wuthering Heights,* a gift from my father, along with a deep love of reading. Like a talisman, I had carried the cloth-covered book, whose spine bore the duplicitous line, tooled in gold, 'by the author of *Jane Eyre*'. We had come across it by complete chance at a flea market in Camden (a secret we could not tell Mother). I would later discover that Emily's English publisher had permitted this misattribution in order to capitalise on *Jane Eyre*'s commercial success. It was not in perfect condition; the cloth boards were worn on the edges and the back one had a v-shape nicked out of it. The pages were coming loose, as the threads that sewed them together were fraying with age and use. But to me, all of these features, including the cigar-smoke smell of the paper, were like a time machine. Perhaps the seeds were sown then. A book is never what it seems. I think my father had hoped my love of books would instil an interest in my schooling, but if anything, it only fuelled my loathing for the classroom. I tended to live in my imagination and so, every evening, I would race home from school and ask him to read to me. He was a civil servant, an honest man with a passion for learning. He always said that books were more than words on paper; they were portals to other places, other lives. I fell in love with books and the vast worlds they held inside, and I owed it all to my father.

'If you tilt your head,' he told me once, 'you can hear the older books whispering their secrets.'

I found an antique book on the shelf with a calfskin cover and time-coloured pages. I held it up to my ear and closed my eyes tight; imagining that I could hear whatever important secrets the author was trying to tell me. But I couldn't hear it, not the words at least.

'What do you hear?' he asked.

I waited, let the sound fill my ears.

'I hear the sea!'

It was like having a shell to my ear, with the air swirling through the pages. He smiled and held my cheek in his hand.

'Are they breathing, Papa?' I asked.

'Yes,' he said, 'the stories are breathing.'

When he finally succumbed to the Spanish Flu in 1918, I stayed up all night by his side, holding his cold hand, reading his favourite story. *The Personal History of David*

Copperfield, by Charles Dickens. In some silly way, I thought that the words would bring him back.

'I refuse to marry a man I've never even met purely to aid the family finances. The whole idea is preposterous!'

Mrs Barrett dropped the brush as I spoke and the sound of metal on marble churned my brother's features. He loathed any loud noises.

'Get out of here now!'

The poor woman had very unreliable knees and it took three failed attempts before she got up and left the room. How she managed to refrain from slamming the door behind her, I will never know.

I continued with my defence.

'If I am such a burden to you both, I will simply move out.'

'And where on earth do you think you would go? You have no money,' my mother pointed out. Now in her sixties, she had always referred to my arrival in the family as their 'little surprise', which would have sounded quaint had I not been aware of her loathing for surprises. Growing up in a household of an older generation only compounded my urge to break free and experience the modern world.

'I have friends,' I insisted. 'I could get a job.'

My mother shrieked.

'Damn and blast, you ungrateful brat!' Lyndon growled, grabbing my wrist as I attempted to get up from my chair.

'You're hurting me.'

'I will hurt you far worse than this if you do not obey.'

I tried to free my arm, but he held fast. I looked to my

mother, who was making an intense study of the rug on the floor.

'I see,' I said, finally understanding that Lyndon was the man of the house now and he would make the decisions.

'Very well.' He still held on to my wrist, his sour breath in my face. 'I said, very well.'

Meeting his eyes, I again tried to pull away. 'I will meet this suitor.'

'You will marry him,' he assured me and slowly he released his grasp.

I smoothed down my skirts and tucked my book under my arm.

'Right. That's settled then,' Lyndon said, his cold eyes looking somewhere just beyond me. 'I shall invite Austin to supper this evening and all will be arranged.'

'Yes, Brother,' I said, before retreating to my bedroom upstairs.

I searched the top drawer of the dressing table and found a cigarette that I'd stolen from Mrs Barrett's stash in the kitchen. I opened the window and lit the tip, taking a long slow inhale like a femme fatale from the films. I sat at my dressing table and let the cigarette rest on an old oyster shell I had picked up at the beach last summer, a carefree holiday with my best friend Jane before she herself got married. Despite the fact that women now had the vote, a good marriage was still seen as the only option.

Looking at my reflection in the mirror, I touched the

nape of my neck where my hair ended. Mother had almost fainted when she saw what I'd done with my long tresses. 'I'm not a little girl any more,' I had told her. But did I really believe that? I needed to be a modern woman. I needed to take a risk. But without any money, how could I do anything other than obey my elders? That was when my father's words returned to me ... *Books are like portals*. I looked again at my bookshelf and took another long drag of my cigarette.

'What would Nellie Bly do?' I asked myself, as I often did. To me, she was the epitome of fearlessness – a pioneering American journalist who, inspired by Jules Verne's book, travelled around the world in a mere seventy-two days, six hours and eleven minutes. She always said that energy rightly applied and directed could accomplish anything. If I were a boy, I could announce my intentions to do the Grand Tour of Europe before getting married. I longed to experience different cultures. Twenty-one years old and I had done nothing. Seen nothing. I looked again at my books and made my decision before I finished smoking my cigarette.

'How much can you give me for them?' I watched as Mr Turton examined my hardbacks of *Wuthering Heights* and *The Hunchback of Notre Dame*.

He was the proprietor of an airless shop that was in reality just a very long corridor without any windows. His pipe smoke gave the air a viscous quality and my eyes began to water.

'Two pounds and that's being generous.'

'Oh no, I need much more than that.'

He saw my father's copy of *David Copperfield* and before I could stop him, he began to leaf through the pages.

'I'm not selling that one. It has … sentimental value.'

'Ah, now this is interesting. It is known as the "reading edition", as Dickens would have read from it at his public readings.' His bulbous nose and tiny eyes gave him the look of a badger or a mole. He sniffed out the valuable book like a truffle.

'Yes, I am aware,' I said, trying to snatch the book back from his greedy paws. He continued with his appraisal, as though he were already selling it at auction.

'Sumptuously bound in full polished red calf. A charming edition; ornate tooling in gilt to the spine; all page edges gilt; original marbled endpapers.'

'My father gifted me that book. It is not for sale.'

He looked at me over the rim of his glasses, sizing me up. 'Miss …?'

'Miss Opaline Carlisle.'

'Miss Carlisle, this is one of the best-preserved examples of these rare issues I have ever handled. '

'And the illustrations by Hablot K. Browne. You see his pen name, Phiz,' I added, with pride.

'I could offer you fifteen pounds.'

The world fell silent, the way it often does the moment before a life-changing decision. On one path lay freedom along with the unknown. The other was a gilded cage.

'Twenty pounds, Mr Turton, and you have a deal.'

He narrowed his eyes and his lips betrayed a grudging smile. I knew he would pay, just as surely as I knew that I would devote my life to getting that book back. As his back was turned, I slipped my *Wuthering Heights* back into my pocket and left.

That was how my career as a book dealer began.

~

Available in paperback, ebook, and audio!

ONE MORE CHAPTER

The author and One More Chapter would like to thank everyone
who contributed to the publication of this story...

Analytics
Abigail Fryer
Maria Osa

Audio
Fionnuala Barrett
Ciara Briggs

Contracts
Sasha Duszynska
Lewis

Design
Lucy Bennett
Fiona Greenway
Liane Payne
Dean Russell

Digital Sales
Hannah Lismore
Emily Scorer

Editorial
Kate Elton
Arsalan Isa
Charlotte Ledger
Bonnie Macleod
Jennie Rothwell
Tony Russell
Emily Thomas

Harper360
Emily Gerbner
Jean Marie Kelly
emma sullivan
Sophia Wilhelm

International Sales
Bethan Moore

Marketing & Publicity
Chloe Cummings
Emma Petfield

Operations
Melissa Okusanya
Hannah Stamp

Production
Emily Chan
Denis Manson
Simon Moore
Francesca Tuzzeo

Rights
Rachel McCarron
Hany Sheikh
Mohamed
Zoe Shine

**The HarperCollins
Distribution Team**

**The HarperCollins
Finance & Royalties
Team**

**The HarperCollins
Legal Team**

**The HarperCollins
Technology Team**

Trade Marketing
Ben Hurd

UK Sales
Laura Carpenter
Isabel Coburn
Jay Cochrane
Sabina Lewis
Holly Martin
Erin White
Harriet Williams
Leah Woods

**And every other
essential link in the
chain from delivery
drivers to booksellers
to librarians and
beyond!**

ONE MORE CHAPTER

YOUR NUMBER ONE STOP

FOR PAGETURNING BOOKS

One More Chapter is an
award-winning global
division of HarperCollins.

Sign up to our newsletter to get our
latest eBook deals and stay up to date
with our weekly Book Club!
<u>Subscribe here.</u>

Meet the team at
<u>www.onemorechapter.com</u>

Follow us!

 @OneMoreChapter_

 @OneMoreChapter

 @onemorechapterhc

Do you write unputdownable fiction?
We love to hear from new voices.
Find out how to submit your novel at
<u>www.onemorechapter.com/submissions</u>